THE DARKEST
OF NIGHTS

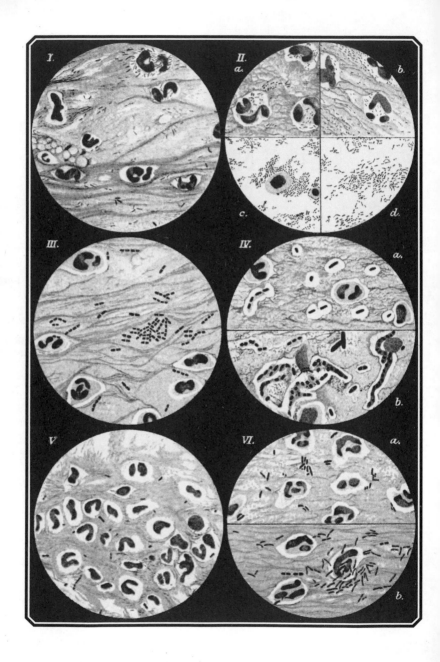

THE DARKEST
OF NIGHTS

CHARLES ERIC MAINE

With an Introduction by
MIKE ASHLEY

This edition published 2019 by
The British Library
96 Euston Road
London NW1 2DB

Originally published in 1962 by Hodder & Stoughton, London

Copyright © 1962, The Estate of David McIlwain
Introduction copyright © 2019 Mike Ashley

Cataloguing in Publication Data
A catalogue record for this book is available from the British Library

ISBN 978 0 7123 5218 5
e-ISBN 978 0 7123 6493 5

Frontispiece illustration from
The Bacteriology of the Eye by Theodor Axenfeld, 1908

Cover artwork: *Tycho Brahe discovering nova*, c. 1971 by Chesley Bonestell.
Reproduced courtesy of Bonestell LLC.

Cover design by Jason Anscomb
Text designed and typeset by Tetragon, London
Printed and bound by TJ International, Padstow, Cornwall

THE DARKEST
OF NIGHTS

INTRODUCTION

A Plague upon Humanity?

ONE THOUGHT GUARANTEED TO CHILL US IS THE THREAT OF a worldwide epidemic and in recent years there have been plenty of possibilities which, thankfully, scientists have managed to keep in check.

There was the Ebola epidemic that erupted in West Africa in December 2013 and though that particular crisis was declared over in March 2016 the Ebola virus remains a potent threat. HIV/AIDS is still a major epidemic, indeed it is regarded as a global pandemic with some 37 million individuals living with the virus.

Humanity has lived with plagues for its entire existence. The most notorious was the bubonic plague, especially the Black Death of the fourteenth century which wiped out about a third of the population of Europe. An earlier outbreak of the plague in Europe in the sixth and seventh centuries is believed to have caused the death of half the population. Other plagues and epidemics over the centuries include smallpox, malaria, typhus, cholera, measles and, of course, influenza. The epidemic of Spanish flu that erupted after the First World War in 1918 caused the deaths of over 75 million people worldwide.

In most years there is a new influenza virus that emerges having mutated and become immune to existing antidotes. In the late 1950s one of the fears was of Asian flu which had started to spread from China in 1956 and is thought to have caused the deaths of at least

two million people, mostly in the Far East. Recurrences of mutations of this virus have surfaced periodically ever since, such as the
avian or "bird" flu recognised in the late 1990s.

Charles Eric Maine gave thought to these viruses and how they
might be affected by nuclear radiation. He had already envisaged
global destruction arising from nuclear bomb tests in *The Tide Went
Out* in 1958. Then he considered whether nuclear fallout, which we
all feared in the 1950s, might cause a virus to mutate in such a form
as to be incurable. In *The Darkest of Nights*, first published in 1962 and
later published in the United States as *Survival Margin*, he postulated
just such a virus that took two forms. The AB version is lethal and
incurable. The BA version is harmless and even confers immunity
against the AB version, but the BA version can't be cultivated on
its own because it immediately breaks down into both AB and BA
and the AB version becomes rampant. Scientists soon realise that
there's every chance that the AB virus will wipe out at least half of
the world's population.

Of course governments try and keep quiet about this whilst
preparing for just such an eventuality, but inevitably the truth leaks
out and social unrest soon follows.

Maine's tense thriller—he preferred to call his novels scientific
thrillers rather than science fiction—follows the research into the
virus and the dawning realisation of the peril facing the human
race and the consequential chaos as individuals panic and rebel.

In all his novels Maine, whose real name was David McIlwain
(1921–81), presented a disturbing set of circumstances and then
explored how a few individuals try and cope with the consequences
as their lives rapidly spiral out of control. In *High Vacuum* (1957),
for example, the first moon rocket has crashed with only enough
oxygen for the survivors for four weeks, or longer if there are fewer

of them! In *The Tide Went Out* (1958), which is also available from the British Library, nuclear testing cracks open the Earth's crust and the oceans start draining away.

McIlwain had been born in Liverpool and in his teens discovered the world of science fiction. Through fandom he contributed to various fanzines and published his own, *Satellite*, with his friend John F. Burke. McIlwain contributed stories to these amateur magazines, but the Second World War intervened before he had a chance to develop a professional career. He trained as a signals officer in the Royal Air Force and fought in North Africa. After the war he continued to work in television and radio engineering, before turning to journalism and editorial work on a television trade magazine.

His links with radio meant that his earliest works were written as radio plays, starting with *Spaceways* in January 1952. To make this story of the first manned flight to the Moon more acceptable to a wider audience he incorporated a murder mystery. He was fortunate that *Spaceways* was picked up by Hammer and, with a script by Paul Tabori, was released as a feature film in 1953. Maine novelised the script, which means that his first outing appeared in three different media in two years. Unsurprisingly Maine soon turned professional and produced a novel a year over the next twenty years, including crime novels under the pen names Richard Rayner and Robert Wade.

Several of Maine's novels were filmed, the best known being *The Mind of Mr. Soames* (1961), about a man who was in a coma since birth and regains consciousness when he is thirty. It was made into a feature film in 1969 starring Terence Stamp and Robert Vaughn.

Other novels by Maine include *The Isotope Man*, which started life as "Time Slip", a half-hour television play broadcast in November 1953, where a man who has died is brought back to life but is now out of sync with his surroundings, by just under five seconds. In *Escapement* (1957), published in America as *The Man Who Couldn't Sleep*, a scientist discovers ways of recording brain patterns, memories and dreams and the protagonist, who suffers from insomnia, finds he can enter a world of his own dreams. *World Without Men* (1958) has an all-female society and explores what happens when the first male baby comes into the world. *B.E.A.S.T.* (1966) has scientists trying to develop a simulation of animal evolution, resulting in a form of "virtual" life.

Time fascinated Maine and he wrote two time-travel novels, *Timeliner* (1955), also based on a radio play, in which an individual is propelled further and further into the future, each time his mind taking over the body of an individual who seems to have some remote relationship with him, and *Calculated Risk* (1960) where people from the future come back to our present to try and stop an impending disaster.

These examples show the fertility of Maine's imagination. Not all of his novels were appreciated in his lifetime, at least not by the science-fiction fraternity, though he was popular amongst general readers. Some of his ideas have dated, but that does not stop his books from challenging our thinking about how we would cope with strange and frightening circumstances, such as when faced with only a 50:50 chance of survival against a deadly virus.

MIKE ASHLEY

AUTHOR'S NOTE

THE GENETIC EFFECTS ON HUMAN BEINGS OF RADIOACTIVE fallout from nuclear weapon tests have received prominent publicity in recent years, but what has not been stressed is that the same process of mutation can equally change the structure and nature of all life forms. This novel sets out to examine the threat to humanity posed by such an eventuality and show how men, being what they are, exploit the situation to their own several ends.

CHAPTER ONE

A S SOON AS IT BECAME OBVIOUS THAT THE PATIENT WAS GOING to die, Dr. Sutaki telephoned the Tokyo office of the International Virus Research Organisation and asked for Dr. Ward, who was director of the local research unit.

The woman who answered the call spoke in a methodical English voice. "I'm afraid Dr. Ward has gone to Los Angeles for three days. Perhaps Dr. Woolner, his deputy, could help."

"This is Dr. Sutaki at the Tanhai hospital. We have a suspected Hueste virus case."

"I'll get in touch with Dr. Woolner at once, Dr. Sutaki. I take it you know the procedure."

"Yes. We already have samples of blood serum and cerebrospinal fluid, and we are ready for immediate autopsy as soon as death occurs."

"Good. Dr. Woolner will probably bring a colleague with him to assist."

"Thank you."

Dr. Sutaki hung up and checked the time. The research unit was fourteen kilometres from the hospital in the northern suburbs of Tokyo, which meant that the English doctor and his assistant could be expected within the half-hour. He smoothed his hands down his white coat to dry the sweat from his palms, and returned to the isolation ward.

Another Japanese doctor stood by the bed in the small room. He glanced briefly at Sutaki as he entered, his dark eyes sombre behind the gauze mask that covered his hair and most of his face. Sutaki donned his own mask and joined his colleague.

"Any change?" he asked.

"Temperature nearly one hundred and seven. Breathing faster, but very shallow. Notice the characteristic gloss of the skin."

Sutaki leaned forward and gently touched the cheek of the patient close to the oxygen mask which was taped across his open mouth. The skin, yellow-grey and shiny, indented a little, then filled out slowly as the finger was removed.

"Epithelial oedema," he said, standing back. "They're sending Woolner but it looks as if he may be too late."

"You're certain it is the Hueste virus?"

Dr. Sutaki considered for a moment. "Yes," he said.

The patient, a middle-aged Japanese male, lay perfectly still beneath the thin white sheet, as if already dead. Only his face was visible, and the colour of his skin was pallid, despite the dry glaze and high temperature. The slight rhythmic movement of his chest as he breathed oxygen from the mask indicated that he was still alive.

High in the wall above the bed an air extractor hummed quietly. Beyond a narrow window afternoon sunshine burned on green grass and cast the red brick wall surrounding the hospital grounds into shadow. The random sounds of distant traffic trembled occasionally in the still air of the room.

"This morning," Dr. Sutaki said, "I spoke to the Area Medical Officer. This is the eighth case in Tokyo and the forty-fifth in Japan in the last two days."

"Epidemic figures. Another hundred in the next two days and a thousand within the week, perhaps."

"I was hoping we would be able to avoid the worst of what is happening in China. *They* were taken by surprise. We have had nearly a month in which to carry out basic research."

"Hueste has made *some* progress."

Sutaki nodded. "At least he proved that it *was* a virus and put forward the mutation theory—but that doesn't help in practical terms. What we need is a breakthrough in the form of a reliable vaccine or serum."

"Well, it may come any time at all. I understand they're using an electron microscope at the research unit to analyse the structure of the virus."

"I give them six months at least," Sutaki said despondently. "In that time the epidemic could engulf the entire world."

They remained silent for a while, staring as if unseeing at the motionless shape of the patient. The breathing seemed quicker but more feeble, and the glossiness of the skin had increased perceptibly.

The other doctor said: "I read somewhere that all this was the result of an experiment in bacteriological warfare that went wrong."

"Not according to Hueste," Sutaki commented. "He attributes it to accidental mutation of an ordinary virus—a relatively harmless virus perhaps related to influenza."

"It could have been a deliberate mutation."

"Perhaps, but that merely complicates a simple theory. It is just as reasonable to suppose that nuclear weapon tests in the Pacific area were responsible at some time past. Menshekin published a detailed study of the effects of ambient radioactivity on simple marine life. I think it is reasonable that over a period of cyclic generations of virus, mutating each time, an extremely virulent strain might be produced sooner or later. In any case the theory is of no practical value. What we need is therapy…"

Suddenly they became aware that the patient had stopped breathing, even though the oxygen was still hissing persistently in the mask over his face. His shiny skin seemed to have set like hard ceramic, but in due course it would dissolve and liquify.

They exchanged glances. Sutaki checked the body temperature and found it a fraction below one hundred and eight degrees. Some minutes later it had fallen to one hundred and five, and it would continue to fall because the body was no longer animated by life.

Having confirmed the fact of death, Dr. Sutaki arranged for the body to be transferred to the operating theatre for an autopsy.

Dr. Woolner arrived at the hospital shortly after the autopsy had begun. A small, tubby man with ginger hair and a bristling moustache, he wore a formal, dark grey suit despite the hot weather. He was accompanied by a young, raven-haired woman wearing a cool white dress whom he introduced as Dr. Pauline Brant, one of the research unit's specialists in bacteriology. Dr. Sutaki himself was engaged in performing the autopsy, and the new arrivals acted principally as observers for the first half-hour, with Dr. Woolner occasionally contributing comment and advice.

As an autopsy it was conventional enough, except that the body was still warm and the blood had been drained off into an electrically heated receptacle for transport to the laboratory. Dr. Sutaki had already opened up the ventral surface from throat to pelvis and was carefully removing parts of selected organs for further pathological examination. Later he sawed through the cranium and took out the brain, then, after stitching, turned the corpse over and slit the cooling flesh down the spine to remove sections of the spinal cord.

That completed the procedure; the rest was up to the specialists with their instruments, reagents and microscopes.

The sheeted body was wheeled out and the containers were taken away on a metal trolley. Sutaki washed his hands and greeted his visitors for the second time, with less abstraction and more cordiality.

"Perhaps we could all have coffee… or something more hospitable, such as saki?" he suggested.

"Coffee would be most welcome," Pauline Brant said.

They left the operating theatre and walked through austere white corridors to an outbuilding which proved to be a spacious and pleasant canteen. Fake bamboo walls were adorned with Japanese tapestries, all highlight and shadow. They drank coffee together at a small corner table.

Dr. Woolner apologised for his late arrival, but Dr. Sutaki pointed out that it was really the patient's fault for dying too soon.

"You'll be letting us have samples of blood serum, and brain and spine sections in the usual way," Woolner said.

"Of course."

"We shall be sending specimens to America, and Dr. Brant"—he glanced at the girl—"will be flying back to England the day after tomorrow, so we'd like to include a comprehensive selection of pathological specimens in her luggage."

"You may take whatever you wish, Dr. Brant," Sutaki said, smiling cordially at Pauline. "I am a strong supporter of the International Virus Research Organisation, and Dr. Ward is a very great friend of mine."

"Dr. Ward is a worried man," Woolner stated. "At this moment he's in Los Angeles discussing the virus threat with Hueste himself and a dozen other experts from all over the world."

Sutaki nodded tersely. "We are all worried men—and women. But I have more faith in Dr. Ward than in Dr. Hueste. The first is practical, and the second is what one might call—a theoretician."

He paused for a moment, eyeing Woolner speculatively, then added: "Have there been any new developments?"

"Not really—except that the IVRO research headquarters at

Brierley—that's near London—seem to think that the Hueste virus exists in two isomeric forms."

"Isomeric?"

"What they mean is that the protein structure as shown under the electron microscope follows an 'A' or 'B' pattern. The one form is a mirror image of the other."

"Is that an important discovery?"

"We don't know at this stage. It may be a step forward. Apparently they've stopped calling it the Hueste virus. In the cable I received yesterday from Brierley they referred to it as the 'AB' virus."

"But surely that is simply a matter of a label…"

Woolner shook his head. "More than that, I think. They're making tests with the two virus isomers to see if they have the same effect. The trouble is that animals don't react in the same way as humans. Apart from certain species of monkeys the virus doesn't seem to be lethal in the animal world."

"We have made tests of our own on monkeys," Sutaki said. "In theory we produced a serum containing antibodies, but it failed to produce immunity in any degree. Half of the monkeys died—but for reasons which seemed to have nothing to do with the serum."

Woolner finished his coffee and wiped his mouth with the back of his hand. "We have a small supply of American vaccine, as you know, Dr. Sutaki. According to Dr. Ward it has achieved a limited success—but on the other hand it is also suspected of causing infection in a number of cases. Frankly, my instructions are to use it only on infected patients when their temperature reaches one hundred and five."

"In other words, when they are inevitably going to die."

"Exactly, Dr. Sutaki. It means you must notify us in good time. Today, for instance, we arrived too late."

Sutaki spread out his slender hands apologetically. "It is difficult to be certain of diagnosis. It is not until the temperature exceeds one hundred and five and grey oedema of the skin sets in that one can be really sure. At that point it is merely a matter of time, just a few hours, to death."

"In the next few days you will have many more cases," Woolner pointed out. "Diagnosis will become easier. If you will keep us informed in good time then together we may be able to do something to keep this plague under control."

He stood up, preparing to leave.

"Thank you for your co-operation, Dr. Sutaki—and for the coffee."

"There will always be plenty of both for you and your colleagues," Sutaki said with a smile. "Meanwhile I will arrange for pathological samples to be put aside for you and Dr. Brant." He bowed slightly towards the girl. "They will be delivered tomorrow."

Dr. Woolner and the girl took their leave and drove back to the research unit. The Tokyo traffic was dense for early afternoon, but it thinned out as they filtered into the outer suburbs. He drove the station wagon in a leisurely fashion, with the windows wide open to neutralise the heat. But even the breeze slipping into the car was warm and unrefreshing.

"In a way," she said thoughtfully, "I'm sorry to be going back to London now that the crisis is beginning to build up."

"You'll be better out of it," he assured her. "How long is it since you were home?"

"Nearly three years."

He stopped at traffic lights and lit a cigarette. "Me—I've got a year to do. My kids won't know me when they see me, and as for the old woman..."

The lights changed and he drove on, the cigarette dangling from his dry lips. "I wouldn't mind doing a spell at Brierley in a cold wet English summer. I imagine that's where you'll end up."

"I don't think so," she said. "I'd prefer to come back to Tokyo as soon as my holiday is over."

"They like to circulate the staff—to get people with field experience on the routine work at Brierley. It makes for fresh ideas." He paused to tap the ash off his cigarette. "And there's your husband, of course."

She stared stonily through the windscreen. The research unit was only four blocks away.

"We're both independent characters and we go our own ways," she said.

"Foreign correspondent or something, isn't he?"

"He used to be. That's how we met—in South Vietnam."

"What do you mean—used to be?"

"He went back to take over a staff job as foreign editor on the newspaper."

"Living in London?"

"Yes."

He swung the car into a small courtyard adjoining the building of the research unit, stopped and switched off the engine.

"At all events it will be a happy reunion for you both," he remarked, getting out of the car.

She made no reply, but smiled wryly, and followed him into the building.

The research unit of the International Virus Research Organisation was staffed by eight people under the general direction of Dr. Alec Ward, who was an American. All were doctors, specialising in virology, bacteriology and detailed research connected with epidemic disease. They came from various countries, including Britain, Germany, France, Denmark and Canada. The unit was one of eighty-two sited at strategic points throughout the world, and administered from New York, where the International Virus Research Organisation, or IVRO as it was popularly known, had its skyscraper headquarters.

The principal research centre, as opposed to administrative, was the Brierley research establishment just outside London, but a great deal of high level research was also carried out in Los Angeles and Paris, and there was an important bacteriological laboratory near Moscow. The smaller research units in the field operated largely as collecting stations for data and samples, although they collaborated with local hospital authorities in applying new therapeutic techniques.

It was Pauline's fifth year with IVRO and her second tour of duty in the Far East. Japan was a considerable improvement on Vietnam, she decided, but on the other hand more than half of those eighteen months in Vietnam had been spent with Clive, before and after the wedding. In retrospect the time took on the quality of an extended honeymoon.

On that first holiday in London together they had rented a flat for three months, and in due course Clive had returned to Vietnam while she had been posted first to Singapore and then to Tokyo.

Within less than a year, as the political situation in Vietnam had eased after the end of the war in Indo-China, Clive had been recalled to London to take over the foreign desk on the *Daily Monitor*, following an internal shake-up of reorganisation and promotion.

In some odd way, it seemed to her, the distance between them had lengthened and time had slowed down. Even his letters came less frequently—and there were things one could read between the lines.

The trouble is, she told herself, that I'm a career woman at heart, and Clive is a career man, and in our particular chosen careers we're only likely to get together once every few years. That is hardly a marriage, and we both know it.

Somewhat disconsolately she finished packing and had a quick meal. There was still an hour to reach the airport. Only three members of the staff were left in the building, the others having gone to the hospital where in the past twelve hours forty-two virus patients had been admitted. She said her good-byes with a certain regret, and as an afterthought telephoned the hospital for a final word with Dr. Woolner.

Woolner himself was not available, the switchboard girl said, but she could get Dr. Sutaki.

"I didn't have a chance to say good-bye to Dr. Woolner," she explained when Sutaki came to the phone. "Perhaps you would be kind enough to tell him I called."

Sutaki seemed to hesitate for quite a long time before answering. "Yes, Dr. Brant, I will tell him."

"Is anything wrong?" she asked, sensing caution in Sutaki's bland voice.

"No... that is to say, Dr. Woolner has been working very hard, and there has been a reaction."

"You mean he's ill."

"In a technical sense..."

"Dr. Sutaki, please tell me the truth. Is it the Hueste virus?"

Again Sutaki hesitated. "How can we possibly know at this stage? True, he has a high temperature and some degree of coma, but one must not..."

"Thank you," she interrupted, hanging up.

She paced the floor for half a minute, fighting indecision. Finally she lifted the telephone again and made a personal call to Dr. Ward in Los Angeles. The connection took ten minutes.

"This is Pauline Brant," she said, when Ward answered the phone. "I want to cancel my vacation. Dr. Woolner has contracted Hueste virus and I feel I shall be needed here."

"I already know about Woolner," Dr. Ward said in his slow American drawl. "Dr. Sutaki rang me about an hour ago. I'm fixing a replacement right now."

"I still prefer to cancel," she insisted.

"Now, look, Pauline," Ward said amiably, "you need that vacation more than we need you. I sure appreciate the gesture, but if you deliberately miss that plane I'm going to be very, very mad. You may think you're needed in Tokyo just because the virus has spread to Japan, but I'll tell you something—that goddam virus isn't going to stay in Japan. We had our first Hueste reported in San Francisco only this morning."

"But what's the good of my going back to London when we can fight the plague at its source?"

"Because," Ward said firmly, "any time at all the virus is going to spread across Asia, Africa and Europe too, and Pauline, it won't matter a damn where you are. In fact, you may be a darned sight more useful to the boys at Brierley because of your field experience—so get on that plane."

"But, Dr. Ward, I'd much rather..."

"*Get on that plane!*" he shouted over the line. "That's an order with no appeal. It's bad luck about Woolner, and I know how you feel, but we still have to run IVRO as a systematic business and not a free for all."

"Well, all right," she said, surrendering reluctantly.

"That's better. Have a good vacation and give my regards to London."

"I will," she promised, and hung up.

From the airliner, flying over the Malayan peninsular, the world seemed an immense, remote place, she thought, passing by in slow motion from the detached viewpoint of twenty-five thousand feet. Humanity had hardly begun to make an impression on the sprawling vista of green and brown that made up the land surface of the planet. A broad winding river was a silver-blue thread and the town at the estuary was little more than a minute area of mottled rash.

Time dragged, as it always does when there is no sense of motion. Oddly enough, she found her thoughts turning to the past rather than the future, visualising red-haired and once lively Woolner lying motionless in the inevitable Hueste coma, his skin dry and greying while his temperature climbed to the inevitable lethal peak, and the virus, meanwhile, consolidating its hold on the tissues of the body—the blood cells, the meningeal skin of the brain, the central nervous system—eroding and dissolving them away. A mere forty-eight hours—that was all the interval granted between the onset of fever and the point of death. The coma came swiftly, and perhaps mercifully, at an early stage.

There had to be new diseases, of course. Medical science was always being confronted by variations and mutations of familiar infections. Sometimes the strains were harmless, and sometimes extremely virulent. Evolution in the world of bacteria and viruses proceeded at a fast pace so that even the latest antibiotic drugs were likely to become ineffective as each succeeding generation of virus built up an immunity according to the classic and most basic law—the survival of the fittest. It had long been recognised in medical circles that a mutated virus, sparked off, perhaps, by ambient radioactivity or even natural cosmic ray bombardment, might leap ahead in the evolutionary scale to a stage where all the devices and techniques of mankind were powerless to hold it in check. The Hueste virus seemed to be of that type.

It had started in Southern China only a few weeks earlier. Perhaps a single radioactive gamma particle falling from the upper atmosphere, long after a nuclear weapon test, had traversed a single virus cell floating aimlessly in the subtropical air, damaging the molecular protein structure and forming a new variant which would in due course reproduce and continue to reproduce its mutated form. Nobody would ever know the true origin of the thing, but Dr. Ludwig Hueste, a German virologist working in China on a quite different project, had been the first to isolate the new virus when the first few hundred victims had been conveyed to hospital to die.

The Hueste virus had thus acquired a name, but not an explanation. Day by day the death roll had mounted at a frightening rate, running through the thousands and hundreds of thousands into, finally, the millions.

The outside world had been sceptical at first. One never quite knew what was going on in China, and there were the old regular rumours of famine and plague that kept cropping up from time to time. But this plague was different, as world health authorities soon began to realise.

Medical organisations in almost every country were combining forces to deal with the threat, principally through the existing organisation of IVRO. At the same time a kind of unofficial censorship was being subtly imposed, and tacitly accepted by information services throughout the world, in order to avoid creating unnecessary alarm and panic among ordinary civil populations. To the masses of people throughout the world the Hueste virus was just another of those Far East plagues, like cholera or Asian 'flu. It would circulate for a while and finally blow itself out like a spent hurricane.

This one is different, she repeated to herself, closing her eyes drowsily, soothed by the incessant vibration of the jets. At least, it's different so far. There hasn't really been time to tackle the problem systematically, and it may be that the solution will prove to be quite simple. Somewhere, somehow, for every virus there is an antivirus, if one knows how to create it. At this very moment the finest scientific brains in the world are seeking the answer. Tomorrow, or in a week, or perhaps a month, they will find it.

Presently she fell asleep, and the jetliner screamed its predetermined course towards Singapore, the first stop on the route that would lead through Karachi, Lydda and Rome to London.

CHAPTER TWO

CLIVE WAS WAITING FOR HER AT LONDON AIRPORT—A TALL, dark Clive with grey eyes and a crinkled sardonic face, who had lost most of his tropical tan and had put on weight over the absent years. Their first embrace was hearty rather than sentimental, but after that they became oddly formal towards each other, almost as if they were shy.

"You haven't changed, Pauline," he said, looking her over, "but you're different just the same. Something about your hair..."

"I had it cut short."

"And you look taller."

"Not taller, Clive, just thinner. It's an optical illusion."

He picked up the cases. "I've got the car outside."

"Wait a minute," she said, taking from him a black metal box with white stencilled lettering on the side. "Pathological specimens," she added, by way of explanation. "There's someone waiting to collect them at Reception."

He shrugged. "Okay, Pauline. I'll wait here."

She took the box to the reception bay where she was duly introduced to an urbane young man in a military style raincoat whose name she didn't catch. They chatted informally for a few minutes, and then she handed over the box.

"It contains samples of blood, brain, body fluids and parts of other organs," she explained.

"I hope they're in good condition."

"They ought to be." She patted the top of the black box. "It's a portable refrigerator, battery-operated and... transistorised—I think that's the word. IVRO have ordered five thousand of them from the Toshibura company in Okawa."

"Hm. Clever, these Japanese," he said laconically.

"Well, I must get back to my husband."

He nodded. "Dr. Youde, our head of research, is hoping you'll look in at Brierley in the next day or two, if you can spare the time. We do realise that you are on holiday, but there's a bit of a flap on, and he thinks you might be able to help."

"Of course," she asserted. "Perhaps tomorrow—but certainly before the weekend."

She said good-bye and returned to Clive. A few minutes later her luggage was stowed in the car and they were driving towards London and home.

During the journey she eyed him covertly, trying to relate the reality to the memory. The three years that had passed formed, in some indefinable way, a transparent barrier between them; there was a sense of renewed liaison, but no deep feeling of reunion.

"How's the *Daily Monitor*?" she enquired presently.

"Booming. Circulation now topping two million, and advertising ten per cent up."

"Good. And the job?"

"No complaints, but I think I liked it better in the old days, when I had a roving commission."

"You're starting to feel restless again," she accused.

He glanced at her sidewise with a half smile. "Not really, but I don't care to be deskbound. Sometimes I envy you your freedom."

"One can be just as deskbound in Tokyo as in London," she commented. "Perhaps not deskbound in its literal sense, but certainly tied to routine and procedure."

Silence for a minute while he manoeuvred the car through thickening traffic on the dual-carriageway.

"As a matter of fact," he said casually, "I've been offered a top executive job with an American television outfit."

"Doing what?"

"Sort of features editor. It's a new venture—a kind of news magazine covering events all over the world. I don't mean hard news of the type that makes the headlines in the daily papers, but rather the undercurrent stuff—the news behind the news, the trends and back-room operations that build up into tomorrow's headlines..."

"But, Clive, you already have a good job. After all those years on the *Monitor*..."

He shrugged. "Perhaps too many years on the *Monitor*. Time won't wait." He glanced at her briefly, almost defensively. "You know me, Pauline—always one eye on the next rung of the ladder."

"Yes, I know," she murmured, but there was an element of regret in her voice. "I only hope it will be worth while, in the long run, I mean."

"I've been promised the equivalent of ten thousand a year. By my standards that's worth while. What's more, I'd be based in New York, and spend most of my time flying round the world with a film unit in a chartered aircraft."

"Yes," she said with resignation. "I can see the attraction. Have you accepted?"

"Well, I haven't signed on the dotted line, but it's all cut and dried. There are certain conditions involved."

"Such as what?"

"It's rather complex. Let's talk about it later, when we've had time to settle down."

"Whatever you say, Clive."

"I'll take you out to dinner this evening," he added cheerily. "Then we can talk at leisure about our respective futures."

Just that one word "respective"—it was like a remote bell tolling for the death of something she was not even able to define at that moment. She looked at Clive and he, sensing her movement, glanced quickly at her, the inevitable smile of charm on his lips. For an instant their eyes met, but there was no feeling of contact. And suddenly she knew that their marriage had come to a stop.

It was a big, ground-floor flat in a secluded road in South Kensington. Cerise curtains shrouded a wide bay window, but glancing through the panes as she walked past she could see a baby grand piano, a tall bookcase crammed with a colourful miscellany of books, and the fleshy green leaves of a rubber plant standing on a small polished table.

Inside, the air of spaciousness was confirmed. Clive had chosen antique furniture which lent elegance and dignity to the living room. The ceiling was high and moulded, and the walls papered in white and gilt. Her feet were noiseless on thick carpets. The only thing out of key was a television set in one corner, but its blank screen was discreetly hidden behind folding doors.

There were two bedrooms and a kitchen that was surprisingly large and modern, with a glass door leading out to a small lean-to conservatory adorned with flowering shrubs in pots and tiny barrels. The bathroom was clean and clinical in décor. Looking over the assortment of male toilet items on the glass shelf under the wall mirror she noticed something which had evidently been overlooked. It was a small gilt tube with a familiar device engraved in red on the side, and she immediately recognised it as a well known brand of lipstick. She made no comment, however, and Clive apparently had not noticed.

After the initial tour of inspection, she made coffee, and they sat for a while in the large living room exchanging reminiscences. Strange, she thought, how after three years there is really so little to talk about—or, rather, how few are the things one seems to have in common as a basis for amiable conversation. Here they were, the two of them, sitting at opposite sides of a spindly glass-topped table, engaging in polite superficial conversation like strangers who had just been introduced.

"The *Monitor* has always been recognised as having the finest foreign news coverage of any national newspaper," Clive was saying, smoking a cigarette in a faintly bored fashion. "Fortunately I realised that right at the start. A lot of the other staff correspondents didn't. That's how I finally got to be foreign editor. I was always determined to be a jump ahead of everybody else."

"I never knew you were so dedicated," she remarked.

"I'm not dedicated. Just single-minded when I happen to feel in the mood."

"You've done very well for yourself, Clive, whether dedicated or single-minded or both."

He shrugged. "I can do better. I'm not one for missing opportunity when it knocks. Take this Asiatic virus story, for instance. I've got a feeling it may be very important."

"For the *Monitor* or the new television job?"

He smiled. "For myself, in either capacity. Lucky thing I've got a wife in IVRO. You wouldn't believe how difficult it is to get reliable information out of official sources."

"I don't suppose I know much more than you do, darling."

"Don't be silly," he said, crushing the stub of his cigarette into a glass ashtray. "What do they pay you for? You must have come across this Chinese plague."

"A few cases."

"Well, then—what's the IVRO verdict on it?"

"I don't think they've reached a verdict as yet," she replied, eyeing him thoughtfully. "You know how it is with virus research. These things take time."

"I'm not interested in research—just the facts as they are. For one thing, I've heard that the death roll in China is already running into millions."

"You must make allowances for exaggeration and a certain amount of sensationalism," she pointed out. "I should have thought you could have obtained accurate figures from the Ministry of Health, or the World Health Organisation, or even IVRO itself."

He leaned forward, studying her with his sardonic grey eyes, lighting another cigarette. "It's a funny thing, Pauline—I can't get any hard facts from anyone. Not even you. We have a man in China, but his cables are chopped to pieces by the censor. No details—no statistics."

"Well, you know how difficult it is to get reliable information from China at the best of times."

"I know something else," he insisted. "There's a great deal of covering up going on. I'd like to know why there have been four emergency meetings of the Cabinet during the past week, and why the House of Commons only two days ago rushed through a Bill authorising the Government to spend one hundred million pounds over and above normal Budget estimates for special purposes, as they put it. And why there's a phoney cold-war scare about Russian troop movements and missile installations just the other side of the Iron Curtain when even our own correspondents in Eastern Europe say there's no truth in it."

"Clive, I really don't know what you're talking about," she said helplessly. "It's three years since I was last in England, so how can I possibly know what's happening in Parliament?"

He gave her a cynical, disbelieving smile that made his face seem oddly sour and distorted. "You're not trying to tell me that you don't really know what's going on, are you?"

She sipped her coffee guardedly. "I suppose I know *something* of what's going on, but I'm afraid it doesn't amount to much at present. When I left Tokyo the research unit was working on the Asiatic plague. It just happens to be a rather virulent and nasty epidemic bug which we haven't encountered before. The backroom boys are trying to find a vaccine or antibody, and they'll probably succeed in the next few weeks—and that's about all one can say."

"Pauline," he said, with a dogmatic air, "you sound just like any spokesman of the Ministry—understating and dodging the issue."

"Perhaps there's nothing to understate or dodge."

"I think there is, for one or two tiny reasons. With my usual proverbial luck I managed to find out from a drunken and indiscreet civil servant that the Ministry of Works has put out secret tenders for the construction of more than two thousand deep underground shelters and a like number of big incinerators all over the country. They're to be built on a crash priority basis during the next few weeks."

"Incinerators?" she queried.

"If you would like me to be more precise—crematoria. But I understand they're described officially as nuclear decontamination centres."

They looked at each other in strange silence for a moment, and then she stood up.

"I'll make some more coffee," she said.

*

In the early evening they went to a Chinese restaurant near Knightsbridge. The lighting was soft and diffused, and the food was good, and, perhaps under the charitable influence of the wine, she found herself mellowing to the man, the comparative stranger, who was her husband.

At an appropriate moment she said: "I like the flat, Clive. It's the kind of place I could really think of as home."

"It's not bad," he conceded.

"One tends to become rootless—living abroad, I mean."

He regarded her solemnly. "I thought that was the kind of life you liked, Pauline."

"It's the kind of life I've become accustomed to, whether I like it or not. It's just—well, living... in the way I live."

He made no comment, and they continued eating for a while.

Presently she said: "This television job, Clive—how imminent is it, if that's the word?"

"All I have to do is sign a contract. I could do it tonight if I felt so inclined, but, of course, I'd need to give three months' notice of resignation to the *Monitor*. That's a nuisance."

"At least it covers my holiday."

"Yes, I suppose it does."

"And after that I suppose you go to New York and I go back to Tokyo."

"That's something we need to discuss," he said, sipping the wine. "To tell the truth, Pauline, I achieved this new post by what you might call influence. If I may be frank..."

"Please do."

"Well, I was offered the job by the president of International Telerama Incorporated mainly because I happen to know his daughter very well."

Something began to smoulder coldly inside her. "I see. How old is... is this daughter?"

"Younger than you, my dear. She's an only child and her father is a millionaire. I don't want to sound cynical, Pauline, but I really do have a chance to pull the right strings and hit the jackpot."

She put down her fork and studied him intently. "Clive, are you asking me for a divorce?"

He contrived to smile in an apologetic way. "Technically, yes. There's nothing personal in this at all, and we both stand to benefit—financially, I mean. I'll make more than adequate provision for you. Let's face it, as things are you and I are hardly married at all, and a divorce wouldn't really make much difference..."

"Clive, what exactly are you trying to say—that you want to marry this woman for the sake of a well paid job and because she happens to be the daughter of a millionaire?"

"There's a little more to it than that."

"Are you in love with her?"

He pouted in an embarrassed manner. "If I knew precisely what love was I'd be able to answer that question. I like her very much. She fascinates me."

"Weren't you ever in love with me, Clive?"

"Yes," he admitted, sighing. "I suppose I was. Looking back, how can I know? Freud said that love is ninety per cent association. We were very close at the time, but since then the years have slipped by. The point is, Pauline, that we can't continue on this basis, living on opposite sides of the world and meeting three times in a decade for an emotional holiday. Frankly, it's immoral."

She smiled, but there was no humour in her heart. "Very immoral," she agreed. "The immorality of marriage, faithfulness and continence." After a brief pause she went on: "I assume you are involved in an *affaire* with this woman."

He nodded slowly, reluctantly. "What else could you expect in three years of separation? I admit liability and plead guilty. Three years is a long time."

"I was never unfaithful, Clive, not in three years—nor would I be in ten years."

"That has nothing to do with it, my dear. Men and women are different, thank God, and in any case this is more than just a casual *affaire*. It's a business proposition. As I see it, the future for both of us is one of separation, of what you might call platonic correspondence by air mail for years at a time. It's not fair to either you or me. Can't you see, it's not so much a question of unfaithfulness as of taking advantage of opportunity?"

"You were always very good at that, Clive."

"I don't blame you for being bitter and cynical," he said with a wry grin. "I'm not even trying to put up a defence. All I'm suggesting is that here is a chance to convert a dead marriage into money."

"What makes you think our marriage is dead?" she asked coldly, knowing, in fact, that it was already dead and buried. "You're not giving me a chance."

"A chance of what?"

"To replan our lives, perhaps. We were happy enough together at one time." She hesitated, thinking. "I could even resign my post with IVRO and settle down to being a good wife—and perhaps eventually a good mother."

"Settle down," he echoed. "Is that what you want to do?"

"I think so, if I could be sure that you were capable of doing the same. The point is, Clive, I'm not prepared to surrender unconditionally."

He reached across the table and touched her hand. "I wouldn't want you to do anything of the sort, Pauline, and I wouldn't respect you if you did." He smiled at her in a kind of sympathetic communion which was largely one-sided, she thought; there was even a hint of smugness in his expression. "We're both intelligent people," he went on smoothly. "I suppose neither of us is really the settling kind. Frankly, I never did understand women who are prepared to humiliate themselves in order to preserve the structure of a marriage that has already crumbled."

"I don't wish to preserve something that is dead, Clive," she said, "but I do want to be sure that it *is* dead. It's so difficult to know when to take you seriously."

"What on earth do you mean by that?"

"Just that I think sometimes you don't even know your own mind. Or rather, if you do, it's a case of what's good for Clive Brant is good for everybody—but it's not always true, you know."

She looked at him with a certain melancholy regret and went on: "While I'm in London for a few weeks, can't we see if we can pick up where we left off? Isn't it worth a try?"

He shook his head wearily. "I'm already committed, Pauline, for better or for worse, but I have great faith in my luck. I think, perhaps, I'm a gambler at heart. There must be a guardian angel looking after me, determining the conditions of my future..."

"We all have our guardian angels," she said bitterly, "for better or for worse. You're a self-centred fool, Clive. The trouble is I still love you."

He looked slightly sheepish and put out. "I don't see how one can love somebody one hasn't seen for three years. It's not human."

"In that case I'm not human."

His expression became more embarrassed. "Can't we be adult and sensible about this, Pauline?"

She took a handkerchief from her bag to dab briefly at her eyes. There were no tears—only the threat of tears.

"It's all right," she said. "You can't expect me to feel cold-blooded about it, but I love you enough to let you have things the way you want them. I think one day you will live to regret it. I'm selfish enough to hope you will."

"Perhaps I will," he admitted, "but one has to take life as it comes. One has to be practical."

"Practical Clive," she said, nodding. "I suppose you realise that I can't possibly stay here in the flat as your wife. That's a very practical point."

"You don't have to," he said, recovering his self-composure. "I've already booked a room in a hotel for you in the Kensington area."

"I see." There was an edge of anger to her voice now. "You really have got it all cut and dried, haven't you?"

"Practical Clive, as you've just said," he remarked.

"I only wish you'd told me about this before. I wouldn't have bothered to come back. My God... when I think of it—at the time they needed me out there..."

He looked at her with a certain melancholy regret. "I couldn't have put it in writing, Pauline—not in a letter. I thought it would be better to talk about it face to face."

"That was very considerate of you, Clive."

He acknowledged the irony of her voice with a rueful grin. "I may be a bit of a bastard, but I do have some principles, you know." He signalled the waiter for more coffee.

"Divorce is always a painful business," he went on. "It's nice to be able to discuss it in a reasonable fashion."

Her resentment sharpened and smouldered. "Yes, Clive, it is nice—*so* nice. To be able to commit adultery and enjoy a free and easy mind, knowing that your wife will be sweet and reasonable and say, 'Of course, darling, if you want to go off with another woman whose father owns a television network, then it's all right by me.' If we could all behave irresponsibly and cast aside decency and duty it would be a wonderful world. We could all do just what the hell we liked!"

"I've already pleaded guilty," he said resentfully. "I'm not trying to make excuses or put up a defence. I'm prepared to admit that it's all my fault, the whole rotten business. All I'm saying is—it would simplify matters for all of us in the long run if you would divorce me."

The waiter brought the coffee and cleared away the plates. For a while there was silence. Clive lit a cigarette and stared pensively at the tablecloth.

As soon as the waiter had gone, she said: "Who is this woman you want to marry?"

"Nobody you know. Her name is Noelle Langstrom."

"How old is she?"

He spread out his hands. "Does it matter?"

"I like to know how strong the opposition is."

"It's not a question of opposition, Pauline, but rather of readjusting the lives of three people."

She laughed tersely, with irony. "How simple you make it sound, Clive. Supposing I don't want to be readjusted. Supposing I choose to stay married and condone the adultery..."

"That would make things rather difficult. In the course of time you might choose to divorce me for other reasons. I can wait."

"I need time to think. After all, we haven't seen each other for nearly three years. We're practically strangers."

"That," he said grimly, "is precisely the trouble."

Later that night she moved into the hotel. The resentment had faded into a morose blankness that hindered logical thought. This was the shadow that had fallen across Clive's letters over the past year, and although the ultimatum had come as no great surprise, it was nevertheless a shock. But like most shocks it contained its own anaesthetising quality that produced a welcome temporary numbness.

Undressing for bed, she looked at herself in the full-length mirror of the wardrobe. I'm still attractive enough, she thought, and young enough at thirty-one, and I have the right kind of figure to wear pretty clothes. Perhaps I married too late, and perhaps I spent too much of my early life in academic study. Certainly a career woman must be difficult to live with, particularly when she's married to a career man. Or perhaps the fault lies in those long years of separation.

I don't think we failed each other in the early days, she told herself. All the same, something was lacking. The love we had was not strong enough to survive the barrier of time and space.

And when you came down to fundamentals, that was the essence of the thing. One could not conduct a marriage by remote control, on a kind of business basis, with husband and wife acting as associated companies in an international merger and holding a board meeting every three years. It couldn't work.

On the other hand, she thought, if I had resigned my job and returned to London with Clive when he was recalled two years ago, the same thing might have happened in just the same way, but with more subterfuge and deceit. That would have been harder to bear.

At least I am left with a sense of independence, she thought, and the humiliation is not so bad as it might have been. I suppose the marriage certificate was already perforated when we got it, and all we have to do now is tear along the dotted line.

"Clive, the hollow man," she said aloud to herself. Some men are like that, she decided—full of charm in a boyish way, with not a malicious thought in their handsome heads, but in a way the con men of the world, single-minded and open-minded at the same time, for whom human relationships are temporary, to be exploited for what they are worth, always meaning well and willing to take the blame for the relationships that don't work out. Men without feeling or remorse, but perhaps sincere enough in their own superficial way.

Feeling more satisfied, she went to bed, but nevertheless she slept restlessly and awoke next morning still tired and despondent.

CHAPTER THREE

THE VIRUS RESEARCH CENTRE AT BRIERLEY TOOK THE FORM of a long brick and glass building partly screened by a low wall bordering the main road to Hatfield. It resembled a small factory crossed with a large greenhouse. Despite its relatively open position it proved difficult to locate, Pauline discovered, because it was flanked by other industrial buildings of similar pattern, and the identifying sign-board was by no means prominent.

After she had paid the cab driver she pushed her way through the double glass door of the main entrance. Two minutes later she was in the office of Dr. Charles Youde, the director of research at the Centre. Youde was a tall, gangling man with thick grey hair swept straight back from a pair of formidable concave glasses. His whispering voice and effete manner were in direct contrast to the alertness of his blue eyes.

"Delighted, Dr. Brant," he murmured with evident enthusiasm, ushering her into an uncomfortable chair. Indeed, the whole office was uncomfortable in its formal austerity, with rectangular, upright furniture and filing cabinets, faded books leaning against each other on varnished shelves, and a general décor of brown, dark green and lifeless grey.

"I was hoping you might find time to look in," Youde added.

She had more time on her hands than he could possibly imagine, but she merely asked a formal question. "Were the samples in good condition?"

"Excellent. We're working on them now—not that we expect to find anything new, you understand. Just for confirmation."

He sniffed and rubbed the back of his hand across his nose. "It's the very devil—this Hueste virus, I mean. All we can do at the moment are blood group reaction tests, and, of course, there's the hen fruit side."

"Hen fruit?"

He smiled apologetically. "A house joke, as you might say. We're using eggs to produce virus cultures, but the bug is proving recalcitrant, I'm afraid. It seems to prefer human blood."

"What are the chances of beating the virus, Dr. Youde?"

"Excellent." He chuckled for no apparent reason. "Given six months—perhaps a year. In that time we may possibly develop a vaccine capable of providing complete immunity. Of course, it will probably take another six months to mass-produce it in any quantity. Say, eighteen months, taking everything into consideration."

She was well aware of the sardonic undertones of his voice, and it seemed to her that she was merely stating the obvious when she said: "All the indications are that it will spread round the entire world in the course of a few weeks."

"Of course it will. We're doing what we can, but we can't perform miracles to order."

She considered for a moment. "If the virus reaches this country, as seems likely, within the next few weeks, and if we have not succeeded in producing a prophylactic vaccine in the time available, what will happen?"

"You mean, how many people will die?"

"Well, yes."

His answer was precise enough. "About thirty million."

She sighed, unable to visualise the figure in practical terms. "Thirty million in just a few weeks?"

"Yes."

"How does one dispose of so many dead bodies in such a short space of time?"

"That is a matter for the Government and local authorities. What did the Chinese do?"

"It's difficult to be sure. There were stories of incinerators and acid pits, but I was never able to differentiate between fact and rumour."

There was an interval of silence while he lit an old battered pipe with a sputtering match. She turned things over in her mind, sensing the darker, serious depths beneath his apparently casual and unconcerned manner.

Presently she said: "This figure of thirty million—how did you arrive at it?"

"As a matter of fact, it was something of an exaggeration. The true figure will probably be nearer twenty-six million—about half the population of the United Kingdom."

"Why?"

"It has to do with the structure of the virus, but I feel sure Dr. Vincent could explain it to you much more clearly than myself. I think, perhaps, I ought to introduce you to Vincent at this point. He's our protein chemistry expert and he knows a great deal about the architecture of the Hueste virus."

He put his pipe carefully on the desk and walked towards the door. "If you would care to come with me, Dr. Brant."

He led the way along a corridor, through a white and chrome laboratory, and then via another corridor to a small glass-walled office. She found herself face-to-face with a dark-haired man in a white coat that was grubby round the collar and stained with coloured fluids and reagents, taller than herself, but not too tall, of wiry build with a lean relaxed appearance.

Youde introduced her to him, mumbled something about the molecular structure of the Hueste virus by way of an opening gambit, then said he had work to do and excused himself. Dr. Vincent promptly produced a packet of cigarettes with a laconic air and offered her one. They lit up together. Somewhere remote a centrifuge whined plaintively.

"I hope I'm not interfering with your work," she said apologetically. "The fact is I'm on vacation from the Tokyo Centre, but I thought I might be able to help in some way."

"I'm sure you might," he said, but there was an air of cynicism in his voice. "How is Tokyo?"

"A sort of poor man's New York."

"And the death rate?"

"Increasing, I'm afraid."

He shrugged. "The Japanese islands were always over-populated. Nature has her own methods of preserving the balance of power among her creatures."

"Does that apply to the rest of the world?"

"Why not? We're all homo sapiens. Occasionally we get taken for a ride by nature, just to put us in our humble place. This is one of those occasions."

"Isn't there anything we can do about it, with all our science and technology?"

He paused, as if to consider his words. "Yes, Dr. Brant, there's something we can do immediately to very good effect." He glanced briefly at his wristwatch. "It is now almost twelve-thirty and we can have lunch together. I know a good pub about two miles down the road where they dish up a thick juicy steak at a working man's price. Do you feel hungry?"

She regarded him amiably. "It's a long time since I had

lunch with a working man, and come to think of it I am rather hungry."

"In that case, let's go," he said, throwing off his white coat and slinging it over a chair.

"Thank you, Dr. Vincent."

"You can call me Vince," he said, opening the door for her. "Everyone else does."

"All right, Vince," she said, warming to him. "In that case, I'm Pauline."

"One of my favourite names," he remarked.

They went out of the building into the forecourt, where he escorted her to an antiquated but immense car.

"Ermintrude," he announced, patting the square bonnet affectionately. "Another of my favourite names. She's old, but reliable. Sometimes does as much as thirty going down a hill."

In fact, Ermintrude proved to be a fast and comfortable car, with a quiet engine and an adequate surge of acceleration.

"She does five miles to the gallon," Vince commented. "Nothing is gained without sacrifice."

It was a big roadside pub with a swinging sign that announced: *The Traveller's Rest*. They went into a spacious lounge bar, where he ordered whiskies and food.

They sat at opposite sides of a small round table, sipping their drinks.

"According to Dr. Youde, you are going to tell me about the molecular structure of the Hueste virus," she said.

He grinned and shook his head. "At this time of day and in this environment the Hueste virus is faintly obscene."

"Obscene or not, we shall soon have to face up to it in all environments at all times of the day and night."

"True," he admitted, raising his glass. "Here's to survival, anyway. The toss of a coin."

"Meaning?"

"It's a reasonable chance—fifty-fifty."

"I'm afraid I'm not up to date on the research side. I've been mainly concerned with the clinical aspects of the virus—syndromes, pathology and so on."

"You're lucky, Pauline," he observed. "I wish I'd had a chance to see it in action. Quite different from analysing blood specimens and fragments of refrigerated brain and liver. One tends to become impersonal about it."

"It's difficult not to be impersonal, anyway. The thing acts with such finality, and once the coma begins…"

"Have you ever known a patient recover from the coma, even for a few seconds?"

"Never."

"How would *you* diagnose a typical virus case?"

She reflected for a moment. "Only by the death symptoms—unconsciousness, temperature rising above one hundred and five, dry skin with grey discoloration. Towards the end there is a pronounced condition of epithelial oedema which makes the skin appear swollen and glossy. At that stage death is only an hour or two away."

"We know that the virus attacks cell tissues," he said. "That accounts for the oedema. As the cells break down the skin becomes turgid with fluid and serum. But the real damage is done long before, when the virus breaks down the meningeal tissue and outer cortex of the brain. That is the point of coma—and the point of no return. Even if one could destroy the virus at that moment, the patient would still die—or remain in a coma for the rest of his life."

She eyed him thoughtfully, her mind suddenly far away. "At Tanhai hospital, just as I left Tokyo, they were keeping a virus fatality for observation after death. I didn't see the body myself, but Dr. Woolner told me that after five days the flesh was almost completely liquified. All that was left was a rather clean skeleton lying in a pool of thick, grey sludge."

"Enchanting," he remarked. "I think that calls for another drink." He refilled the glasses and announced that food would be ready in five minutes.

"No more shop talk," he said. "Tell me about yourself."

"There's really nothing to tell, Vince."

"Married?"

She smiled wryly. "Past tense, I think—or perhaps future imperfect."

"Bad luck. What does your husband do for a living?"

"He's a journalist."

He nodded. "I can appreciate the basic conflict. Doctors and journalists don't go well together."

"I can't really understand why."

"Simple enough. They're both jobs demanding single-minded dedication. Journalists and doctors should marry simple, undedicated people. Few marriages can cope with two careers."

"Are you talking from experience?"

His expression became rueful and defensive. "I haven't reached the divorce stage yet. I see my wife occasionally on an astringently platonic basis, but we live apart."

"She's a career woman, too?"

"Unfortunately. She's a writer. Does adaptations for television and radio, and so on. She has a small flat in Chelsea and is deeply involved with the cravat and long-haired set. By pounding a typewriter occasionally she makes more money than I do, and with much less effort."

"Why do people behave so perversely?" she asked, sighing deeply. "It seems to me that there are no standards left in the world any more."

"There's more freedom, and a looser moral climate," he said. "People behave as they want to behave—and, after all, what are standards? One tends to think of standards as some kind of arbitrary code of behaviour imposed by society, but it isn't so at all. Standards are strictly personal. We all try to justify our actions, however illegal or immoral they may be, and every justification becomes a standard on its own level."

"Certainly there's a conflict between human behaviour and the law," she agreed. "I suppose if people accepted the standards and conventions imposed by society there would be no need for laws at all."

"Society does not impose anything," he pointed out. "One can behave as one chooses, but there are certain penalties for antisocial behaviour. Society can penalise it, but cannot prevent it."

"You're taking a rather pessimistic view."

He finished his drink and shrugged. "In fact, Pauline, I'm an optimist at heart. There's good and bad in all of us, and I like to think that the good wins out in the end. But standards are always changing, from year to year, and sometimes from day to day. In a crisis most of us would find out just how flexible standards can be. Take the Hueste virus, for instance…"

He was not able to pursue his theme, for a call from the bar announced that the food was ready. Vince collected it and brought it over on a tray. Steak and chips and peas, with mustard. Simple and unimaginative, but hot and appetising.

They abandoned the confusing ethics of living and concentrated on the more immediate matter of nourishment.

After lunch Pauline went back to the Research Centre with Dr. Vincent and spent an hour wandering round, observing the organisation and the work in progress. Despite an abundance of equipment, a surfeit of staff and a pervading atmosphere of efficiency, there seemed to be little sense of urgency. It was understandable, of course; the Hueste virus was still many thousands of miles away, and one could afford to follow routine procedure in a methodical, matter-of-fact way.

In the basement of the building was a small cinema, with a screen four feet by three and a tiny projection box. Dr. Vincent arranged for the showing of some short lengths of film and a number of slides illustrating various aspects of the virus research programme, including pictures taken with the aid of an electron microscope. The virus itself was so small as to be at the limit of visual resolution, and only by peering intently at the screen could one distinguish a cluster of ovoid cells, apparently featureless, looking rather like a cargo of elongated eggs spread across a black floor.

Sitting in the darkness, watching the slides, Vince said: "Each cell has a distinctive protein structure in molecular terms, probably based on the DNA spiral, but lop-sided in an odd way, as if part of the structure had been obliterated. That is, incidentally, the basis of Hueste's radioactive mutation theory."

"Logical enough," she agreed.

"I think Hueste is almost certainly right. We know these mutations are going on all the time due to radioactive particles in the air. Fortunately the vast majority of mutant strains simply fail to survive, or can't perpetuate themselves. The interesting thing is that in this case the virus exists in two isomeric forms. One kind of cell is a mirror image of the other, with the lop-sidedness reversed, as it were."

"Have you found an explanation for it?"

"We think so. Making a statistical count, we discovered that both types of virus cell are equally prevalent. Basically the cell has an 'AB' structure—that's purely a coding convention. What happens is that when reproducing itself the cell divides into two isomeric cells, one an AB type and the other a BA type."

"Is that important?" she asked, wondering how such abstract research into the basic composition of the virus could help to prevent the spread of the killer plague.

"It happens to be vitally important—for one simple reason. You see, the AB virus is lethal, while the BA type is quite harmless. And what is more, the BA type infection will confer immunity against the AB type."

She stared at him in the semi-darkness of the cinema. "In that case, why can't we arrange to infect everybody with the BA virus to make them immune against the AB type?"

"It's not so simple. For one thing, you can't cultivate a virus in an inanimate medium. It will only reproduce in living matter."

"I know that, Vince."

"So we're using live eggs as a medium, but this particular virus has an extremely strong cytopathogenic action. It destroys the surface membrane of all living cells. Every time we get to the stage of establishing a living virus culture, the egg dissolves and dies."

"But surely not with the BA type?"

"There's no way of differentiating. Even if you start with a pure BA strain, the moment it begins to reproduce it breaks down into isomeric BA and AB types and, of course, you're back where you started—with the lethal AB."

"But if the BA type gives immunity…"

"That's the tricky part. It does to the individual, but he then acts as an AB carrier. The mechanism of the thing, so far as we understand it, is that the infecting virus, whether AB or BA, is absorbed into the tissues of the body. But in reproducing it splits into isomers, and the body becomes the carrier of the opposite isomer to the one which started the infection."

She considered this for a moment. "You mean that the AB patient—that is, the one who will die—becomes a harmless BA carrier, and vice versa."

"Just so."

"In that case, since the AB victims die very quickly and the BA cases survive, surely the lethal AB type must gain the upper hand in time, because there will be more and more carriers around."

"One would think so, but in fact the infectious phase of the virus only lasts about ten days. After that time the carrier ceases to be a carrier. The virus gives up, as it were. In addition, the sheer virulence of the thing has a levelling-off effect. Statistically, in any large group of people, approximately half will contract AB virus and the other half BA—which means that half will die and the other half will survive to become AB carriers for two weeks. It's a vicious circle."

"You mean that if this epidemic spreads throughout the world, half of humanity will die."

"I'm afraid so."

"But why can't we isolate the BA patients who are carriers of the lethal AB. Perhaps quarantine them for two or three weeks?"

"Because the mild BA infection is difficult to recognise and diagnose," he explained. "The symptoms are slight—a transient fever, temperature rising to about one hundred for an hour or two, and perhaps a headache. That's all. Without complex laboratory tests on blood samples, diagnosis is virtually impossible."

"Then there's nothing we can do about it."

"Well, we're doing all we can, Pauline, and that's precious little. Cures and prophylactics for virus disease usually take years of patient research. The Americans are working on the mutation theory—that is, they are bombarding samples of Hueste virus with hard radiation in the hope of creating a stable BA type which will form the basis of an immunising vaccine. It's all highly speculative, and there's always the possibility that a vaccine might have undesirable effects, perhaps lethal, on people who had unknowingly contracted BA infection. In other words, there might be trouble with antibodies, rather like the Rhesus reaction in blood groups. We're still working very much in the dark."

They saw the last of the slides and left the cinema, returning to Dr. Vincent's office. He lit a cigarette and smiled at her gloomy expression.

"Cheer up, Pauline," he said, patting her cheek gently. "It's a fifty-fifty chance for each of us. If we keep our fingers crossed we might achieve a breakthrough before the damned bug reaches this country. Meanwhile, to get down to more important matters, will you have dinner with me tonight?"

"Have you considered, Vince," she said with due solemnity, "that I may be a virus carrier myself? After all, I have been in close contact with AB cases in Tokyo."

"We estimate the incubation period at around ten hours. If you haven't had a temperature since you left Japan…"

"No." She smiled, and regarded him archly. "In which case I'll be glad to join you for dinner."

"It's a date," he said.

Later she called in Dr. Youde's office to make an official request for a job. He stroked his thick grey hair and peered at her through his concave glasses.

"It's rather irregular, Dr. Brant," he said, with a hint of apology in his voice. "I mean, the fact that you are on official vacation. I don't think the IVRO executive would be willing to grant any additional remuneration other than, say, a small *ex gratia* payment just as a token."

"I'm not asking for additional pay," she said. "The fact is I didn't particularly want to take this holiday at all—not at the present time. If I could do something in a voluntary capacity, perhaps on a part-time basis."

He pulled a sheet of blank paper across the desk and began to doodle on it with a ball pen.

"I'm sure we can arrange something, though at this stage it would be largely routine. Classifying blood groups and clinical samples, for instance, and perhaps making some cytological tests."

"That would be excellent, Dr. Youde."

"Later, of course, when things begin to warm up, there will probably be a great deal of liaison work with the evacuation centres. That's where your field experience in Tokyo will be most useful."

"Evacuation centres?" she echoed questioningly.

He opened his mouth to speak, hesitated, then smiled in slight embarrassment. "I'm afraid I mentioned the unmentionable, Dr. Brant. I trust I can rely on your discretion to repeat nothing, absolutely nothing, that you may hear casually during your visits to

Brierley. There's a great deal of precautionary work going on behind the scenes, and most of it is under a strict security embargo. Obviously the Government has to take steps to prepare for the coming emergency."

"You mean—disposal of the dead, for example…"

"That will certainly be one of the major problems when you consider that the normal death rate in the United Kingdom is around three hundred thousand people a year. When the virus strikes we anticipate that some thirty million will die in roughly a month—equivalent to the rate of three hundred and sixty million in a year."

"I hadn't quite thought of it in that way," she admitted, "but I do realise the size of the problem. In China…"

"I don't think we need worry about China," he interrupted. "By the time the virus reaches us the Chinese crisis will be well and truly over, and the immediate task facing the Government will be how best to dispose of some two million tons of dead bodies in an orderly and sanitary way. Then there's the vast financial poser of insurance. The liability of the insurance companies could amount to several thousand million pounds during the period of the crisis."

"But, surely, if the Government takes over responsibility for disposal of the dead there won't be any need for death payments…"

"It will require legislation. I imagine the Government will rule by decree during the crisis, anyway."

She stared at him thoughtfully for a moment. "This statistical business—just how accurate is it?"

"I don't quite follow you, Dr. Brant."

"I mean the AB and BA business. Theoretically every other person must die, but that doesn't necessarily mean one in two in a small group of people."

He adjusted his glasses and leaned back in his chair. It was evident that for Dr. Youde the impending Hueste epidemic possessed much of the abstract intellectual interest of a cleverly compiled crossword puzzle, and held the promise of absorbing figures and statistics in which the entire human tragedy could be crystallised and analysed. In a way he reflected the attitude of IVRO itself, objective and dispassionate, collecting data and specimens, methodically carrying on routine experimental work in virology as if it were an academic exercise not immediately related to matters of human survival. Research always tended to be like that, she realised. Beyond the laboratory walls the world was a remote place that seemed to have little substantive existence, and reality was under the tiny cover slips on the glass microscope slides. That was where the true struggle was taking place; until the life and death of the almost invisible virus cells was fully understood, the life and death of humanity ravaged by those same virus cells was almost an irrelevant side effect.

Youde said: "The statistics apply on a mass basis. In a group of, say, a million people, half a million will die, plus or minus a dozen or so. When you come down to smaller groups the equation is much more uncertain." He tapped his fingers ruminatively on the desk. "In a group of a hundred people the death rate might vary between forty and sixty. Among ten, the limits would be wider—from three to seven, perhaps. Among five people, all might die or none. But in the mass, you understand, the figures will average out—it will be one in two as near as makes no difference."

She sighed. "I suppose all we can do, any of us, is keep our fingers crossed and hope we catch the innocuous BA infection."

His lips narrowed into an enigmatic smile. "There are other things we can do, too. The virus will come and go over a period of six to ten weeks, and after it has gone there will be no further danger. It is by no means impossible to seal oneself off from the world and from infection for a few weeks. One would need a supply of food and sterilised water, of course, and the air would have to be filtered or reconditioned in some way."

"I suppose that's a possibility."

"I would regard it as more of a probability. However, we shall see in due course."

He stood up, wiped his glasses, and came round to the front of the desk.

"What's the use of speculating?" he asked. "We are all very ignorant, and the future is anybody's guess. Do let me assure you, Dr. Brant, that if you really wish to work with us during your vacation, you will be more than welcome."

"There are very good reasons why I should prefer to work," she said.

"In that case you are at my service." He chuckled genteelly at his witticism. "If you could allow me a day or two in which to work something out for you…"

"Of course. I'll come back in two days, Dr. Youde."

"Excellent."

She took her leave and made her way back to London and the hotel.

CHAPTER FOUR

WITHIN A WEEK THINGS BEGAN TO HAPPEN IN AND AROUND London, and elsewhere throughout the country. The bigger parks were arbitrarily closed to the public while, almost overnight, giant earth-moving machines and teams of men moved in, setting up generators and floodlights and building temporary camps of wood and asbestos huts so that work could continue on a shift basis round the clock. Similar manoeuvres were taking place in other towns and in certain rural areas, and soon an army of excavators and bulldozers was hard at work, scooping enormous holes in Britain's subsoil.

While the machines were digging, other gangs of men were erecting prefabricated buildings in secluded parts of the country-side—buildings with high brick walls and tall chimneys. Some of the trucks bringing supplies and materials were loaded with what appeared to be great rectangular steel tanks, but they were always well shrouded by tarpaulins so that it was difficult for the casual observer to attempt to guess their purpose.

To Clive Brant, witnessing these unexplained events from the news centre of the *Daily Monitor*, it seemed that an enormous deployment of manpower, machines and materials was being carried out with all the ruthless efficiency of a major military operation, and with much the same kind of secrecy. On the surface the explanation was obvious enough, although there had been no official statement: at last the Government had decided to do something practical about atom-proof shelters and decontamina-tion centres in the event of a nuclear war. Nobody really believed that such a war was either imminent or even possible, but it was thought that the Government had decided on a policy of taking a number of practical defensive measures on the principle that it was better to be prepared before the event than to be caught napping after it.

Meanwhile the news agency wires continued to bring in reports of alleged missile activity in Eastern Europe, and the Soviet press carried similar stories of suspected American missile consolidation in Britain and Western Europe. Of the progress of the Hueste virus there was little mention. In Japan a state of emergency had been declared and a tight censorship was now in operation. It was known that the virus had spread into Malaya and parts of Siberia, and also the western seaboard of the United States, but hardly any factual information was available.

Clive found himself becoming rather perplexed by the increasing degree of inconsistency in news reports and cabled stories from foreign correspondents, and having to face critical questioning from the news editor of the paper, a small, wiry man named McAllan who claimed to have spent nearly forty years of his life in journalism. Certainly McAllan knew his job, but he was an intense, dedicated individual who had little to say, and when he said it invariably succeeded in ruffling his audience.

There was a minor row, for instance, over Thomson's wire from Singapore. To evade local censorship Thomson had telephoned his report to Macey in Calcutta, who in turn had cabled Wyatt in Cairo, and so, by a devious route, although admittedly at third hand, the story had finally reached London without cuts.

After vetting the wire, Clive had passed it to McAllan as a legitimate news story. Ten minutes later the intercom buzzed on his desk. He pressed a switch.

"Mac here," said McAllan's astringent voice. "That Singapore wire—I don't like it."

"Thomson's a good man," Clive pointed out.

"Thomson, Macey, Wyatt—they're all good men. But what we've got is a report of a report of a report. Besides, it conflicts with other reports which have official corroboration. I think we'd better talk about it, Clive."

"I'll be right in," Clive said.

McAllan in effect ran the paper. It was he who decided whether a story rated as news or not, whether it would be written big or played down, whether reporters would follow it up, whether it would justify a tie-up feature, whether it was front-page, inside-page or diary material. His superiors—the editor, the managing editor and the editorial director—were mainly concerned with broad policy matters, and occasionally politics. Perhaps McAllan's greatest virtue and asset was an instinct for accuracy; he was a stickler for the facts. An inaccurate fact wasn't a fact at all, it was a lie, he would frequently tell reporters who had failed to check some apparently insignificant detail in their stories.

He was chain-smoking menthol cigarettes as usual as Clive went into the office, which adjoined the newsroom. A large glass ashtray on the massive, battered desk contained at least fifty stubs, and by the end of the day it would be nearer a hundred, but McAllan's salary could sustain the expense. In any case, what he spent on cigarettes he saved to some extent on food, and he had never been known to drink anything stronger than a cold lager on a hot day.

McAllan, in shirt sleeves and braces, leaned back in his chair and frowned at Clive across the paper-strewn desk. He picked up a sheaf of stapled teletypes and riffled through them.

"Two thousand tents," he said, quoting flatly from the report. "Patients stacked on wooden shelves mounted on steel racks. Lime pits for disposal of the dead… and not only the dead."

"I know it sounds fantastic," Clive admitted, "but after all, it's an eye-witness report, and Thomson is a reliable man."

"This isn't Thomson writing. It's Wyatt in Cairo interpreting a wire from Macey in Calcutta interpreting a phone call from Thomson in Singapore."

"I still think it has the ring of truth," Clive insisted. "By European standards it couldn't happen that way, perhaps, but in the East things are rather different—there's an attitude of fatalism, for one thing. It seems logical enough to me that they might consider a comatose patient who has no chance of recovery dead enough to be thrown into a lime pit."

"Have you checked with IVRO and the Ministry?"

"Yes. They both say they have no information on the subject— but they don't positively deny it."

"I don't like it," McAllan reiterated. "Thomson quotes a death roll of over one hundred thousand already. What do the Ministry say?"

"Just under three thousand."

McAllan grimaced and scratched his chin in uncertainty.

"After all, it *is* an eye-witness report," Clive pointed out.

McAllan struck the desk with the palm of his hand. "I don't give a damn if it's an eye-witness report or not. All that concerns me is whether it's true. The only possibility is a negative story—the Ministry deny that living patients are being thrown into lime pits in Singapore—and I don't like negative stories because they're bad journalism. A journalist's job is to present the facts, not publish denials of rumours and allegations."

"I could telephone Thomson direct for verification," Clive suggested.

"You mean verification of Wyatt's report from Cairo."

Clive grinned wryly. "At least he could confirm or deny the facts and figures before the censor cut him off."

"All right," McAllan said. "Phone him now, will you? We can't afford to waste time on this story. If it's true, it's important."

Clive telephoned Singapore within the hour. Mr. Thomson had taken ill very suddenly, they said. He was now in hospital. They were sorry, but they did not know which hospital. Was it the virus? How could they possibly know? He was ill, and beyond that they had no further information.

He hung up with a sense of foreboding and reported back to McAllan.

"I rather think we've lost our man in Singapore," he announced. "He's in hospital. Probably the virus."

"Damn!" said McAllan, spreading his stubby fingers over the blotter on his desk. "In that case I think we'd better forget about the whole thing. It's too risky."

An idea occurred to Clive—an idea with exciting possibilities and distinct personal advantages, if it could be put over in the right way. "Look, Mac," he said. "The way censorship is tightening up on the virus situation we're not likely ever to get a story we can print—outside of official handouts. We've got more than enough competent correspondents out East, but they're not allowed to communicate without using subterfuge. Seems to me the only way to get a true picture of the situation in Singapore is for someone to fly out there and take a look around for himself."

"Are you volunteering for the job?" McAllan asked, frowning.

Clive shrugged. "I know the area and I've got a lot of contacts. Don't forget that my wife has worked with IVRO in the Far East for some years."

"You realise there's a personal risk involved."

"It's a risk we'll all be facing sooner or later. Funny thing, I was a war correspondent at one time and somehow I lacked the imagination to think of personal risk."

"It might be a good idea," McAllan said, "but it's not for me to decide. Better have a word with Wardale first. Tell him that as foreign editor you think it would be a good move to spend a few days in the Far East to assess the local situation at first hand. I'll back you up if necessary."

"I'll do that right away," Clive said gratefully.

Wardale, who was the editor, proved to be lukewarm on the project. "For one thing, Brant," he said, adjusting his rimless glasses, "we know that censorship is in force in the virus areas, and we also know that the British Government supports the censorship on policy grounds. In fact, we've had a directive from the Ministry asking for our co-operation—not only us, but the press generally. And there are stringent travel restrictions in force in the East. You may find yourself unable to move outside the airport buildings, wherever you land."

"There are a few strings I can pull," Clive said. "My wife is a qualified virologist with IVRO, and I've got connections on that side. In any case, I've got a good reason for wanting to see our Singapore correspondent, Thomson, if he's still alive and conscious."

"Yes, yes," Wardale put in hurriedly. "I've no doubt you will be able to pull the right strings and perhaps see the right people, though it may not be so easy as you imagine. My point is that even if you came back with a major front-page story based on first-hand observation, we might not be able to print it. The Ministry want us to clear all virus stories with them before publishing, which means in effect that for the present we're restricted to official handouts."

"You mean that censorship is already in operation in this country?"

"I'm afraid so, though not officially. It's not just a question of Singapore. Other things are going on behind a security screen. The deep atom shelters and the decontamination centres for radioactivity—you'll hardly find a reference to them at all in any newspaper. You yourself see only one aspect of the news, namely, the foreign side which has generally been censored at the point of origin. McAllan acts as a selective filter, but he doesn't fully realise the developments that are taking place behind the news. He's a good fact man, which means that a fact from an official source carries more weight than an alleged fact from a distant correspondent. Thomson is probably right about Singapore, but his story conflicts with other reports put out by Government departments and official organisations such as IVRO. Our policy is quite clear—we pay lip service to authority in the best interests of society generally."

"So you don't think I ought to go to Singapore?" Clive asked.

Wardale eyed him steadily. "I think perhaps you should go, not because it will give us a story which we can't use, but because it may be our last opportunity to send a staff man abroad before communications close down altogether. It will also provide us with valuable background information against which we can assess and balance the official news releases. Yes, Brant, you can go."

Clive played his final card. "Thank you, Mr. Wardale. It occurred to me that while I'm in the Far East I might as well look in on Tokyo and the west coast of America, where they have virus trouble too."

"Why not? On the other hand, remember that we're running a newspaper, not a travel agency."

"Quite. What I have in mind is a brief series of quick stopovers at key points in the virus area, probably taking about four days. It would probably be simpler to make a round trip, flying back via New York. That way I could also pick up something of the climate of public opinion in the US where the virus is concerned."

"All right, Brant," Wardale said amiably. "As you wish. Best of luck."

That same evening Clive telephoned New York.

"Long time, no see, darling," Noelle Langstrom said in her quiet American voice.

"Too long," said Clive, "but I've got good news. I'll be seeing you in a few days."

"But, Clive, that's wonderful. How come?"

"I'm flying to Singapore—tomorrow if I can get a reservation. It's a follow-up on the Hueste virus story. After that I'm moving on to Tokyo, San Francisco and New York. I should be able to spend a day and a night with you, depending on the timetable."

"You may run into trouble at Tokyo, Clive. So far as I know there's no in or out traffic at all apart from high priority stuff and mail."

"I believe," he said, trying to remember the exact details of the air embargo, "that the airport is open for refuelling and so on, but passengers are not allowed to disembark. On the other hand they may make a special concession for a journalist."

"Not with censorship the way it is."

"Well, it's worth a try, anyway. I've got to produce results of some sort to justify the trip."

"Have you signed daddy's contract yet?"

"No, but I will very soon. I'm just getting things sorted out—principally the question of divorce."

"Won't she co-operate?"

"Yes, given time. I'm not in a position to force the issue. It might do more harm than good."

The girl sighed audibly into the telephone. "Please don't stall for too long, darling. Daddy's almost ready to start operating his Telerama company."

"Don't worry," he said reassuringly. "We'll talk about it in a day or two when I'm in New York."

They said their good-byes and he hung up, feeling very self-satisfied. His personal guardian angel was obviously in a benign, benevolent mood, organising the pattern of his future in the best possible way. A sense of exhilaration began to possess him.

He poured himself a whisky, then went to the kitchen in search of a snack. There was part of a cold chicken in the refrigerator, and some oddments of salad, but on an impulse he slammed the refrigerator door and decided to telephone Pauline and take her out to dinner. More than a week had gone by since he had last seen her, and the need to re-establish contact seemed suddenly very urgent.

Pauline's voice over the telephone was cool, but not unfriendly. With some reluctance she accepted his invitation when he made it clear (not without a little harmless exaggeration) that he was on the point of setting off on a world tour and that there were certain things they ought to discuss before he left for Singapore.

After a wash and a shave, he picked her up in his car at her hotel and drove into Soho. The journey took place for the most part in an embarrassing silence, and the few outbursts of sporadic conversation were formal and trite. Clive outlined the nature of his round-the-world assignment, without mentioning New York, while Pauline briefly mentioned that she was now working for the IVRO Research Centre at Brierley.

"That's a bit much," Clive commented. "I mean, to have to work while you're on holiday."

"I don't have to. I choose to work. Anyway, it's not a holiday so far as I am concerned—not any more." There was no mistaking the bitterness in her voice. Clive began to experience misgivings about the wisdom of attempting to entertain his wife under the shadow of divorce. Surely, he thought, adult people can behave in a friendly, sensible fashion under such circumstances, without backbiting and recrimination.

They dined in an Italian restaurant near Soho Square. To Pauline it seemed that Clive was appeasing his conscience; having made the matrimonial break he was now eager to maintain a liaison with her, if only to prove that basically he was a reasonable individual and not bloody-minded. This savoured of hypocrisy, she thought, particularly as he seemed to make a point of exhibiting his guilt complex.

"I do want you to understand that there's nothing personal in this, Pauline," he said at one point. "It's just that—well, the marriage never really had a chance, and I got caught up in things I couldn't control."

"Like a millionaire father-in-law," she said with cynicism.

He grinned ruefully. "That's my girl. Always quick with the repartee. Not that I blame you, of course—you have every justification. But you must admit that I've never attempted to put up a defence."

"But you have, Clive—the best defence of all—the defenceless defence."

"What exactly do you mean by that?"

"You know very well what I mean. The man who admits every-thing, who says I know I'm a bastard, it was all my fault and all the rest of it. That's a defence, Clive. It's a voluntary shedding of responsibility."

He licked his lips thoughtfully. "But, after all, what else *could* I say? There's no blame attached to you."

"But there is, you know," she said. "A marriage is a partner-ship, and when the partnership breaks down then both parties are responsible to some extent. In a way I'm as much to blame in that I failed to hold you as a wife."

"Don't you think this idea of *holding* is just a little Victorian?"

"Perhaps, but will Miss Noelle Langstrom feel the same once she's your wife? It's not so easy to be wise before the event."

"Noelle is a fairly sophisticated woman. I don't think she has many illusions—about me or anything else."

"Is that a good basis for marriage?" she asked.

He shrugged. "Why not? All cards on the table. If one has no illusions, then one can hardly be disillusioned."

"I see," she said. "A marriage of disillusionment. I suppose it could work, in this day and age. Disenchantment is very fashionable."

As an evening it was not a great success, although it did demon-strate that Pauline was settling down to a new kind of independ-ence, though with cynical overtones. On the whole, however, things seemed to be working out all right.

Over coffee he ventured to mention the subject of divorce, and found her surprisingly matter-of-fact about it.

"I don't want to rush into it, Clive," she said, "because I want to be quite sure that you won't change your mind. There are big changes coming up in the world we know, and we may all find ourselves living completely different lives."

"You're referring to the virus?"

"Yes. There will come a point, perhaps in just a few weeks, when any kind of long-term planning may be utterly futile. If we're going to reorganise our lives, I think it would be better to wait until the crisis is over."

"Crisis?" he questioned. "Do you really believe the virus will cause a crisis in Britain?"

"I know it will."

He eyed her sceptically. "I know there's trouble in the East, but we're a bit more civilised and advanced this side of the world. I dare say there'll be a serious epidemic, but we still have to live our lives and plan ahead." He paused, choosing his words carefully. "I do want you to realise, Pauline, that if it were purely and simply a question of divorce I'd leave the whole thing to you, to act in your own time, using your own judgement. But, frankly, there's a business proposition involved which will be to your benefit as well as mine, and it does rather hinge on the question of a quick divorce. I'm not trying to push you, but I'd appreciate your co-operation."

"All right, Clive," she said after a long pause. "If it means so much to you, I'll give you what you want. The only thing I'm afraid of is that when you've got what you want you may regret it."

"That's *my* worry," he said. "The point is that while I'm making this round-the-world trip I'll probably call in to see my future employer in New York. Can I truthfully tell him that you are starting divorce proceedings immediately?"

"Yes, Clive, you can tell him that, and Noelle, too. That should make her a happy woman—or is girl the more accurate word?"

When he took her back to the hotel an antiquated black car was parked outside the main entrance. The man sitting in the driving seat was dark and rather gaunt in appearance, and smoking a cigarette. It was only after he had said goodnight to Pauline and was actually driving away that he saw the man get out of the car and walk over to her at the hotel entrance. Her manner seemed cordial, as if she had been expecting him. A moment later, already accelerating down the road, he observed in the wing mirror that they were going into the hotel together, arm in arm.

His annoyance was transient. If she has already got a boy friend, it's a good thing, he decided—a very good thing indeed.

CHAPTER FIVE

H E ARRIVED AT SINGAPORE THREE DAYS LATER, AND IMME-
diately ran into difficulties with the authorities. Under a
new emergency decree air transit had been blocked, apart from
certain restricted categories of priority passengers. At the airport
a uniformed official explained the new regulations in a kindly but
firm manner.

"Unless you have specific business to transact that has been
authorised by the Government, or unless you are a resident, or
have close relatives in the area, or if you are a doctor acting under
the auspices of the International Virus Research Organisation…"

"My wife is a member of IVRO," Clive pointed out.

The official smiled and shook his head. "In that case your wife
could no doubt obtain an entry permit, but as a journalist you
yourself would be barred."

"My main purpose is to see our local correspondent—a Mr.
Richard Thomson—who was taken ill a few days ago."

"A virus case?"

"I have no idea."

"I'm afraid that whatever the nature of the illness you would
not be allowed to see him unless you were a close relative. If he
contracted virus, then he will be dead by now. If some other illness,
then he will be segregated in an isolation hospital to keep him away
from virus carriers."

Clive reconsidered his plan of action. "Would it be possible to
talk to a responsible medical officer who could give the true facts
of the situation in Singapore?"

The official shrugged. "You must realise that the medical authorities and personnel are very busy. They are working day and night.
In any case, they could not give you any information other than that
which is already being released through the normal news channels."

"I do not believe the news channels are giving a true picture
of the situation," Clive said. "That is the reason I came here. My
paper suspects that vital information concerning the spread of the
virus is being suppressed."

The official took a large white handkerchief out of his pocket
and mopped his brow. The interior of the airport building was
like an oven in the sunglare, and swinging fans merely circulated
the hot air without cooling it. Beyond the horizontal window a
white airliner taxied slowly across the tarmac towards a distant
runway.

"That is only partly true, sir," the official said. "All available
information is being passed to the people concerned at official
levels—the governments of the world, medical authorities, and so
on. After all, they have to take the necessary steps to deal with the
virus when it eventually strikes. But there would be little point in
releasing all the horrific details—and believe me, they *are* horrific—
to the ordinary people. It would only cause unnecessary alarm, and
perhaps uncontrollable panic."

"I'm perfectly willing to go through the proper channels,"
Clive insisted. "I would like to make a formal application to the
Government of Singapore for permission to interview certain key
people on behalf of my newspaper."

The official eyed him dubiously, as if uncertain as to whether he
could stretch a point or not under the circumstances. "You might as
well accept my word, Mr. Brant," he said. "However, I do not wish
to seem unreasonable, and in view of your status as foreign editor,

I am prepared to allow you to use a telephone to make whatever arrangements you can."

"Thank you," Clive said.

"You may use the telephone in my office, and, of course, you must not leave the airport building."

Clive spent the next three hours telephoning unwilling officials concerned with administrative and medical services and made precisely no progress whatever. They were all very sorry, but under the present conditions of emergency it would not be wise to admit casual observers. In any case, adequate arrangements had already been made for news bulletins to be transmitted to the outside world, and to admit independent journalists would merely complicate matters. Furthermore, to raise the ban for the benefit of one unauthorised visitor would establish an unwelcome precedent that would perhaps make it difficult to prevent others from gaining entry to the emergency zone.

At one point Clive found himself speaking to a doctor named Lennox whom he had known some years earlier in Vietnam. Lennox was an IVRO man—an acquaintance of Pauline's rather than Clive's—but the connection was sufficient to enable some of the formal barrier of red-tape and non-communication to be broken down.

Lennox was amiable enough, and asked after Pauline. Clive made a non-committal reply, and for a minute they politely played remember-when. Then Clive got down to the real business of the telephone call. Lennox regretfully admitted that he could not help in any way, nor could he supply information.

"I'm not asking for a report on the situation," Clive emphasised, "but there are certain facts and rumours which I should like to have confirmed or denied, if it's possible."

"Such as what?"

"One hundred thousand dead—that was four or five days ago. By now the death roll should be much higher—perhaps double or treble."

"I really haven't got any figures," Lennox said after a pause. "There have been a considerable number of deaths, of course, but I wouldn't like to estimate how many."

"What about tented hospitals which are reported to be nothing more than collection centres for the dying?"

"Well, we've had to use tents, naturally. Our existing hospital accommodation is swamped. As for collection centres—that's a bit of an overstatement. We *are* concentrating the virus cases in tented treatment centres, but purely as a matter of expediency."

"What about lime pits for the dead and dying?" Clive persisted.

"For the dead, certainly. I don't know what you mean by the dying."

"Virus patients who are still alive but regarded as dead for all practical purposes."

"That sounds cynical," Lennox remarked, "and most unfair on the medical administration, don't you think? There's nothing wrong with lime pits that I can see. We haven't got the facilities for mass funerals and cremations, and in this hot climate, with people dying at an accelerating rate, we can't afford delays."

"I'm not offering criticism, just checking an eye-witness report," Clive said.

"Well, don't quote me. Censorship is pretty tight round here just now. We're doing the best we can under very difficult conditions, and it's easy enough for an outside observer to distort the facts."

"Don't worry," Clive assured him. "We've got censorship troubles of our own, too, and we wouldn't be allowed to print a word of it, anyway. All we're trying to do is build up a general picture of the world situation. My next stop is Tokyo, and then the States."

"You won't get anything out of Tokyo, except a quick turn round and take-off."

"We'll see."

Clive hung up with a cordial farewell. At least Thomson's report had been accurate enough, and might even have been an understatement. Lennox had obviously been whitewashing the situation with a faintly injured air, and it could well be that a more ruthless approach to the problem of mounting virus cases was being implemented.

Later, he reported to the airport official, who eyed him questioningly.

"Any luck, Mr. Brant."

"No. Singapore seems to have sealed itself off from the outside world."

The official nodded. "That is the way it will be everywhere as the virus spreads. It is not a happy prospect, but there is, perhaps, no other alternative."

"Maybe not," Clive agreed. "My problem now is to get to Tokyo and from there to Los Angeles or San Francisco."

"That may be difficult. Passenger flights to Tokyo are few and far between. We may be able to route you through Okinawa, perhaps tomorrow, if there's a reservation available. Your best plan would be to check with bookings at once."

"Thanks, I'll do that," Clive said.

But first he went to the airport bar to buy himself an iced beer.

He flew to Tokyo the following morning and within an hour was on his way to Los Angeles in a fast jet. At the airport he had snatched a brief opportunity to telephone the Tokyo IVRO centre, using

Pauline's name to secure a bona-fide introduction, but the doctor at the other end of the line had been relatively uninformative.

"It's just as well your wife is out of it, Mr. Brant," the disembodied voice had said. Strange, he thought, to be listening to a reedy voice in a telephone receiver that belonged to someone who knew Pauline better than he did, who had worked with her for almost as long as they had been married.

"I can't comment on the situation here," the voice went on in reply to a direct question from Clive. "We're very busy, and the virus is at its peak. We think that in a week or two things will begin to ease off—in Japan, that is. I wish I could say the same for the rest of the world."

"What's the score on deaths?" Clive asked.

"I'm afraid you'll have to go to official sources for that. Pauline could probably tell you, if she's still in touch with the statistical side. On the other hand, there *is* a kind of security blanket in force, and she may not be free to reveal information of that kind."

"You've obviously managed to survive the crisis," Clive said. "Would you care to sum up briefly your first hand impression of it?"

"Frankly, no. I survived because I was lucky enough to contract the BA type virus which is harmless and gives immunity. For that I'm grateful, and that's the only impression I can pass on."

"Well, thanks anyway," Clive said, and hung up.

At Los Angeles all passengers were subjected to a clinical blood test which caused a delay of more than two hours while blood samples were vetted for Hueste virus. Nothing was said, and he was unaware if any passengers had been segregated from the rest, but at least it looked as if the Americans were approaching the problem in a methodical way.

He night-stopped in Los Angeles and telephoned Noelle.

"Clive," she protested, "how dare you stay away from me for a whole night?"

"I couldn't get a plane reservation before this afternoon."

"Hell, if I'd known you'd already arrived I'd have got daddy to charter a private plane."

"It's just as well you didn't, honey. The last thing I want to be is a hole in daddy's pocket."

"Don't be silly, Clive. You're practically an executive on daddy's payroll, and all the best executives are expensive. You have to think big."

"I haven't signed daddy's contract yet," he pointed out, "and until I have I prefer to think around medium size."

"How soon will you be with me, Clive?"

"Around midnight, I think."

"I'll wait up for you. Don't be any later."

He agreed to try not to be any later.

Los Angeles seemed normal enough. It was busy and noisy, and the streets were alive with bustling traffic. He walked leisurely downtown, bought himself a newspaper, stood in a quiet bar reading the headlines to the accompaniment of a double whisky.

Russia shows missile muscle, the front page announced, followed by a story purporting to come from a Leipzig correspondent on new missile bases reportedly under construction in East Europe. The editorial leader—a terse tract on "H-manship"—ought to have been disturbing if one were not in some vague way aware that missile plots and politics were probably a subterfuge, perhaps even agreed at high diplomatic level between East and West, to distract attention from the more sinister Hueste virus.

On an inside page was a brief reference to "earthworks" in progress at a number of points outside the city centre, as part of the

Government's "long-term plan for civil defence". But the remainder of the paper consisted of the usual run of news and pictures—two murders, a grand larceny trial, divorce, birth, death and people generally. In this particular edition there was no direct reference anywhere to the virus.

He looked at the title of the paper: *Los Angeles Sentinel*. On an impulse he finished his drink and hailed a cab. A few minutes later he alighted outside a semi-skyscraper that housed the *Sentinel* offices.

He entered the building and was promptly whisked up to the fifteenth floor in an elevator. A tall brunette with butterfly glasses intercepted him in the reception foyer, and for a minute or two they had a heart-to-heart talk. Yes, she guessed, the editor, K. A. Schuster, would sure be glad to meet a colleague from across the Atlantic. How was London? Why, only last year she'd spent three weeks, she and a girl friend, in a small hotel in Earls Court, having a hep time. Bad luck they'd just missed the June heat-wave, but even the London rain seemed warm and friendly. If Mr. Brant would care to sit down while she gave K. A. a buzz...

Clive eased himself into a plush armchair in the glass-walled room and waited. Presently he was ushered into the office of K. A. Schuster.

Schuster was a small man, squat in build, with glossy black hair that fitted his head like a skull-cap. He wore rimless pince-nez glasses with a fine gold chain fitted to one lens that clipped behind his right ear. He was coolly dressed in light grey, matching the clinically grey and white walls of the office.

"Glad you dropped by, Clive," he said cordially, standing up to shake his visitor's hand. "We don't much get the chance to meet our opposite numbers from the British press."

"I'm on a circular tour of the world," Clive said. "The idea is to check on the Hueste virus, but so far I've drawn a large blank. It seemed to me that one way of getting an overall picture of the situation in California would be to compare notes with a newspaper editor like yourself. At least you sense the atmosphere of public opinion."

Schuster perched himself on the corner of his desk and looked solemn.

"Blank is the operative word round here, too," he stated. "There's an invisible veto on every news channel, not to mention a strong directive from State Department in Washington that amounts to censorship. Naturally, we do have inside information, but we can't publish it."

"It's the same in Britain—a kind of invisible black-out on virus news."

"You haven't got the virus over there yet," Schuster pointed out.

"It's only a question of time. Preparations are going ahead."

"Such as what?"

"It's difficult to be certain. Excavating and building under the heading of nuclear defence."

Schuster snapped his fingers demonstratively. "Precisely the position over here, Clive. You want to know what they are? Surface incinerators and underground hideouts."

"I'd figured something like that," Clive said thoughtfully. "How priority will be allocated, I can't imagine."

"So far the problem hasn't arisen. The virus has only just begun to sink its teeth in on the West Coast. Five thousand deaths, I'm told, but accelerating. I guess you'll realise we're not allowed to publish that."

Clive considered for a moment. "It looks as if the pattern of events in the States is going to follow that of China and

Japan—sealing itself off from the world in order to deal with a big internal problem."

Schuster stood up, took a box of cigars from a drawer in the desk, and offered it to Clive. They both occupied themselves for a while in lighting short fat Havanas. Then Schuster said:

"It won't be the same pattern. That kind of thing may happen in China and Japan where they've got too big a population and too low a standard of civilised living. We've got more in the way of medical and scientific know-how and resources. We'll find the answer any day now. After all, we've got our top brains working on the virus."

"So have we."

"Then there's nothing to worry about, is there? You know what I think? Some of those deep excavations are going to be turned into underground laboratories where the bacteriologists can really get to work without worrying whether they're going to catch a dose of Hueste AB or BA. It may take a week or two, but we'll pull the rabbit out of the hat, don't worry."

"I hope you do, and I hope it will be more than just a conjuring trick."

Schuster smiled confidently. "There'll be casualties, of course—maybe a million or more—but what's a million in two hundred million? Half of one per cent. It may be a good thing at that. It may help solve the labour problem and start an upturn in business generally. I haven't noticed any fall in the Dow Jones index since the virus hit the States."

"I can see you're an optimist," Clive remarked. "Personally, I don't think it will be quite so easy as that. I think your one million dead may rise as high as fifty-million…"

"That's some theory, Clive!" Schuster said with a genial laugh. "What the hell do you imagine we could do with fifty million cadavers? You're assuming that America is going to sit back passively and let this goddam Hueste bug have its own way. Well, I can tell you, it won't be like that at all. There's another little bug called *homo sapiens*—a clever little bug, and a darned sight cleverer than that Hueste bug when it comes to the point. The virus may have beaten the Chinese and the Japanese—so what? The US is a tougher proposition."

"Could be," Clive said with restrained scepticism. "What's the position in Russia?"

"We have a correspondent working on espionage terms near Moscow. He works a secret radio transmitter. According to him the virus has gotten a strong hold in the east—the parts of Siberia bordering on China and Korea. He estimates the total deaths so far at around twenty million."

"That's more than *Tass* or *Pravda* have admitted."

"Naturally. What do you expect?"

Clive felt suddenly depressed. "I wonder," he said, "what the end result will be. Humanity is covering up in a big way, concealing the truth, playing it down, pretending that everything is under control. I wonder—I just wonder."

Schuster patted his shoulder in a brotherly way. "You worry too much, Clive. Tell you what—let's have a bite together. That way we can talk informally and off the record."

"Kind of you," Clive said, nodding briefly.

Schuster put on a battered trilby hat and together they went down into the streets of Los Angeles.

It was eleven thirty-five when the airliner touched down at New York. A few minutes later Clive was in a cab speeding towards the western suburbs of the city.

The Langstroms lived in a big sprawling bungalow set well back from a quiet road some fifteen miles from Manhattan. The house was pseudo-cubic in style, with wide horizontal windows and grey stucco walls resembling, if anything, a suburban maternity clinic. The double garage was an obvious extension to the original build- ing, and its flat concrete roof had been converted into a rather ostentatious patio-style garden, with ornamental plants in tubs, and fluorescent lights mounted on dural columns.

They were all waiting for him as he arrived at about ten past midnight: Edgar himself, black-haired and fleshy, his moist mouth shaping an enthusiastic greeting beneath its overhanging but neatly trimmed moustache; Mrs. Langstrom, slight and pale and faintly mystical, smiling an ethereal benediction; and Noelle herself, blonde like her mother, but essentially lively and practical, with clear blue eyes and a face that was not so much beautiful as fascinating, in the Scandinavian fashion.

"Welcome, Clive," Edgar announced in the tone of voice that implied he might be about to make an after-dinner speech. "This sure is a surprise. I could hardly believe it when Noelle told me you were dropping by on a global tour. They do you proud on that newspaper of yours, I guess."

"The dropping by part was not officially on the programme," Clive said, "but I couldn't resist making a small diversion on the way back from Singapore."

He kissed Noelle in a perfunctory manner, rather put out by the eager and observant presence of her parents. She, however, clung to him unselfconsciously and rubbed her cheek against his with characteristic lack of inhibition.

"Clive, my dearest darling—it's so wonderful to see you again. I've missed you such a lot, you've no idea…"

"That's right," Edgar confirmed buoyantly. "The girl's been as neurotic as a hard-up junky who can't afford a fix."

"Neurotic, neurotic, neurotic, because I love you, love you, love you," she murmured dreamily, to Clive's embarrassment.

"Almost rushed her off to a psychoanalyst," Edgar added with a chuckle.

Mrs. Langstrom stood silently to the rear, observing the scene with quiet satisfaction in her serene eyes. A happy woman, Clive thought, or perhaps not so much happy as placid and contented—or even simply resigned to making the best of it. How difficult it was to assess human character at a glance.

"A drink," Edgar pronounced solemnly. "Whisky, vodka, gin, rye…?"

"Thanks. Whisky, I think, with just a little water."

Edgar went over to a triangular cocktail cabinet set in a corner of the room and fussed over an assortment of bottles and glasses. Clive looked around, beginning to feel composed and more at ease now that the awkward preliminaries of introduction and reunion were over.

It was a big room, but the ceiling was low, lending a claustro-phobic air. The décor was jazzy, with some walls papered in bright patterns and others flatwashed in pastel colours. Globed wall-lights provided a diffused illumination, reflecting dully from the polished surfaces of slender, modern furniture which seemed to have been designed for show rather than solid practical use. The pale green carpet was probably of nylon fur. The inevitable television set stared blankly and moronically from a hideous fake antique cabinet in an angle of the room, and elsewhere there was a glass-fronted bookcase, a miniature piano with pink and green keys, and an enormous electric convector heater resembling a miniature power station (mercifully switched off) which was presumably intended to reinforce the central heating system if the temperature of the room happened to drop below heat-wave level. So far as Clive was concerned, the dry warmth of the air was already enervating enough, and he began to understand why Americans invariably put ice into their drinks.

Noelle said: "I wish you could stay for a while, darling. Say, four or five years."

"So do I," Clive agreed, "but there's some unfinished business to attend to in the sceptred isle."

Edgar brought a small tray with four drinks into the centre of the room and set it on a spindly, glass-topped table.

"Help yourselves," he urged.

"Apart from which," Clive went on, taking his glass of whisky, "I'm still working for the *Monitor* until the Eye-Witness project comes into operation."

"Cock," said Edgar with jovial brusqueness. "Eye-Witness is already a reality. I've got the staff lined up just waiting to go. Have you made up your mind yet?"

"Yes."

"Okay—where's the signed contract?"

"Still unsigned, I'm afraid. There have been certain difficulties and things are still unsettled."

"Cock," Edgar repeated sharply. "Nobody ever settled anything by stalling. Every problem demands action, and until it gets action it remains a problem."

Clive smiled uneasily. "There's an intermediate stage between problem and action, surely—and that's thought."

"Thought never helped anyone. Judgement, maybe—shrewd, intuitive judgement—but not thought. The thinkers of the world tend to go on thinking, but never get around to doing anything unless they're pushed into it. I hope you're not that type, Clive."

"Not quite. I can sort out my own personal problems quite well, but I can't resolve other people's problems at the same time."

"That's their own business."

"Not always. Sometimes one makes problems for other people, and then one has a certain responsibility."

"I never heard a man talk about problems so much," Edgar said, swallowing his drink.

Noelle affected a smile of patient boredom. "Daddy, I know exactly what Clive is talking about, and I think it's something he and I should discuss between us. Why don't you be a good boy and push off to bed?"

"Always trust a woman's judgement," Edgar said with a chuckle, glancing quickly at Clive. "Remember, it's *judgement* that matters, not thought. We'll take this up in the morning. When are you off?"

"Tomorrow evening—Idlcwild to London Airport."

"Okay, Clive. We'll talk business tomorrow and I'll put you in the picture on the latest developments. I've got my lawyer to register a company in the UK and have already assigned a camera unit. You'll have Ross and Beigal, they're both experienced boys, and I figured that with you and Noelle working executivewise we could get started on covering the virus angle. The way I see it, there are bound to be restrictions on travel any day at all, so the chances of using a mobile camera unit are remote. Instead, I've got half a dozen teams set up to cover the major continents, if we can get co-operation from the governments concerned. I tell you, Clive, the Hueste crisis is going to be the biggest story of the century. We've got to beat the censorship and get it on record, then one day, when it's all over, we can consolidate and edit all the miles of film we've shot and really produce a significant contribution to the archives of human history. We've already got teams working in the Far East using miniature Japanese movie cameras not much bigger than a cigarette lighter, and if you ask me…"

"Daddy, nobody's asking you," Noelle interrupted in a voice that implied reproof. "I thought you were going to talk business tomorrow."

Edgar glanced at his wristwatch. "I guess it's already tomorrow, but I see your point," he said apologetically. "Pleasure before business—that's the modern way. Times change. Why, when I was a boy…" He broke off and grinned. "Well, goodnight you two. Don't stay up all night. Tomorrow's a busy day for all of us."

After her parents had retired, Noelle licked her red lips with the tip of her pink tongue and moved slowly and easily into Clive's arms.

"At last," she whispered, "I've got you all to myself."

"For a little while."

"Let's make the most of it, Clive, my darling."

Yes, why not? he thought, kissing her firmly and with gentle expertise, only too aware of the tension of her slim body as she responded to him. Then she pulled him down on to a divan and wound her arms around him, her eyes misty with pleasure and surrender.

"Do you love me?" she asked.

"You know I do."

"That's not the right answer, Clive. You must say yes or no."

"Yes."

She pouted a little. "And you're not supposed to sound so matter-of-fact and formal."

"Sorry," he murmured, kissing her again.

"If we were married we could do this all the time," she said presently.

"If we were married we probably wouldn't want to."

"Now you're being cynical."

He grinned. "Just realistic. After all, there would be other things to do, like work and household chores, and eating, and going out to see shows and visit people."

"I can do without all the other things. Just keep on kissing me, my love."

He did so in a leisurely fashion, methodically, enjoying the nearness of her and observing almost objectively the slow, inevitable surge of his own emotional excitement. The old captivation returned, and once more he was caught in the familiar hypnosis that had possessed him so many times before, during the long evenings in his flat when Noelle had been in London—the long months of adultery. It would have been so easy, so inevitable, to let nature take its course, but a vague sense of guilt nagged at his mind; the opportunity was there, but it was not the only factor to be considered. In some strange indefinable way the environment seemed to be quite wrong, as if, illogically perhaps, he owed it to his future employer not to abuse his hospitality while staying in his home.

Abruptly he sat up and said: "I think I could use another drink. How about you, honey?"

The look she gave him was withdrawn and sad, but understanding. "Yes, please, darling."

As he went over to the cocktail cabinet, she asked: "How is the divorce progressing?"

"Slowly but surely. She needs time to settle down to the idea."

"But, Clive, she's had time—at least two weeks."

He restrained an ironic smile. "That's not really *time*, Noelle. The point is that she's back for three months, and she'll have to take action before her vacation is over—that is, within the next few weeks."

"I can't see what she hopes to gain by delaying," she said in a sulky manner. "I suppose you're still great friends, you and her."

He paused while he splashed whisky into the glasses. "Not exactly, although she's taken it very well. There's a trace of bitterness now and then."

"She can't do much else but take it well, Clive. No wife in her right senses would desert her husband for the sake of a career in Japan."

He brought the drinks to the divan and sat down beside her. "I think she realises that," he said.

"I can't help feeling you're being a bit feeble about it, darling. Remorse and sentiment and all that boloney."

"I don't think so," he said, smiling wryly. "I'm being as tough as I can reasonably be. The trouble is I can see her point of view, and in a way I do feel sorry for her—but there's no question of remorse or sentiment. I've been firm enough, but I don't want to rub it in more than I have to."

"Does she still love you?" she asked.

"I don't know. It's irrelevant, anyway."

"But it's not, Clive. If she loves you then she's not likely to divorce you. I'm a woman, and I understand these things."

"She's probably suffering from injured pride more than anything else," he said in a matter-of-fact voice. He glanced briefly at his wristwatch. "I think it's time we got some sleep."

"Not until you've made love to me," she stated flatly. "I need to be reassured."

"Wouldn't it be rather indiscreet, here, in your own home?"

There was a sardonic edge to her laughter. "Do you imagine mom and dad don't know? Why do you suppose I practically ordered them to retire?"

He raised a quizzical eyebrow and said: "My relationship with your father has been mainly professional. I really don't know how sophisticated he is."

"Sophisticated like a rabbit, Clive. Mom made up her mind to tolerate his girl friends years ago. She traded monopoly for security, and she still has the status so she doesn't really mind."

He moved closer to her, spinning his thoughts for the right thing to say. "Noelle, my sweetheart, I had every intention of making love to you, but I thought daddy might disapprove if ever he found out."

"Fool," she whispered. "Foolish, naïve Clive. What are we waiting for?"

He finished his drink. "Nothing at all, Noelle. Nothing at all."

CHAPTER SIX

CLIVE SPENT MOST OF THE NEXT DAY AT THE HEADQUARTERS of the Langstrom organisation near Times Square. Here the administrative offices were grouped together in one building, the studios being located elsewhere in the city. The organisation, Edgar Langstrom explained, was principally engaged in producing television shows and series on a packaged basis; these were recorded on film or videotape and subsequently sold to the networks. More than twenty programmes were on the current schedule, including quizzes, shopping magazines and play series and serials from domestic situation comedy to space opera. Most of them received a high audience rating and had acquired good sponsors.

The proposed Eye-Witness project was the company's first venture into serious documentary television. Langstrom's original plan had been to set up a special unit with its own editor and staff, equipped with all available channels of information, on the lines of a newspaper. The unit would be mobile and international in concept.

Unfortunately the plan had had to be modified in view of the virus threat and the imminent embargo on travel and communications. His intention now was to set up a number of small, autonomous film units which would gather material independently from all parts of the world. The films and commentaries would later be collated and edited when it became possible to form a central production unit, which might not be until after the virus epidemic had subsided.

In the ordinary way, Langstrom said, the Eye-Witness project would have been postponed until times became more settled, but the crisis in itself was news—and more than news. He felt that now was the right time to make a positive start with a big story. It offered a unique opportunity to observe human society, and in particular human government, facing up to a universal threat, and it was an opportunity which could not be missed.

He admitted that the project would be costly and might show a financial loss at first, but the foreign editions were expected to swing the balance sheet into the black within a few months. Eventually Eye-Witness would build up into something big, he felt convinced—a kind of television version of *Time Magazine* put out on a world-wide basis. Ultimately he visualised a daily programme, part film and part live, which would embrace not only off-beat news stories, but also informed comment on the arts and sciences.

A suite of offices had already been allocated to Eye-Witness personnel, and engineers were in the process of installing telephone and teleprinter services.

"How soon do you want me to start?" Clive asked.

Langstrom, who seemed to have everything cut and dried in his mind, said: "Immediately. I'd put you on the payroll today if you were free."

"There's the small matter of the existing contract on my present job. It would take me at least three months to get clear—legally, I mean."

"Ditch it. If they go to law for breach of contract, I'll settle the bill. You've got to remember, Clive, that the important thing is continuity. Once we start we're committed—we have to keep on producing, week after week, a top quality programme. That calls for long-term planning, and that's why I'm anxious for you to join us at the earliest possible moment. We've got to have groundwork, and plenty of it."

"I'll do what I can," Clive promised, "even at the risk of litigation."

"Well, you'd better do something, and fast. I'm aiming to get a two-man film unit over to you in a few days—Noelle too. Meanwhile you'll need to get busy negotiating with government departments for permission to shoot newsreel material."

"That may not be so easy," Clive said, frowning. "There's a subtle form of censorship in operation, and a great deal of subterfuge and false news—like the East-West missile tension, and suppressing the truth about the virus."

Langstrom's manner became sterner and more businesslike. "That's what I'd suspected. Can you substantiate it?"

"Only by experience, instinct and observation."

"You *don't* believe in the missile Cold War?"

"I don't believe all I'm told in official handouts. The missile business and the trouble in Africa is small beer compared with the Hueste virus. And don't forget that the Russians themselves have already been hit quite seriously."

"How seriously?"

"Twenty million dead, I've heard."

"You mean you believe what you hear off the record, but you don't believe official handouts, as you put it. To most ordinary people that would seem to be a perverse attitude, like rumour mongering."

Clive shrugged. "Not at all. I believe the things which seem eminently reasonable—which seem to fit into the pattern of events as they exist. I believe that the number one crisis in the world today is the Hueste virus—not nuclear war."

Langstrom peered at him intently for a moment, clearly thinking up a new line of questioning, as if he had suddenly decided that this was the ideal moment to vet his new executive on matters of policy and politics.

"I understand your first wife is an IVRO scientist, Clive," he continued. "You must know a great deal about IVRO's work in this crisis."

"Very little, I'm afraid. IVRO operates under a very tight security blanket. As an international organisation responsible only to world governments it is in a sense a law unto itself—like a kind of medical secret service."

"*Medical—secret—service.*" The words were echoed slowly and with emphasis. "Clive, what precisely do you *mean* by that?"

"Just that IVRO operates as an extension of world governments on a confidential basis. One might suppose that the organisation has a duty to mankind as a whole, out in the open with no discrimination, but in practice it behaves as a government department, smothered by security."

"That's interesting," Langstrom said, reflecting for a moment. "That's the kind of thing I want for Eye-Witness—a crusading exposure of arrogant bureaucracy—but it has to be backed up by hard evidence. It's not enough to make allegations. You're suggesting that IVRO is anti-humanity. I like that. It's good controversial stuff, but it has to be proved beyond reasonable doubt."

"I didn't say that exactly," Clive protested. "All I suggested was that IVRO appears to be pro-government in policy."

"But you're implying that government internationally is anti-humanity."

"Government is always pro-itself. The Establishment instinctively protects the Establishment, and humanity doesn't enter into it. The government that professes humanitarianism will in the next breath attempt to justify atrocities against humanity."

Langstrom raised one eyebrow. "You're something of a cynic, aren't you, Clive?"

"I don't think so. I have an objective outlook, and as an experienced journalist I've learned not to trust authority. Perhaps I'm a sceptic rather than a cynic."

I'm playing it well, Clive thought. Sooner or later the big policy quiz had to come, when E.L. would want to dig below the surface of the executive he plans to hire and accept as a son-in-law. All I have to do is to say the right things—controversial things with the right amount of cool scepticism. He is an iconoclast at heart—a nonconformist out to destroy traditional symbols. You've only got to look at the tasteless furniture and décor of his home to realise that. Basically he's an agitator, and he may even have political aims. Television as a medium of mass influence could easily be exploited and twisted for political ends.

Langstrom's next question was expected; the interrogation was descending towards more basic levels. He said: "What *is* authority?"

"Ordinary people, like you or me, but able to pull the strings of civil and military power. People backed by the police, the judiciary and the armed forces, able to make decisions that affect the lives of the masses. Just human beings with the usual selfish motives, making up their minds, right or wrong, like all of us."

"You mean you favour anarchy?"

"No—I simply favour honesty, either as an individual or as a government." But not always the truth, he thought, with a sense of irony. There was also such a thing as diplomacy, and the truth as such was not always welcome, anyway.

"In other words," said Langstrom, frowning, "you believe that governments throughout the world are not telling the truth about the virus crisis."

"I think that's a fair statement."

"And you're suggesting that those in authority in every country are united in a conspiracy against the ordinary people."

"That's rather exaggerating the position. I see it more in the proverbial sense of pulling the wool over the eyes as a form of international control to prevent panic and mass hysteria."

"Isn't that a worthy motive?"

"It's dishonest."

Langstrom's tense face relaxed and he seemed to breathe more easily. "Okay, Clive—you're on the right lines. If I had to make what was a statement of policy I'd say this: never take anything for granted, always ask questions, and never assume that authority is automatically right. That's going to be the policy of Eye-Witness—a forthright policy aimed at dragging out the truth, however deeply it may be buried. We may be shot down in flames on occasions, but in the long term we must win through, provided we maintain our integrity."

All very well in theory, Clive thought, but in practice there could be innumerable snags. A government which preferred to have the truth suppressed could legislate to that end, and the Eye-Witness project could be killed before birth. In any case, no crisis would ever be accepted by the mass of the population without an official pronouncement from authority, and even then there would be sceptics and super-optimists. The lone wolf howling his virus warning might just as well be predicting the arrival of little green men from Mars for all the serious attention it would receive. Humanity was always indifferent to danger before the event.

Later in the day, after a drug-store drink and lunch with Edgar Langstrom, he bought a newspaper. A small headline in the bottom corner of one of the inside pages announced: *Virus in Europe?* The story began: *Unconfirmed reports from Paris and Bonn indicate that the Hueste virus may have reached Europe. The French newspaper* Le Figaro *yesterday stated that at least six cases of AB virus had been diagnosed. Later editions published an official denial.*

At a medical conference in Bonn, Dr. Hoerter-Weiss, the eminent bacteriologist, said that blood specimens from four hospitalised patients who had died suddenly seemed to indicate virus infection. These had been sent to the International Virus Research Organisation for identification.

In London thirty-six passengers arriving by air from Cairo were quarantined for medical examination and blood tests after an Israeli businessman had collapsed and died during the flight during a short period of coma. The cause of death is not yet known, but Hueste virus is suspected.

Clive grimaced mentally to himself. It was starting, as it must inevitably start, and at first there would be the official denials and the glib untruthful explanations; then as the thing built up the barriers would close, and nations would cut themselves off from the world, one by one, until the thing had run its course and the dead had been disposed of, whether in lime pits, incinerators or mass graves.

In a few weeks we shall all be in the middle of it, he thought. For many of us there will be no escape, and that is why planning for the future seems futile. Better, perhaps, to wait and see—then those of us who survive the plague can settle down to reorganising the chaos, but with greater intelligence and more humanity than before.

At the airport, waiting to board the plane for London late that evening, a female voice over the public address system announced: "Will all passengers for flight fifty-one please report to room E2 at once. All passengers for London on flight fifty-one must report to room E2 immediately."

He was drinking whisky at the bar with Noelle when the announcement was made. The time was approaching eleven-thirty, and take-off was less than fifteen minutes away.

"Now what?" Noelle asked.

He shrugged. "I'd better find out. Keep an eye on my drink until I get back."

Room E2 proved to be a large office on the first floor of the airport building, overlooking the tarmac. Passengers were already queueing in front of four tables behind which airline officials sat, checking papers and passports. He joined one of the queues.

Presently the smartly dressed young woman ahead of him reached the table and became involved in a heated argument with the official. "Of course I'm an American," she was protesting indignantly, "but even a US citizen has to go abroad for business reasons."

"What business?" the official asked.

"I'm a textile buyer for the Merlin Fashion Corporation. There's a hundred-thousand dollar deal tied up in this trip."

"Is that your only reason for visiting Europe, mam?"

"Isn't it a good enough reason—or would you rather I was taking a vacation?"

The official shook his head with an air of melancholy. "I guess that wouldn't be any good either. You'll have to postpone your trip, mam."

"Like hell I will!" Now she was angry. "My flight is booked and my fare paid and nobody's going to postpone anything so far as I'm concerned."

"Sorry, mam. The position is that from midnight the British and American governments are imposing restrictions on travel. Business comes under the non-essential category, unless you've got specific written authorisation from the US Department of Commerce or the British Board of Trade. Would you be kind enough to report to Mr. Deverel in room three-B—just across the corridor?"

She glared at him speechlessly for a moment, then stamped out of the room, eyes flashing and head held high, to tell Mr. Deverel a thing or two.

Clive moved up to the desk, producing his passport and air ticket on request.

"British citizen," the official remarked. He was a relatively young man, with neat fair hair and a methodical, almost lethargic, manner. "You resident in the UK, Mr. Brant?"

"Yes."

"What's your job?"

"Foreign editor, London *Daily Monitor*."

The young man glanced sharply at him, but made no comment.

"Reason for travelling to London?"

"I'm going home, that's all."

"How long have you been in the States?"

"One day. I'm on the final leg of a round-the-world business trip."

The official looked at him in a dead-pan manner. "Got any credentials?"

Clive produced a business card and his N.U.J. press card.

"Okay, Mr. Brant, I think you're clear. Now if you would be good enough to go to room eight-A for a quick medical check, I think you'll make that plane."

"Take-off in four minutes," Clive pointed out, glancing at his wristwatch. "Is it really necessary to waste time in this way."

The young man grinned amiably. "There won't be any take-off until we say the word, Mr. Brant—so not to worry. Room eight-A, please."

In room eight-A he was questioned by an elderly doctor while a white-coated nurse took a sample of blood from his arm.

"Any fever recently?" the doctor asked. "Something like a slight cold, perhaps?"

"No."

"Travelling alone, or with your family?"

"Alone."

They took his temperature; it was normal.

"You'll appreciate that this is just routine," the doctor said. "A whole lot of people are virus carriers without even realising it. You wouldn't want to feel responsible for spreading infection."

"Naturally," Clive agreed, with faint irony.

"We'll have the result of the blood test ready in about ten minutes. It doesn't necessarily clear you. A complete test would take about two hours. But it will establish that you're virus-free for as long as it takes to fly to England. When you get there you'd be well advised to have a full blood test."

"I'll remember that."

"Meanwhile, if you'd care to wait in room fourteen-D downstairs…"

He waited in room fourteen-D, along with a score of other passengers. Conversation had broken out between them in a sporadic, resentful way. What the hell goes on? they wanted to know. What right had the Government to interfere in the personal arrangements of individual citizens, all because of some obscure oriental bug? Clive said nothing. He felt that he knew most of the answers, but he was not in the mood for answering questions.

At intervals a chic blonde in blue uniform would come into the room and call out a name, and in due course his turn came round. The girl gave him a buff-coloured card in the form of a medical clearance certificate, and also his passport and air ticket. He went back to the departure lounge, where Noelle was fidgeting anxiously and looking pale and weary.

"You were away over half an hour, darling," she complained. "What was it all about?"

"Virus trouble," he said, outlining what had happened and why. "It's already past midnight," he concluded, "so from this moment on international travel is banned except for nationals returning to their homeland, and certain priority cases carrying official sanction."

"Oh, God," she sighed. "I can't believe that the virus threat is all that serious."

"I'm afraid it is, honey."

"You mean—I may not be able to come over with the film unit in a week or two…"

"Neither you nor the film unit, if things get really tough. Edgar may be able to pull a few strings, of course."

"Daddy's very good at that. He'll fix it."

"I hope you're right. Daddy may be a good fixer in normal times, but when a crisis blows up the fixing takes place on a different level."

She stared at him in a melancholy fashion. "Clive, why do you have to go back at all? You could stay here in New York, and send a cable to your newspaper office to say you'd resigned."

He acknowledged the suggestion with a wry smile. "Of course, honey. It's the obvious simple solution, but it can't be done."

"But why not? The *Monitor* couldn't do anything about it. They'd just have to write you off as the foreign editor who never came back. You could even tell them you'd died of virus."

"Yes, I could indeed. I can just imagine McAllan's face on the receiving end of a transatlantic phone call. Sorry, Mac, I can't come back—I'm dead."

"Don't be stupid, Clive. Someone else could send the message, and you could change your name. You could tell your wife you were dead, too, and then we wouldn't need to go through the dreary business of divorce."

"I'm sure Pauline would accept that as a very plausible statement of fact," he said sardonically. "A cable from New York, where her husband's other woman lives, saying Clive is dead."

"I don't like being referred to as the other woman," she protested sulkily. "I don't *feel* like the other woman. In fact, I regard your wife as the other woman."

"I see what you mean," he admitted, "but frankly, Noelle, I don't think I can reasonably die by proxy, as it were. Let's face it—a sly subterfuge followed by a bigamous marriage is not the brightest of futures for either of us."

"What a pessimist you are, Clive."

"I don't think so. In my own slow way I'm rather practical. I have to do things the way I see them, and I can't act to specification. Do you understand, honey?"

After a reluctant pause, she said: "Yes, I do understand, though I don't agree. It doesn't really matter, Clive. Daddy will fix things. I'll be with you again soon."

The public address system announced in metallic tones: "Will authorised passengers for flight fifty-one for London please take their seats in the aircraft. Flight fifty-one for London. Passengers should join their aircraft immediately."

Clive finished his drink and said: "Well, good-bye for now, Noelle."

"So long, Clive."

"We'll keep in touch."

"Yes—if we can."

"Not to worry," he said, patting her cheek.

He left her sitting at the bar, holding a half empty glass of whisky. Oddly enough, as he walked across the tarmac to the airliner, he was aware of a subtle sense of liberation, of freedom, emerging from the descending melancholy. To be oneself, free from pressure, duty and obligation—that was something, even though the uncertainties of the future seemed suddenly to have multiplied, and Britain had become a cold, forbidding place.

The take-off was nearly an hour late. Once airborne it seemed to him that he was in a different world entirely, and presently he fell asleep.

On the morning of Clive's arrival in London, Pauline was summoned to Dr. Youde's office at Brierley Research Centre. Youde seemed nervous and fidgety, making heavy weather of concentrating his attention on a sheet of typewritten paper on the desk in front of him.

"I don't know if you've seen the newspapers this morning, Dr. Brant," he began.

Pauline nodded. He eyed her uncertainly through his concave glasses.

"Then you must realise that the Government have started the wheels turning, so to speak, in their antivirus programme. The pattern is similar to that being followed in other countries."

"I know," she said.

"There is an absolute ban on travel—except in particular circumstances. This does, I regret to say, affect you personally."

"You mean... I can't go back to Tokyo."

"That is the position. I have confirmation from the IVRO executive. Their instructions are that as soon as your official vacation terminates you will be automatically transferred to my staff here at Brierley."

"I see," she answered. "Obviously there would be little point in moving staff to Tokyo when the crisis there is over, and when it is about to start in Britain."

"The virus is already with us," Youde stated solemnly. "You won't find it reported in the press, but there have been nearly one hundred cases of confirmed AB type during the last few days. Of those more than eighty have already died."

"What will I be expected to do here, Dr. Youde?"

"Acknowledging the fact that there is little one *can* do at this stage, I think perhaps you could play a useful role in preliminary diagnosis at one of our major evacuation centres. On the other hand…"

He broke off, eyeing her with a certain degree of thoughtful speculation.

"Yes," she prompted.

"On the other hand, there is also a possible opening for you in what we might call—the underworld." He smiled narrowly.

"I don't quite follow."

"I am referring to the classified isolation centres," he explained. "Perhaps you haven't heard of them referred to in that way, but you must certainly know of their construction."

"You mean the underground excavations?"

"Precisely. Some of them are already in occupation. Essentially they are sterile living quarters, completely self-contained for food and water, with virus-free air pumped through pressure filters. They are designed to allow human beings to survive in reasonable comfort for some three months in virus-free conditions."

"Yes," she murmured reflectively, "I remember some talk about virus shelters, though it was difficult at the time to differentiate between fact and fiction."

Dr. Youde interlaced his fingers in a pious manner. "In the absence of a vaccine it is the only measure the Government can reasonably take to ensure the survival of those who are important to society. Obviously there are many thousands of individuals of high executive level whose survival is vital to all of us."

She frowned. "You mean—vital to those who are left behind after the virus has taken its toll."

"Quite. So far as administration goes, each virus centre has to have medical staff of at least one qualified virologist with some diagnostic experience, capable of dealing with any infection ruthlessly and efficiently."

"I can see that," she said, "but what I don't quite understand is the question of priority—in other words, who decides which people are entitled to survive in the virus shelters?"

"Why, the Government and local authorities, of course. Who else?"

"On what basis do they make their choice?"

That silenced him for a few seconds, while he contemplated his thoughts and analysed policy. Then he said: "I think the key survival factor is what you might call social utility, if you know what I mean. At all events, that is something we can safely leave to the good judgement of those whose task it is to make what must be a very difficult and harrowing selection. For ourselves, the problem is simpler. An underground research centre is being constructed on virus-proof lines about three miles north of here, and we hope to move into it in the course of a few days. So, whatever happens, we shall be all right."

"Jack," she added with irony.

Dr. Youde blew his nose on a large green handkerchief. "I know how you feel, Dr. Brant," he said, "but after all, one has to be practical. If half the population of Great Britain is to die, then authority might reasonably be expected to take the necessary steps to protect those whose survival is a matter of some social importance."

"It depends what you mean by social importance."

"What I am trying to put to you is simply this: I can arrange for you to be attached to one of the classified isolation centres as a resident virologist. You would have to live underground for several months, but you would be guaranteed almost one hundred per cent protection from virus infection. Your sole duty would be to make regular blood tests of the others assigned to the centre—just in case the virus managed to seep in, in some way."

"And the alternative?"

"To take your chance with the rest—perhaps join the staff of a hospital or evacuation centre, where you would be handling AB virus cases, and, of course, risking infection."

"But always with a fifty-fifty chance of survival, surely, Dr. Youde."

"Of course."

She thought it over for a moment, then said: "Could I have time to make up my mind?"

"Yes, but please don't take too long. Things are starting to move very quickly."

"I'll give you a decision tomorrow morning."

"Very well, Dr. Brant."

He stood up, came round the desk, and patted her on the shoulder. "Don't be influenced by what you feel to be ethics," he advised. "In times of crisis ethics are of little practical use. After all, ethics are of negligible value to a corpse."

"Yes," she said, with a sad smile. "Or thirty million corpses for that matter."

Later in the day she discussed the proposition with Dr. Vincent.

"I was hoping you'd be retained on the Brierley headquarters staff," he said. "At least that way we could go underground together for a while."

"I have the chance to go underground, anyway, Vince," she said, "but I'm not sure that I want to."

"Why ever not?"

"Well—because the morality of it confuses me. I can't really see why a privileged few should be granted absolute protection against the virus while the mass of humanity has to take its chance on a fifty-fifty basis."

"Why worry about the mass, Pauline? Any one of them would jump at the chance to escape an even-chance death. Take the long-term mass view—do you really want to be one of the thirty million who must inevitably die?"

"No, Vince, but…"

"But nothing! You've got your moralities confused, Pauline. One's first duty is to life itself, to survival. You can't argue with the cold fact of death, whether you believe in heaven, hell or flying saucers. So why not take the necessary steps to ensure survival and argue about the morality of it afterwards, just as they did when they dropped the first atom bomb on Hiroshima?"

"I see what you mean. In times when survival matters, common humanity goes by the board."

"I'm afraid it does, Pauline. But there's another angle. In the last war they provided air raid shelters."

"For everybody—not just the selected few."

He lit a cigarette. "True," he admitted. "But let's be realistic. When it's impossible to provide adequate protection for the masses, then what's wrong with becoming one of the privileged few, as you call them, if the opportunity exists?"

"All right, Vince. Why not? I suppose a sense of morality cuts deeper than mere practical issues, and at a time like this one ought to be practical at all costs."

"Now you're being sensible," he said, smiling. "I think you ought to accept Dr. Youde's offer of a post in an isolation centre. I want you to stay alive for a very special reason."

She said nothing, but regarded him questioningly, half knowing what he was about to say. His lean face seemed paler than usual, and there was a vulnerable quality in the set of his brown eyes.

"Yesterday," he went on, "I instructed my solicitor to file a petition for divorce."

"I'm glad," she said quietly, after reflection. "On the other hand, I rather got the impression that you didn't feel very strongly about divorce."

"I had no immediate incentive to start proceedings—until I met you, Pauline."

"Oh," she remarked, unable to restrain a smile.

"I was wondering," he continued hesitantly, "if you... as we get on so well together..."

"Vince," she interrupted, "if you're thinking of asking me to marry you..."

"I am."

She touched his hand gently. "Please, don't. Not yet."

He looked crestfallen, and for a moment she studied him objectively—gaunt but rugged, quiet and methodical, and personable enough in his own reserved way, but still virtually a stranger. But then, Clive was in effect a stranger, too. All people were strangers to each other, and it was the mere fact of going to bed together that qualified them for the status of marriage. This man could be my husband, she thought, but do I want him as my husband? He is not even my lover, and the relationship between us is amiable rather than amorous. On the other hand, that could well prove to be a sound basis for marriage, to be concerned with common interests rather than mutual passion. At least the interests tend to survive, while the passion is all too likely to fade or change its direction.

"Let's arrange it this way," she continued. "I'll start divorce proceedings, too. Then, when we're both free and able to commit ourselves, we'll make our final decision."

"Logical," he said in a melancholy voice, "but not really reassuring to a man. What with all the uncertainty about the virus…"

"That's another reason for waiting, Vince. If we could be sure of what the future holds, we could reasonably plan ahead, but as things are…"

"I hope you'll keep your promise."

"What promise?" she asked, momentarily taken aback.

"To start divorce proceedings."

"Yes, of course. In a day or two."

"All right, Pauline. I can wait, however long it may be. But please take Dr. Youde's advice and go underground."

"I'll probably do that," she agreed, "but, honestly, Vince, it's something I must work out for myself."

"Fair enough," he commented.

They left it at that.

CHAPTER SEVEN

FOR CLIVE THE PROSPECT OF RESIGNING HIS POST AS FOREIGN editor of the *Daily Monitor* posed certain problems. He felt that he needed a reasonably strong excuse, if only as a face saver, so that the abdication would appear to have a more justifiable motive than mere self-interest. The trouble was that he had no grounds for criticism of the management or the job whatever; both were congenial and his employers had always been considerate and fully co-operative.

It would not have been so bad, he felt, if he could have tendered the agreed three months notice of resignation, but to walk out immediately—or at least in a few days—was more than a breach of contract, it was also a breach of loyalty, and this worried him a little. Edgar Langstrom might talk blandly about meeting the costs of litigation in the event of legal proceedings, but the material issues were relatively unimportant. The first and biggest hurdle was to tell Wardale, the editor, that he was leaving, not in three months, but today or tomorrow or the day after.

Better to angle it, he thought, to leave Langstrom and the television job out of it and find another plausible reason on grounds of policy. Censorship, perhaps—a conscientious journalist might well object to working within narrow terms of reference prescribed by a censor, even though the restrictions were being applied without discrimination to all newspapers. But, then, what would a conscientious journalist do with himself once he had resigned? Live on the dole?

In the end his doubts and tentative soul-searching proved to be unnecessary, and the problem was solved for him in an unexpected way. On the day following his flight back to England he reported to McAllan. As soon as he entered his office Clive could sense that McAllan was in a strange, cold mood. Inevitably he was sitting at his desk in shirt sleeves and braces, a menthol cigarette dangling from his lips. His face seemed more sour and shrunken than usual, Clive thought, as if it had been pickled and partly dehydrated, but more significant was the fact that McAllan, who usually exhibited a certain Scottish forthrightness and would stare one bleakly in the eye for as long as was necessary, had developed an apparent evasiveness and was concentrating his attention on various scraps of paper strewn on his desk.

"Nice to see you back safe and sound, Clive," McAllan said without looking up. "How was the trip?"

"Smooth, depressing and not very informative."

"Did you dig up anything new?"

"Yes and no. I confirmed Thomson's story from Singapore, even though I couldn't get any hard facts and figures. Reading between the lines, I'd say his report was accurate. Also, I think I can show that the Government—all governments—are acting with cold-blooded irresponsibility in this crisis."

McAllan screwed up a piece of paper and flung it into the waste-paper basket beside his desk.

"You think you can, eh, Clive?" He grimaced, still staring at the papers on his desk.

"Something on your mind, Mac?" Clive asked.

McAllan looked up for the first time, and sighed. "Nothing on my mind, particularly, but I fancy Wardale's got something on his. He wants to see you."

"Okay," Clive said, "but just between you and me—what's it all about?"

McAllan pouted his lips in a melancholy fashion. "Oh, hell, Clive—it has nothing to do with me. I'm only the bloody news editor." He hesitated, looking Clive straight in the eye. "Off the record I think it has to do with flying to Singapore via New York."

"You mean returning from Singapore via New York."

"Something like that."

"Well, what's the difference? Wardale agreed it, anyway."

"Perhaps so, but you obviously haven't seen this morning's edition of the *New York Times*."

Clive began to experience some misgivings. Edgar Langstrom, he thought. The Langstrom publicity set-up, cutting the ground from under my feet to make sure I don't stall any more.

"What about the *New York Times*?" Clive asked.

"Why don't you ask Wardale? It's really none of my business."

"I will," Clive said.

He went back to his own office and buzzed the editor on the intercom.

"Ah, yes," Wardale said, quite affably. "Could you see me now, Brant?"

"I'll be right round."

Wardale was polishing his rimless glasses with an immaculately white handkerchief, and there was a half smile frozen to his thin lips.

"How was the trip, Brant?" he enquired in a formal tone of voice.

"More informative than the British press," Clive said with deliberate irony, sensing a showdown of some kind and trying to facilitate it by adopting a faintly belligerent attitude so that there would be the minimum of embarrassment on either side.

"Indeed? In what way?"

"I learned enough to confirm my suspicions as to the scope of the tragedy in the Far East. Let's face it, Mr. Wardale—the press in this country and in most countries has been playing it down in a big way."

"Why not?" Wardale asked mildly. "Is there anything to be gained by playing it up?"

Clive chose his words carefully. "In all honesty, I feel that I cannot endorse a policy which seems to me to be calculated to present a completely false picture of world events. If people are going to die in millions, then I believe they're entitled to know."

Wardale put the palms of his hands together as if he were praying. "Wouldn't it be better for them to die quietly and peacefully, believing that everything possible was being done? Or would you prefer to see riots and insurrection?"

"I don't think it would come to that."

"I hope you're right, Brant, but informed opinion at government level takes rather a different view." Wardale propped his chin in his hands in a bored fashion. "Did you learn during your tour just how many people in Japan and Malaya, and China for that matter, were shot for what we might call—mutiny?"

"No."

"Would you like me to tell you?"

"Yes—if you will also tell me where you got your information from."

Wardale smiled coldly. "We are not so uninformed, you know. Running a newspaper is a responsible job. Frequently it's not so much a question of what to publish as what *not* to publish. I'll tell you this much—the management of the *Monitor* is in close touch with the Government on this crisis. We are expected to co-operate. That includes not only myself, but every other member of the staff."

"In other words—censorship."

"Yes. In times of crisis it is inevitable. One has to control the thinking and the morale of the masses."

This, Clive recognised, was an opportunity of the kind he had been seeking. Wardale's attitude was still obscure, and there was McAllan's mysterious reference to the *New York Times* to be clarified, but on the question of censorship one could reasonably justify a resignation.

He said: "Frankly, Mr. Wardale, I don't think I could work under such conditions. It's like moving from journalism into public relations. Instead of telling the truth one has to create good will."

"That sums up the position quite neatly," Wardale commented. "But I'm afraid censorship is with us for a few months whether we like it or not. We have to make the choice: truth or public relations. As from yesterday, when the travel ban was imposed, all newspapers and publications came under a new government department, euphemistically entitled the Press Services Bureau. It means that we have to take all news concerning the virus, politics and international affairs from the Government, and we're not allowed to comment. You realise the implications, Brant."

Clive considered for a while. "International affairs. That means no foreign correspondents, and possibly no foreign editor."

"You're quick on the uptake," Wardale said with a nod. "Of course, in the ordinary way as a newspaper we would naturally redeploy our staff. The people handling foreign news would be absorbed elsewhere in the organisation, though there might be some redundancy on a small scale. But in your case…"

"Yes?"

By way of answer Wardale handed him a newspaper—the *New York Times*, he recognised. It was open at page four, and a down-page news story had been ringed in red ink. The headline announced:

British Editor for Eye-Witness. The first paragraph of the story stated: *Clive Brant, foreign editor of the London* Daily Monitor, *is to head the new Langstrom Eye-Witness TV organisation, scheduled to start operations in the near future. Brant's first assignment will be to cover the Hueste virus situation in the United Kingdom.*

Clive read the report through three times before he had composed himself sufficiently to meet the cool, critical gaze of Wardale's eyes. The news story went on to outline Langstrom's policy, and gave a brief history of his organisation's television achievements to date.

Finally he put the newspaper down on the corner of the desk. "Under the circumstances, Mr. Wardale…"

Wardale seemed to smile sardonically. "The circumstances seem to be about right for both of us, Brant. Coincidentally, at the point in time when we no longer need a foreign editor, due to official policy, our foreign editor has found himself another appointment. The least one can say is that the arrangement is convenient."

"Well, I must admit that I felt rather guilty about having to resign at short notice," Clive said with relief. "Even now, although a foreign editor might not be needed for a few months, there must come a time when things will get back to normal."

"Don't worry about that. As I understand it, after the virus has had its way, we shall be looking for replacements for about half of our staff. There will be a tremendous reorganisation of manpower throughout the country, and the *Monitor* will be just as deeply involved as the rest."

Clive nodded. "Yes. It's on the cards."

"Having said that," Wardale put in briskly, "I must add that although the virus offers what we might call extenuating circumstances, it is my own personal feeling that you have behaved in a rather devious and unethical manner. In a responsible executive post such as yours, Brant, I should have thought you might have warned the management that you were planning to leave. After all, competent foreign editors are hard to find."

"You're perfectly right, Mr. Wardale," Clive agreed, pleased that the anticipated criticism had finally been expressed, and knowing exactly how to deal with it. "As a matter of fact I've been reproaching myself for weeks past, and even now my mind is only partly made up. It's a difficult decision to make, particularly in view of the virus threat. The trouble is that I'm also involved in personal matrimonial difficulties." He paused to consider his words. "I'm forced into the position of having to divorce my wife, and it did seem to me that a new job in a new country might—well, enable me to forget the past and make a fresh start."

Wardale pursed his lips sympathetically. "I understand, Brant, though of course I did not realise…" He stood up and came round the desk. "I hope things work out as you want them to."

"I feel sure they will," Clive said, with just the right amount of wistful doubt in his voice.

"I didn't mean unethical in the ordinary sense of the word," Wardale explained. "But as you know, on the *Monitor* we do enjoy extremely good relationships between management and staff, and…"

"Of course, Mr. Wardale. If it hadn't been for my own indecision and confusion I would have taken you into my confidence a long time ago."

"When do you plan to leave us?"

Clive shrugged. "It's not a matter of urgency. How soon would it be convenient for you to release me from my contract?"

"Under the circumstances, whenever you wish."

"At the end of the week, perhaps?"

"Very well."

Clive said thank you and began to walk towards the door of the office, when Wardale spoke again in a more businesslike way.

"Naturally, Brant, since we are allowing you quite a considerable concession in waiving the contractual period of notice—three months, I believe—there can be no question of salary beyond the date of leaving."

"Of course not," Clive said with a smile. "One good turn deserves another."

That same evening Clive booked a transatlantic telephone call to Noelle Langstrom in New York. The operator was dubious and pessimistic. All transatlantic lines are busy with priority traffic, she explained, and it may be several hours before we can connect you, and even then your call may be interrupted and cut off. Nevertheless he insisted on booking the call, and settled down to wait, feeling unsettled and uneasy.

He poured himself a drink and switched on the television set as an antidote to gloom. The sound built up and then the screen brightened in the middle of a commercial. "Yum, yum," said a smooth, persuasive voice, "delicious!" A cartoon face seemed to be chewing something. "And don't forget, there are eight different flavours."

"Choosey—the *chic* chewing gum," a female voice interposed.

"Buy some tomorrow," the original voice added.

The commercial faded and a panel game took the air. He watched it in a desultory fashion, not amused, his thoughts elsewhere. His guardian angel was still very much in evidence, he decided; events were working themselves out in a precise way that could only be regarded as satisfactory. Even the Hueste virus itself seemed to be lending a helping hand, facilitating a speedy resignation from the *Monitor*, and bringing the new job to him, complete with camera team, instead of obliging him to uproot himself and migrate to New York. It was a time to feel pleased and possibly smug, but oddly enough his mood was one of vague depression. The future was casting a dark, shapeless shadow across the surface of his mind.

He poured himself another whisky. The panel game gave way to more commercials—*The petrol that gives you more drive—Electronic luminance tests prove conclusively that Bozzo washes ten per cent whiter— The pale blue cigarettes that give you the ice-cool smoke, so kind to your throat—For taste and tenderness try Taurus quick-frozen steaks—*and then the panel game again pursuing its inane trivialities.

The telephone rang abruptly, momentarily startling him. He turned down the sound on the television set and answered the call. It was not the New York booking as expected, but Pauline.

"Sorry to disturb you, Clive," she said, "but I've finally made up my mind. I'm going ahead with the divorce."

"I see. Well, it had to come.."

"There's one other thing. I am taking up a new appointment in IVRO which is likely to keep me very much out of contact for two or three months. If there's anything we need to discuss at this stage…"

"I suppose there must be—on the other hand, perhaps the less said the better. Supposing we have dinner together, say, tomorrow night."

"All right, Clive."

"I'll pick you up at the hotel, around seven-thirty."

"I'll be waiting."

He said goodnight and hung up thoughtfully. Once more luck was on his side. Suddenly in one day he had been presented with freedom, both professional and matrimonial, and all the problems that had been bothering him only a few hours earlier were now resolved. And yet there was no great feeling of satisfaction inside him, but just a tacit acceptance of the events as they happened, as if he were in some strange way detached from the outside world and merely observing it objectively. Trauma, he thought. Stress reaction resulting from mental and emotional conflict. In a day or two I'll settle down and begin to respond to things in a more optimistic way.

The panel game had finally ended, and the commercials burst into noisy exuberance once more. *Daddy knows best, Daddy insists on Cornucopia breakfast cereal—Is your hair dry and lifeless, strangled by dandruff?—Easy come, easy go, with a car like this, and easy to pay for, too, on our new step-by-step credit plan...* and then came the news.

The news reader, lean and handsome with a tiny moustache, looked solemn as he glanced quickly at his dummy script then fixed his eyes on the teleprompt device above the camera. He said:

"This evening in the House of Commons the Prime Minister declared a state of emergency. The Cabinet is to be immediately reconstituted on a coalition basis to represent all political parties for the duration of the emergency. This move closely follows the ban on international travel imposed last night, and is a logical step in establishing an effective defence against the Hueste virus epidemic which is now prevalent in Europe.

"The Government is now empowered to act by decree in the event of military action by the Eastern bloc to secure a tactical advantage while Western Europe is preoccupied with measures to deal with the epidemic.

"The Prime Minister emphasised that although the virus has not yet established a bridgehead in the United Kingdom, it is neverthe-less essential to take precautionary action to localise any outbreaks of the epidemic should they occur.

"A number of emergency regulations come into effect immedi-ately. From midnight tonight all travel between individual counties in the United Kingdom is prohibited, whether by road, rail or air, other than by permit, which will only be granted on a priority basis for urgent business or personal reasons. Applications for travel permits should be made to local road licensing authorities, railway stations and airports."

Clive lit a cigarette and watched the television screen in a mood of sour disaffection.

The news reader continued: "A special department of the Ministry of Health has been set up to deal with all virus cases. Because of the extreme virulence of the epidemic it is most important that anybody suspecting infection should report to a doctor or go to the nearest hospital without delay. The initial symptom of virus infection is a rapid increase in temperature. The Ministry stresses that anybody whose temperature rises above one hundred degrees Fahrenheit should seek medical advice immediately.

"Under another emergency decree, all communal gatherings are banned for the duration of the emergency in order to minimise the potential spread of the virus. This means that all entertainments will close down, including cinemas, theatres, stadiums and meetings generally which are not classified as essential." The news reader smiled sardonically. "Television entertainment will continue, however."

He went on: "It is emphasised by the Government that these are simply precautionary measures. While it may not be possible to escape the epidemic entirely, the Government believes that it can be restricted and held to a negligible level if people will observe three simple rules. They are:

"Stay at home so far as is possible. Avoid mixing with other people, especially crowds. Report to your doctor, or the nearest hospital, the moment you think you have a temperature. In other words, keep yourself to yourself and rely on the medical services available."

A pause, then: "The President of the United States today made a tour of the West Coast of America where a number of Hueste virus cases have been reported. Later, at a press conference, he said that the situation was under control, but as a temporary measure to prevent the spread of the virus all inland travel would be restricted. In addition, theatres, cinemas and sports would close…"

Clive switched off the set with a feeling of morbid irritation. Clearly the crisis was building up, and it was frustrating to be on the receiving end of governmental manoeuvring, observing the shift in emphasis from the supposed nuclear threat behind the Iron Curtain to the more immediate and real threat posed by the Hueste virus. Fiction and fact, he thought, but it was difficult to disentangle the two. That was where Pauline had the advantage; she was, in a sense, one of the organisers behind the scenes, those who really knew what was going on behind the locked doors of security and administration.

Restlessly he poured himself another drink, waiting all the time for the telephone to ring. It was nearly ten-thirty before his call to New York came through. The operator warned him that the call would be limited to two minutes because of priority traffic.

Noelle's voice was clear and distinct, as if she were speaking from a call box round the corner.

"Hello, Clive, darling. How wonderful of you to call me so soon." A brief pause, then: "I hope there's nothing wrong…"

"Nothing wrong," he confirmed. "I've ditched my job with no trouble and my wife is divorcing me."

"Clive, I'm delighted."

"Apart from the virus situation, things couldn't be better. I'm rather worried about the travel ban."

"It's all right. Daddy will fix things. Television is top priority right now, since they've closed the movies and theatres."

"That may be okay for daddy, but it doesn't help you or me."

She laughed across the Atlantic. "Silly Clive. I'm already a top executive on daddy's payroll. Business is business, and he's got influence in the right places. As soon as he can get the papers fixed I'll be coming over with the film unit boys."

"How soon will that be?"

"I can't be sure. Maybe two days, maybe two weeks."

"Good girl," Clive commented happily. "All the same, I'm not sure that London is a safe place to be at present. The Government's gone all emergency."

"It's the same over here, Clive, and the virus risk is the same in London as in New York, I guess. The important thing is for me to get to England as soon as possible, before they tighten up the restrictions."

"Well, all right, honey. I look forward to seeing you and to starting my new job as daddy's…" He stopped speaking because he suddenly realised that the line was dead. "Damn," he said aloud, then "Hello, hello, Noelle…"

He flicked the telephone rest. "Hello, operator."

The line remained silent, but he kept on flashing. Eventually the operator's voice came sweetly over the line. "I'm sorry, sir, We had to cut you off in favour of priority traffic after one minute and forty seconds. You will be charged pro rata, of course."

The line clicked and went dead again. He hung up in exasperation. "To hell with it!" he exclaimed. "Anyone would think we were at war."

He poured himself another drink and chain smoked for an hour, then went to bed.

CHAPTER EIGHT

THE NEWSPAPER HEADLINES THE FOLLOWING MORNING MADE mildly amusing reading, Pauline thought, though they all toed the official line so far as editorial comment was concerned. *FULL STOP*, announced one tabloid, adding in a sub-heading: *Britain goes into deep freeze to beat the virus.* One of the right-wing popular dailies declared: *Government stonewalls virus*, and started the lead story in terse imperatives: *Don't travel. Don't mix. Buy a thermometer and use it. With this advice, backed up by emergency decrees, the Government plans to beat the Hueste virus epidemic that is now sweeping Europe.* A Communist newspaper stated: *Virus moves pose anti-Soviet threat.* The *Times* staidly said: *Emergency measures to counter epidemic—Government restricts travel.* And the *Financial Times*, pinkly on the ball, ran a bigger than usual front-page headline: *Shares slide on virus vetoes*, with an informative inside feature, illustrated by graphs, entitled: *What the Hueste is it all about?* But on the whole the newspapers published speculation rather than information.

Pauline reported to Dr. Youde at the Brierley Research Centre around mid-day and told him that she had decided to accept a tour of duty in a classified isolation centre. From her experience in Japan, she explained, it seemed to her that she could perhaps achieve more in protecting the protected than in trying to cure the incurable.

Youde stroked his thick hair in a preoccupied manner and peered at her through his concave glasses.

"Sensible and practical," he remarked, referring to a green-backed file. "For administrative purposes the United Kingdom has been divided up into some two thousand or more independent zones, each with one or more underground isolation centres, depending on the number of people to be protected. The zones will be controlled by area committees, rather like local councils, and they too will be located underground, of course. All the committees will be directly responsible to a central emergency authority based in London."

"Also underground, I suppose," she said.

Youde's pale lips framed a half smile. "Naturally. The essence of the scheme is to set up a network of administrative centres throughout the country which are fully protected from the epidemic and so can function continuously through the crisis."

He picked up a propelling pencil and tapped the point several times on the blotter, as if the motion helped to marshal his thoughts.

"The only thing left to decide," he went on, "is where to send you."

"As close to London as possible," she suggested.

"Mm—but the trouble is that the London centres are already staffed. You see, the virus is spreading from the south, and one has to allocate a certain priority."

He stopped tapping the pencil and referred to the file again. "I assume you would prefer an urban posting. That's where the potential danger will be greatest. Somewhere like Manchester or Liverpool…"

"Is there nowhere closer to London?"

"A few rural districts and some of the smaller towns." His expression brightened suddenly as he scanned the typewritten pages in the file. "How about Colchester?"

She shook her head. "If it can't be London, then I'll settle for Liverpool."

"Excellent," Youde beamed, writing something down in the file. "Zone M45 in Newsham Park. It's one of the biggest in the country. It holds nearly two hundred people."

"When do I have to go?"

"As soon as possible. Perhaps tomorrow, if I can get the necessary documentation completed in time."

"Very well."

Youde closed the file with an air of satisfaction. "Come and see me tomorrow, Dr. Brant, around mid-day. By then I should have your papers ready."

After she had left Dr. Youde's office she went off in search of Dr. Vincent, and eventually found him in his small laboratory surrounded by wooden crates into which he and two assistants were packing instruments and equipment.

"Can I lend a hand?" she asked, by way of introducing herself.

Vince looked up and grinned. "Hello, Pauline. Moving day is almost upon us, I'm afraid. Tomorrow we start transferring the equipment to the new underground headquarters, and before the weekend we move in for the duration."

"I've been posted to Liverpool," she stated.

His expression became lean and gloomy. "Hell—couldn't old Youde find anywhere nearer than that? The chances of our getting together are going to be rather remote for a few months."

"We both knew that, anyway. Even if I'd stayed in London…"

"There would have been ways and means, with the aid of a little wire-pulling in the right places."

She sat down on one of the packing cases. "Vince, I've got a feeling that this is one crisis where wire-pulling won't work. When the storm really breaks, nobody with any sense is going to risk coming out of his rabbit-hole, even if it were permitted."

"There's bound to be some movement between the centres on official business—or in some cases unofficial business."

"And a chance of not being re-admitted if one picks up infection while outside."

"Not a chance, Pauline, but a certainty. The whole object of the shelters is to keep the virus out." He shrugged, picked up a handful of paper shavings from a box and packed it around a chrome equipment case in one of the crates. "We can only see how things go. It may not be so bad as we imagine."

She eyed him despondently. "I think it will be worse."

"When are you going?" he asked.

"Tomorrow, if Dr. Youde can arrange it. Zone M45."

"That's quicker than I expected. Let's have dinner together this evening."

"I can't, Vince. I've already arranged to have dinner with Clive."

He fitted the wooden lid to the crate and tightened the corner screws. "Can't you put him off?"

The dejection in the set of his face made her feel guilty and slightly ashamed, as if she had deliberately let him down. After all, on this, the final evening, the proposed meeting with Clive seemed to possess little real priority. For an instant she was tempted to change her plans, and then a compromise occurred to her.

"I think it would be better for me to see him, Vince. There are certain things we ought to thrash out, but I'll cut it short and come round to see you afterwards—say, around ten."

"Good girl," he said, pleased. "I'll be waiting."

The restaurant near Leicester Square was almost empty, as was the West End of London generally. The gaily flashing signs of Piccadilly Circus performed to deserted roads. A few taxis, mostly empty, and a handful of sombre cars hurried through the clear streets, as if surprised and slightly startled at the unexpected disappearance of London's usually chaotic traffic. Here and there pedestrians walked almost stealthily past dark, silent cinemas and theatres. Through the slatted blind on the window of the restaurant Pauline watched a bus trundle slowly by carrying only two passengers. A moment later an ambulance sped past, but its bell remained silent in the quiet road.

It was quite obvious that people were taking the state of emergency seriously, although the present desolation might well be due to a first shock reaction. During the day a number of new decrees had been announced. All schools had closed, and offices were required to provide a specified minimum working space for each member of their staffs to avoid overcrowding. Working hours were to be staggered on a scale never before attempted in order to ease pressure on public transport. No standing on Underground trains or buses; no overcrowding in shops and restaurants; admission to all kinds of premises to be restricted forthwith.

Clive, who during the meal had been digging for inside information about the progress of the virus, was sceptical about the new arrangements. "So far as I know the thing isn't directly contagious, it spreads through the air and through water supplies. It's not going to make much difference whether there's overcrowding or not."

"Off the record," she said, "there are other measures in hand which haven't been announced yet. Millions of breathing filters are being manufactured for mass distribution, and tablets are to be issued to sterilise water supplies—though boiling is still advisable."

"Sounds like a psychological gimmick to me," he commented. "Are these filters any good?"

"Some filters are good. The best are those which are so non-porous that the air has to be pumped through under high pressure.

I'm afraid the breathing filters they're going to issue will be much simpler—a kind of impregnated gauze mask—but they may help a little, and they might reassure people."

"Exactly my point." He made a wry grimace. "And the tablets?"

"Well, the only certain way to sterilise water is to distil it into sterilised containers."

"But the tablets may reassure people, as you put it," he said sardonically. "What's the betting that the so-called atom shelters are fully equipped with water distillation plant and pressurised air filters?"

"I imagine so."

"There's going to be trouble about those," he warned. "Rumours are getting around that they are simply virus shelters for the Establishment and Top Brass."

She considered for a few moments, anxious to side-step the subject in a plausible way. "Actually, they're administration centres," she explained, speaking the truth if not the whole truth. "Command posts, if you like. After all, underground bomb-proof headquarters were common enough during the war, and there was no trouble that I can recall."

There was a hint of irony in his slow smile. "I think a lot is going to depend on the people chosen to man these command posts, as you call them. This afternoon, for instance, some twenty-thousand workers at a big engineering concern came out on strike because they learned that the chairman and a selected few of the top management had set themselves up in a local virus shelter for the duration. There are likely to be more strikes as the news spreads round."

"It's really none of my business, Clive," she said impatiently. "I can only assume that whoever is responsible for making the selection of those to be protected feels that top management and scientists and industrial leaders are the kind of people the country will need most when the crisis is over."

"The trade unions are taking a different view," he said. "They believe there's a great deal of influence, wire-pulling and protection for the old pals involved. They want to know why people for virus protection should not be chosen by ballot from all levels of society."

"But, Clive, there aren't enough shelters…"

"They realise that. All they're asking is a fair and equitable distribution of protection."

She was about to reply when the waiter brought the coffee. The time was already nine-thirty, and remembering that she had arranged to see Vince at ten, she decided to change the subject very firmly.

"Clive, we didn't meet to talk about the virus situation," she said. "In any case, it's obvious that you know more about what's going on than I do."

"I still have my Fleet Street contacts, and you have your IVRO contacts. Between us we could work the thing out in detail."

"What would be the point? We're not in control of things. Let's talk about a matter which we can control."

"Such as divorce, I suppose."

She nodded. "I saw my solicitor late this afternoon, and he doesn't think anything can be done until the state of emergency is over. It will mean a delay of three or four months."

"I see," he said, clicking his tongue.

"I am citing Noelle Langstrom as co-respondent. I assume it will be undefended."

"There's nothing to defend, Pauline."

He reached across the table and touched her fingers. "I'm sorry, old girl. It should never have come to this, but now that it has, we may as well be sensible about it." With an amiable wink, he added: "Try to get your solicitor to hurry it up, even if it means extra costs."

For a long time she looked at him, taking in the firm rugged lines of his face and the cool humour of his sardonic grey eyes. He had charm enough, she knew, but beneath the charm was a vacuum, and she found herself wondering whether he had ever known, or would ever know, the true meaning of love beyond the superficial level of mildly sensual infatuation. And suddenly she felt sorry for him because something fundamental in him was rootless and drifting, and he would always be moving on and on, finding stagnation in stability and discarding those to whom he felt tied. It would be the same with Noelle once a further new horizon had opened up beyond the one to which he was now striving.

"I'll do my best," she murmured.

"And let's keep in touch from time to time," he suggested.

"I don't think that would be advisable, Clive. In any case, I shall be taking up a new post in Liverpool tomorrow, and it would be almost impossible for you to communicate with me at all other than through official IVRO channels."

"I think I understand. Protection for the privileged. Well, it couldn't happen to a nicer person."

"I merely obey orders." She glanced quickly at her wristwatch. "I'm afraid I have to go. I've got an appointment at ten. Thanks for the meal."

"You're welcome any time. See you after the crisis, presumably."

"Let's keep our fingers crossed," she said.

It was not her first visit to Dr. Vincent's flat; indeed, it had become customary for her to come back with him after dinner or a show for a late night drink and a short session of shop talk. The flat was one of a big apartment block near Maida Vale. Located on the third storey, it was small and rather austerely furnished, but the décor was colourfully amateurish and the walls were bedecked with a variety of framed paintings of abstract shapes and patterns which he produced from time to time as a form of relaxation on a do-it-yourself basis.

On this evening Vince had already been drinking when she arrived. Despite his air of assumed gaiety there was, however, an element of melancholy in the gaunt lines of his face.

He kissed her with ardour and immediately poured her a drink.

"Tonight, my love, we're going to get tight," he announced with exaggerated solemnity.

"Celebrating something, Vince?"

"No, no. We're going to…"—he hesitated, seeking the quotation that hovered elusively at the back of his mind—"to drown the memory of this impertinence."

He picked up his own glass and emptied it. "The fact is, Pauline, I'm fed up with this bloody virus, with all the official bans and decrees, with the great carve up that's going on—the Government's protection racket. I didn't realise until today, walking round the empty lab after they'd moved the crates out, just how deep this thing is cutting across our lives—all of us."

"There's no point in worrying about it, Vince."

"I'm not worrying. I'm just angry."

He went over to a small corner table near the window bay and poured himself another drink. She watched him speculatively. There was a certain carelessness in his movements, in the way he splashed whisky into his glass, which made her think that he had already succeeded in drowning a sizeable proportion of "this impertinence". She smiled to herself; it wasn't quite like the passive, pipe-smoking Vince to let his hair down so much.

He came back to her. "Drink up," he ordered.

She raised a questioning eyebrow, but obeyed the instruction.

"To you and me in three months time," he toasted. "Older, wiser, mellower."

"And alive, we hope."

He crossed his fingers briefly. "How was Clive?"

"Oh, much the same as usual. A little mixed up, I think. He's busy pursuing the ethics of the situation."

"You mean—he doesn't think divorce is ethical?"

She uttered a terse laugh. "*That's* ethical enough. I meant the virus. He went on about industrial strikes—trade union demands for equality of protection…"

"Well, if *that's* all he's got to worry about…"

"Being a journalist he's naturally interested. I think he has some idea that there might be a kind of general strike. I suppose he has what you might term a nose for news—before it happens."

Vince looked surprised. "What on earth would be the use of a general strike in the middle of a virus epidemic?"

"It's no use asking me, Vince. It wasn't my idea."

He put down his glass on the mantelshelf and took her in his arms. "Why are we talking about Clive, anyway? This is our last night together for a long time to come."

"Yes," she agreed. "Time always runs out faster towards the end."

His cheek against hers was bristly, and he smelt of pipe tobacco, but in some odd way these things were pleasant. He turned his head so that his lips found hers, and kissed her eagerly and artlessly. Fingers moving gently down her back made her shiver, but she drew herself closer to him and allowed herself to ride, with a certain caution, the surge of warm amorous feeling that overcame her.

"Pauline," he whispered presently, close to her ear, "why not stay here tonight?"

"Darling, what would be the use?" she said with a sigh. "We would only be making things more difficult for ourselves in the long run."

"Could be we'd make things easier. There would be a more positive link between us during the months to come."

"Either the link already exists or it never will," she said with a smile, still held tightly in his encircling arms. "If I were to stay, it wouldn't really prove anything, other than that you're a man and I'm a woman."

"It would prove we're in love."

She withdrew from him a little. "You ought to know better than that, Vince. It doesn't prove we're in love if we go to bed together."

"It doesn't prove we're not if we don't," he said, releasing her and sipping his drink.

"Exactly. It doesn't really prove anything."

"The truth is," he stated, looking at her with the intensity of drink in his eyes, "that deep down inside you're still in love with Clive."

"I don't think so. Let's put it this way. I'm still in the process of sorting out my emotional life and in many ways I'm confused." She put her hand gently on his arm. "So you see, Vince, you can't really expect me to make major decisions on which the whole of my future life may depend. I need time, darling."

"Yes," he agreed morosely, "I suppose that's all we need right now. Time—time and a half—double time. Nevertheless…"

He kissed her again, gently and with an air of thoughtfulness.

"Stay with me tonight, Pauline," he insisted.

"I've got things to do, Vince. Packing and preparing for tomorrow, letters to write…"

"They can be done in the morning."

"It's nearly morning already," she said, glancing at her wristwatch. She played her final card, the one she knew must succeed with a man like Vince. "It's not that I don't want to stay, darling, but I honestly don't think I should. I can't even give you adequate reasons because I find it difficult to express obscure instinctive feelings. But if you really do insist—if it's so vitally important to you—then…"

He shook his head, as she knew he would. "Not on those terms, my dear. You can't blame me for trying to persuade you, but I would be the last to insist. If we have any future together, it must be on a partnership basis."

"I knew you'd understand, Vince."

He picked up the two empty glasses. "That's the trouble. I'm probably the most understanding individual in the Western Hemisphere. It doesn't seem to get me anywhere, but perhaps it will in the long run."

He refilled the glasses.

"Pauline, the big seduction scene is over, and it wasn't a first night, after all. Let's start a new party. We'll play some music and dance."

"All right, Vince," she said. "But just for half an hour, then I really must be off."

"Good," he exclaimed. "In half an hour we can still get very tight, and you may still change your mind."

She smiled ruefully as he crossed the room to a record player standing on a small table in a corner of the window. He put on a record of soft, dreamy dance music, and came towards her expectantly.

The dancing was pleasant, and he made a number of determined verbal passes, but in the end she left half an hour later, dead on schedule, to face a new kind of future in Liverpool.

CHAPTER NINE

THE ONSET OF THE HUESTE AB-TYPE VIRUS, ESTIMATED TO have an incubation period of some twenty-four hours, was always difficult to diagnose because the accepted blood test was essentially negative; that is, it could demonstrate the absence of AB virus, up to a point, and prove the presence, or former existence, of the harmless BA-type infection. This in itself was useful enough, however, since BA patients were known to act as AB carriers for a period of up to ten days after the temperature peak, and steps could be taken to segregate and isolate them until the infection had run its course so that they were no longer acting as carriers.

The test, which Pauline was required to carry out on all two hundred inhabitants of the Newsham Park underground shelter in Liverpool, was simple in essence. It relied for its efficacy on the fact that BA patients automatically developed immunity to the lethal AB strain due to the formation of antibodies in the blood serum which prevented the AB strain from dissolving away the cell membranes and ectoblast tissues. It was necessary to remove a sample of blood by means of a syringe inserted in the arm or thigh, and the blood was then centrifuged to separate the red and white corpuscles from the straw-coloured serum.

The separated corpuscles were then smeared on five microscope slides. To each sample smear was added one drop of serum from each of the five main blood groups, all taken from patients who had died of AB virus infection. The five test serums had, of course, been sterilised so that no live virus was present; indeed, at no time outside specially equipped laboratories did serologists ever handle live Hueste virus as the risk of infection was considered to be too great.

The purpose of using five test serums was simply to save time in cases where the blood group of the patient or subject under test was unknown. The method enabled the serologist to ignore the agglutination factor in the corpuscles so that one or more slides, regardless of blood group, would show a negative or positive Hueste reaction.

The procedure was then simply one of waiting and watching. In a virus-free patient the test serum would, after an interval of between two and four hours, dissolve the cell membranes of the red and white corpuscles so that the smear on the slide would, observed under the microscope, degenerate from the characteristic grainy appearance of healthy blood into a smooth red paste of free haemoglobin. This merely demonstrated that the person under test had not had virus in the past, and that was all.

If, however, the corpuscles failed to dissolve into a paste but retained their individual form, then it could be assumed that the patient had at some time contracted the BA form of virus, and might still be a carrier of the deadly AB type. At this point the presence of live virus in the blood could only be conclusively demonstrated with the aid of an electron microscope. Segregation was the simpler and less costly method of dealing with the problem, unless the date of the BA infection with its mild symptoms could be established beyond doubt. Many emergency hospitals had been set up purely for the purpose of imposing two weeks of quarantine on suspected AB carriers.

The main difficulty arose in attempting to identify those who were in the very first stages of virus infection, during the short incubating period. Here the blood test offered little assistance, for the corpuscles merely dissolved in the same way as for a virus-free patient—but with one important difference which only became apparent about half-way through the incubation period, when the infection was some twelve hours old. In this case, the corpuscles in the blood sample—and in particular the white corpuscles, which had been actively engaged in fighting the virus—were already in a state of semi-dissolution. Consequently the breakdown time after the application of the test serum was measurably less, although it varied from one individual to another and depended to some extent on the actual blood group.

Generally speaking, however, a blood sample in which the haemoglobin paste formed in less than two hours was regarded with suspicion. Statistically, in nearly ninety per cent of blood tests showing such a result, the people concerned were correctly diagnosed as AB patients and, of course, inevitably died. The remaining ten per cent were usually former BA patients (or BAX types, as they were officially designated) in whom some blood group irregularity produced spurious results.

It was on this basis that Pauline began screening the men, women and children who had been fortunate enough to be allocated living quarters in Zone M45, Liverpool. Her instructions were quite precise: all confirmed BA cases were to be quarantined (but not in the underground shelter, of course), while all suspected AB victims were to be immediately hospitalised.

Only the remainder, the virus-free individuals whose blood samples showed a haemoglobin reaction in not less than two hours, were accepted for the full term of virus protection.

Even so, it was realised that there were likely to be a few cases where AB infection had been unidentified (or unidentifiable), for one reason or another, producing the invariable Hueste syndrome of high temperature and coma the following day. Such cases, if they occurred at all, would show all the virus symptoms within twenty-four hours, and arrangements had been made to secure quick removal of the victims concerned.

But perhaps the biggest danger lay in the acceptance of potential BA cases, whose symptoms were so slight as to pass unnoticed, but who would nevertheless act as dangerous AB carriers. Here the procedure laid down by the IVRO authority was ruthlessly applied. Everybody in Zone M45 (and for that matter all other zones) had to have an hourly temperature check during the first two days. The slightest recorded increase in temperature, however innocuous the cause, would result in immediate removal of the subject to hospital. Authority was not prepared to take any chances with the protection facilities offered by the virus shelters.

The Newsham Park shelter—or classified isolation centre, to give it its official title—was built on the honeycomb principle, occupying two levels some fifteen feet below the surface of a big field near the centre of the park. Consisting of simple terraced flatlets, the honeycomb comprised small rooms and narrow corridors, with walls and partitions of prefabricated concrete slabs and asbestos and hardboard sheets, but there was electricity and radio and television, and an efficient system of oil-fired central heating.

The domestic apartments occupied the entire lower level and slightly more than half of the upper level, the rest of the space being taken up by offices, laboratories, storerooms, an assembly room with a cine projector and a sound amplifier, a communications room containing teleprinter links and code and cypher machines, and, of course, a well equipped clinic.

Pauline was slightly surprised to find that the centre was run by the army. The key man, responsible for all administration, was

a Captain Villier, who commanded about twenty military personnel, including a lieutenant, and several NCO's, and there was also
a number of civilians engaged in specific duties concerned with
maintenance of the technical services, including air conditioning,
water sterilisation, catering, sanitation, and so on. She realised
that Zone M45 was, in fact, being run rather on the lines of a self-
contained army camp, but with civilians on the receiving end of
administration and discipline instead of troops.

The civilian residents at the centre appeared to be mainly of
executive status in industry, commerce and local government, consisting of family groups complete with children. During the courses
of clinical screening, hardships inevitably arose. Twenty-two adults
and seven children had to be rejected on the evidence of blood tests
and sent to a surface hospital under the inflexible rules of procedure.
The families of the infected individuals were given the option of
contracting out of the protection scheme to avoid separation, and
in most cases they did this, but a few others accepted the inevitable
fact of separation in a more practical manner.

It was interesting to note, Pauline thought, that in those instances
where a child had failed its blood test, the parents had elected to
return with it to the surface and face the virus risk, even though
they knew the child would be removed from them and perhaps die.
Voluntary separations, where they occurred, were usually in child-
less families in which one partner had chosen to remain protected
while the other was hospitalised.

Inevitably, of course, virus infection broke out in the centre
within two days of the official "sealing in"—the sealing was notional,
meaning simply that the centre was now closed to the outside world
and that all air and water sterilising equipment was in full operation. There were three cases of AB virus and one of BA. All were

removed to hospital within an hour of the preliminary diagnosis, and the next morning four new candidates were admitted to the centre, where they were kept under strict observation in a small isolation ward adjoining the clinic until it had been ascertained that they were virus-free.

After that there was no further trouble. So far as Pauline was concerned life began to settle down to a dull and rather monotonous routine of regular temperature checks and blood tests.

"Frankly, I'm not sure that I should choose to save any one of them," Captain Villier was saying. "Apart from the children, of course, and then only on sentimental grounds. But I have my orders and it's not my job to ask questions."

"I hardly know any of them at all as individuals," Pauline said.

They were sitting together in a corner of the austere canteen. The meal had been plain but acceptable, and the coffee was not worse than the usual cafeteria standard. Villier was a tall bony man with a pinched face bisected by a straggly ginger moustache several shades lighter than his lank brown hair. He had a crisp manner of speaking which lent him an air of authority, but there was nothing arrogant in his personality. The mid-day catering session was nearly over, and not more than half a dozen people were left in the canteen.

"They're not individuals," Villier said flatly. "They're classified important executives—in theory, at any rate. How many of them got in here because they happen to know the right people is any-body's guess. For example, Mr. A. is legitimately selected because he happens to be the managing director of a big international concern in engineering—nuclear power, electronics, and all that kind of pri-ority stuff. So what happens? He appoints his brother Mr. B. to the board of directors so that he can get protection as well, complete with family. Mr. B. doesn't need to know anything about engineering. He might be a road sweeper by trade. But he happens to have the right kind of relative who can lend him an executive status for a few months. When the crisis is over and he goes above ground again, he'll be asked to resign from the board and go back to road sweeping, or whatever it is that he does for a living."

Pauline shrugged. "You're stating an imaginary hypothetical case, of course."

"I could also state real cases, and give you name, rank and number."

"Well, human nature is like that. Every system is liable to abuse, however well planned. I don't think a few gate-crashers matter very much."

Villier puffed out his cheeks like a hamster and blew exasperated air through his moustache. "It's bad luck on the Toms, Dicks and Harrys who can't gate-crash and who aren't on executive level."

"Not necessarily, Captain Villier," Pauline said. "They're not all going to die. There's a fifty-fifty chance of survival, and when you get down to individual cases, like your Mr. A. and Mr. B., both could well survive on the surface."

"Or both die."

"The odds are still equal."

He fingered his chin pensively. "I wonder how they're getting on up there," he murmured.

After four days underground the world had already split into two levels, she thought: up there and down here. Up there was a part of society abandoned by authority, in the process of breaking down, stalked by death and industrial paralysis. And, if events followed the pattern of other countries, the threat of famine, martial law, and even civil war. It was better to be underground, not merely to escape the virus, but also to avoid the chaos and confusion of a world completely disrupted by sudden plague.

"I suppose if I were a Cabinet minister I should have planned things in much the same way," Villier said. "Obviously the Establishment—as much of it as possible—would have to go underground. What interests me most is the aftermath—what will happen when the Establishment tries to come to the surface again?"

"You think there might be trouble?"

He smiled gloomily. "Trouble? That is probably the understatement of the century."

It was a long memorandum on pale blue paper headed *Department of Home Affairs*, with an embossed governmental insignia, and it had been rubber-stamped *Strictly Confidential*. Dr. Youde adjusted his concave glasses and switched on the desk light so that he could read more clearly the close lines of typewritten instructions.

> *For the attention of grade 'A' executive staff of IVRO, United Kingdom Division*, it began. *Important: this memorandum must be destroyed by fire immediately after reading.*

It continued:

> The Department of H.M. Government responsible for internal security and the maintenance of law and order has recently completed a survey of the current domestic situation in the United Kingdom following the first three weeks of the Hueste virus epidemic.
>
> The object of this survey is to enable the Government, and in particular the Home Office, to anticipate changing

trends in the morale and political behaviour of the civilian population not assigned to classified isolation centres, and to determine official policies which will enable swift and efficient action to be taken, where necessary, to preserve internal security of the State.

It was foreseen that the measures taken to protect classified important executives by means of underground isolation centres would provoke a degree of hostile reaction, manifesting itself principally in industrial terms through trade union organisations.

The position at present is that over forty per cent of UK industry and commerce is strikebound, and there is evidence that certain factions among industrial workers and less responsible trade unions are combining forces with a view to active subversion against the State. If this trend should develop it could have serious ramifications.

IVRO officials will realise that the steps taken to protect classified important executives are essential to preserve the basic structure of our society in the face of a world disaster of unparalleled magnitude.

It will be understood that as the Hueste virus spreads among the unprotected population, the number of deaths due to AB infection can be expected to increase at an accelerating rate towards the final climax, but at the same time and at the same rate the number of BA cases must also increase. The latter, having acquired immunity from further virus infection and being guaranteed survival, can generally be expected to behave in a stable and rational manner. They will normally be favourably disposed towards the maintenance of law and order.

The Home Office has, therefore, been authorised under an Emergency Decree to recruit and establish a special security militia force to supplement the police and the armed forces.

The force will consist exclusively of BAX-type virus patients who are out of quarantine and are duly certified as no longer AB-type carriers. Candidates for the force will be screened politically, psychologically and medically. On enlistment they will be remunerated for their services at an attractive level, and may receive other privileges.

Simultaneously, other essential measures will be introduced to discourage the present wave of strikes and industrial unrest, which is seriously dislocating the nation's supplies of food and materials.

Rationing of foodstuffs, fuels, and all consumer goods is to commence forthwith. Ration cards will be issued to all British citizens resident in the UK, with the exception of workers on strike.

At the same time internal currency is to be substantially devalued to strengthen the economic reserves of the Government. The police, armed forces and the new security militia force will, however, receive increased emoluments together with supplementary rations in acknowledgement of their added responsibilities, so that there will be no significant reduction in their standard of living.

In this way it is expected that a high level of recruitment for all forces of the Crown will be achieved, while workers in industry will have reduced incentive to strike or continue to strike.

IVRO officials at Grade 'A' level are consequently required to establish special units at recruiting stations to carry out medical examinations and blood tests on candidates for all security forces, and in particular the newly formed security militia.

Candidates, in order to qualify, must be of the BAX type, i.e., ex-BA cases out of quarantine. Political and psychological screening by independent units will follow the clinical tests for those who pass.

Appended is a list of recruiting centres which are to be opened throughout the UK during the next few days. Two qualified personnel, preferably a doctor and a serologist, will be required for each centre for a period of four to six weeks. Preferably they should be BAX types, but where this is not possible, volunteers should be sought.

The Government wishes to state that these measures are being introduced with considerable reluctance and on a temporary basis to meet existing conditions. They are to be implemented without delay, and are considered essential for the preservation of traditional democratic institutions in the UK.

It is pointed out that they are in line with similar measures which have been put into effect throughout Europe, and are about to be decreed in the USA.

There was more, of course—several pages of it. Appendices outlining the more detailed points of the proposed security militia organisation, and long tables of statistics on virus deaths, compulsory cremations, man-hours lost through strikes, percentage falls in industrial output, crime and murder figures (nearly thirty per cent up), and so on.

When he had finished reading the memorandum, Dr. Youde made a note of the recruiting centres nearest to Brierley, then folded the sheaf of blue papers and ceremoniously ignited it with a match, according to instructions. Then he sent for Dr. Vincent.

Vincent was looking more haggard than usual. Several weeks in an underground laboratory pursuing a hopeless and perhaps impossible quest tended to exert a depressing and dispiriting effect, he found. In addition there had been bad news, or perhaps good news, whichever way you looked at it. His wife had died of AB virus. It was a remote objective fact that had haunted him for days past; it had been presented to him as a *fait accompli* in the form of a printed advice note on buff paper (rather like an invoice, he thought), after the coma, after the death, after the cremation. There had been a phase of remorse and a subsequent period of reflective melancholy which still persisted. Despite her faults she hadn't deserved to die, not so casually and so abruptly—she had possessed too much of life itself, its zest and energy. But the virus was quite impersonal in its choice of victim: liveliness was no antidote to death.

"Sit down, Vincent," Dr. Youde said.

Vince sat down. He pushed his pipe between his teeth, but did not bother to light it.

Youde said: "How are things progressing in the lab?"

"Sideways."

"I see. How would you like a change of job?"

"Doing what?"

"Carrying out BAX tests on civilians. It's a Government assignment."

Vince frowned. "What's the point?"

Youde outlined the requirements of the Home Office order concerning the proposed security militia force. He added: "They want to recruit BAX types who have no further virus fears, and they want a number of doctors from IVRO to man the recruiting centres for a few weeks."

"Sounds ominous to me," Vince said with a frown. "Is human society really in such an advanced state of disintegration?"

"It's only a precautionary measure. There's a threat of a general strike, and a certain amount of underground subversive organisation going on. Naturally the Government wants to keep the essential services functioning, and take steps to prevent possible sabotage. It's a question of reinforcing the police and military with a security force of people who are immune to AB virus. How do you feel about it?"

Vince considered for a moment. "Frankly, I'd feel happier if I were a BAX type myself."

"There is a risk, admittedly," Youde said, taking off his glasses and polishing them. "You're entitled to decline, of course. The call is for volunteers."

"Just how serious is the situation?" Vince asked, after a pause.

"It's difficult to be precise. We know from IVRO statistics that the death roll in Great Britain now exceeds three million. I've been informed that something like forty per cent of British industry is paralysed by strikes. There have also been several outbreaks of organised violence, mainly attempts to break open the underground isolation centres. For instance, a shelter near Northampton was attacked by an armed mob who managed to break open the air lock, poured about fifty gallons of petrol into the gap, and set fire to it. Seventeen people died and thirty-two were seriously injured, including the IVRO resident doctor. Those who tried to escape from the fire into the outside world were beaten up by the mob, and two died later in hospital. By the time the police and military were able to intervene it was virtually all over."

"I see what you mean."

"That kind of violence is likely to increase. The Government has to choose between maintaining authority or surrendering to mob rule."

Vince smiled grimly. "Personally, I'm in favour of maintaining the old status quo. I want things to get back to what they were, though I realise only too well that they never can. All the same, if it's any help, I'm willing to go along with the Home Office."

"That means you accept?"

"Yes. After all, I really have no choice."

Dr. Youde seemed immensely satisfied. "I was hoping you would say that. Let's face it, the vaccine research programme is going to take a devil of a long time to get anywhere at all. Now that the virus is with us it's no longer an abstract matter of research. There are more practical issues to be decided, and I can't help feeling that IVRO must play its part in the less abstract matters of politics and security."

"Yes," Vince agreed after reflection. "You're quite right."

"The Home Office has asked for a doctor and an experienced serologist. Is there anyone you could suggest?"

Vince spent nearly a minute in earnest consideration. "Wyatt," he said finally. "He's a competent serologist, and I believe he's a BAX type, too. He would need to be blood-tested, of course."

"Very well, I'll have a word with him this afternoon. Meanwhile, just carry on as usual. By tomorrow I should be in a position to give you full instructions."

Vince nodded. "I'll be waiting," he said.

CHAPTER TEN

IDLENESS WAS A PROBLEM FOR CLIVE. FOR MOST OF TWO WEEKS he mooned about the flat, reading newspapers with cynicism rather then interest, watching television in a mood of bored deflation, and occasionally drinking beer very slowly in the local pub. Every day he booked a transatlantic telephone call to New York, but on each occasion it was cancelled at the last minute in favour of priority traffic. Nor was there any communication from Noelle or the Langstrom organisation, so that his new job began to take on something of the quality of an hallucination.

To occupy his time and collect background material for future television work, he began making notes and pasting newspaper cuttings into an improvised scrapbook. He also called in at the *Daily Monitor* building where his ex-colleagues made him feel welcome enough, but were relatively uninformative in response to his more searching questions about the virus—probably because they were equally in the dark, he decided.

The broad picture of events throughout the country was one of strikes, protest marches, incidents of mob violence, and a devastating slump in share prices on the Stock Exchange. Public services were still running, though erratically, but there was talk of a national railway strike and a threatened shut-down of electricity power stations. Troops had taken over the docks and the civil airports. As if subjected to newsprint rationing, the newspapers had drastically reduced their number of pages to as few as four in some cases, while many weekly magazines switched to monthly publication, or ceased altogether.

It was as if the pace of industry and commerce was slackening to something around half of its previous level in anticipation of the destruction of half the country's labour force.

One afternoon the man and his wife occupying the flat immediately below Clive's were taken away in an ambulance. Looking out of his bay window he observed that the woman was already in a state of coma while the man, also on a stretcher seemed apathetic and glassy-eyed. Less than one hour later his doorbell rang. He opened it to find himself confronted by a short bespectacled man in a bowler hat accompanied by a nurse in trim blue uniform. They insisted on invading his home and taking a sample of his blood.

"There's virus in the building," the doctor explained tersely. "For your own sake we have to make sure you're not infected."

"Suppose I was infected. What could you do about it?"

"We would take the necessary steps."

"Such as a plastic coffin and a reservation at the nearest incinerator?"

The doctor eyed him dubiously. "You know, it isn't necessarily like that at all. There are two kinds of virus, and if you caught the mild type it would merely mean ten days in quarantine. After that you would be completely immune to both types."

"Then why not inject everybody with the mild type to confer immunity?"

"An excellent idea," said the doctor, smiling, and then proceeded to explain why it could not be done, adding: "There are experimental vaccines, of course, and if you would like to volunteer…"

"You make it sound like volunteering for certain death."

"By no means, but candidly, the vaccines we've tried so far have made negligible difference—statistically, that is. It would only confuse you if I were to attempt to explain the way in which the virus is divided into two strains..."

"I know about the AB and BA business," Clive said. "My wife works for IVRO."

The doctor raised his eyebrows in surprise. "Indeed. Well, you probably know more about it than I do."

"In some respects, perhaps. How's the death rate progressing, doc?"

The doctor's chatty affability faded somewhat. "There aren't any figures. But it's going up, I fear. Safest thing is to stay indoors, Mr. Brant. Mark time until it all blows over."

He closed his bag and departed with the nurse. Clive stood by the window and watched them drive off in a black station wagon. For a while he stared out and down at the deserted road, and then, suddenly, two ambulances drove by in quick succession, to be followed by a third a few minutes later.

In the early evening the doorbell rang again. Reluctantly, half expecting a return visit of the doctor and nurse with ominous news, he found himself face to face with Noelle. Surprise momentarily robbed him of speech, and it was the girl herself who broke the silence.

"Lordsakes, darling, aren't you glad to see me?"

"Sorry," he said, recovering his composure. "You're the last person I expected. Come on in."

She was wearing a grey coat over a green dress, and her blonde hair had been cut short in a new boyish style. Her lipstick was, if anything, a little too scarlet, but her blue eyes were as lively as ever. He embraced and kissed her with a certain diffidence, still not quite accepting the indisputable fact of her presence. Then she took off her coat and flung herself wearily into an armchair.

"God, what a journey! What with blood tests, interrogation, cancelled flights and a ten-hour delay at Shannon due to engine trouble. It would almost have been quicker by sea."

He poured two drinks. "Noelle, it's good to see you. How did you manage it?"

"Just like I explained on the phone, darling. Daddy made me an executive of International Telerama and started pulling wires like mad. It took time, but I finally got an official travel permit from State Department—also an authorisation for Joe Beigal and Dave Ross, two of our best cameramen, not to mention a crateload of movie equipment and tape recorders."

"Hm. Daddy's obviously got more pull than I gave him credit for."

"You can say that again. I've even got a personal letter of introduction from Cleary of the Federal Communications Commission to a Mr. Danninger at your Central Office of Information here in London. It's all cut and dried."

"Just precisely *what* is all cut and dried."

"The archive project."

He regarded her blankly.

"That was the only way daddy could swing the deal, by agreeing to make movie records for official archives. The Government is even subsidising part of the cost. Some of the material may go on television after it's been vetted by authority, but we figure most of it will be classified and restricted. Every country in the world is doing the same kind of thing, just as they did in the war. Your own Information Centre has got film units in Europe, the States and the Far East."

"Fine," Clive commented, "though it hardly sounds like a profitable commercial venture."

"It's groundwork, Clive. After the epidemic it will pay off for years to come."

He finished his drink and refilled the glasses. "Just where do I fit into this picture of archival enterprise?" he enquired.

"That's all fixed. Daddy's lawyers have registered a company over here named Telerama Great Britain, Ltd. You're to be executive director. There's also a business account open at a City bank for all running expenses until we can get salaries lined up. We're to liaise with the Security Division of the Central Office of Information and get as much down on film and tape as we can."

"Oh," he remarked. "I started with a wrong impression—that the archive set-up was a plot to wangle travel permits rather than a legitimate project."

"It's a bit of both when you figure it out," she said, smiling sardonically. "You'll find out why in due course. Daddy always has a card left up his sleeve."

"Meaning?"

"Wait till we get together with Beigal and Ross. We've got to talk policy and practice first. We're all staying at the Astoria Hotel in Piccadilly, and we'll hold our first meeting there tomorrow. But for tonight…"

He eyed her questioningly.

"Clive darling, do you think we might go out somewhere to eat—just the two of us?"

"Of course, though I ought to warn you that eating out is a rather dreary process nowadays, and there's always the risk of virus infection…"

"That applies, anyway. I mean, for all you know I may be a virus carrier here and now, or you, for that matter. What's the point of living like hermits?"

"Well, sometimes it's difficult to be so objective about it. We'll eat out and then I'll take you back to your hotel."

She looked at him through half lowered eyelids and finished her drink. "Wrong, silly Clive. Beigal and Ross can look after themselves. Tonight I stay here with you."

They went out for dinner.

The Security Division of the Central Office of Information proved to be grudging so far as issuing photography permits was concerned, Clive found, and in the end the applications had to be referred back to higher authority. After a delay of more than a week qualified permission was granted, but all film footage had to be processed and vetted by the COI, and tape recordings were liable to arbitrary censorship. In addition, a detailed shooting schedule had to be submitted each day to Danninger or his assistant for approval so that the Telerama plans could be scrutinised in advance by officialdom.

Clive, Noelle, Beigal and Ross spent many hours in conference at the Astoria working out a practical programme of action. At this stage the virus epidemic was building up to frightening proportions, and the strikes had increased dramatically as a result of the latest Government measures—rationing, currency devaluation, and the establishment of a security militia.

"The thing we have to decide," Clive said at an early meeting, "is what we're trying to put on record. Is it to be merely a documentary record of the virus epidemic from a medical point of view, that is, with the accent on clinical research and therapy, or should we attempt to make it a complete social record showing policies and politics in action?"

Joe Beigal, a swarthy man with crew-cut black hair, wearing a loose light-grey suit, lit a long filter cigarette and blew a jet of smoke straight at Clive. "It's gotta be complete to be any good," he pronounced. "E.L. won't stand for half measures."

"The trouble is we may run full tilt into censorship," Clive pointed out. "Any implication that the Government is acting in an arbitrary, irresponsible way…"

"We don't have to imply that at all."

"But if we're to prevent a balanced view…"

Beigal spread out his hands questioningly. "What *is* a balanced view, Clive? Your view? My view? Or the view of one of those protectees in the deep shelters? Or the view of one of those workers without a ration card having to line up at a street kitchen every day for bread and soup?"

Noelle, who throughout the discussions, had displayed shrewd, level-headed qualities that had rather surprised Clive, said: "It's not our job to have views of any kind, balanced or unbalanced. All we're required to do is report what we see, objectively, like we were cameras ourselves, with no feelings. We leave it to others to draw conclusions and comment."

"That's policy," Clive stated, "but our problem is politics. We're operating by permission and under sanction. If we don't play our cards right we may run into an absolute veto. We want to stay in business, don't we?"

Dave Ross, a thin acidulated man with rimless glasses and lank brown hair, said: "Clive's right. We've got to play ball with the COI, and that means we've got to assume the Government over here knows what it's doing—and that what it's doing is right."

"Whether we believe it or not," Clive added.

Noelle frowned. "I don't think daddy will go for that. He wants the truth. That's what he told me before we came away. Eye-Witness presents the truth—no more, no less."

"Even an eye-witness is entitled to an opinion," Ross murmured with a sad smile.

"The truth is what Danninger, the COI and the Government permit it to be," Clive stated flatly. "Our best plan is to work out a film schedule embracing every possible aspect of the situation, submit it to Danninger, then go ahead as far as we can after he's chopped it to pieces."

Beigal's lips moved into a cynical twist. "That's a fair statement, Clive, but in the long run it makes no difference. What they chop out in London can be put back in New York. E.L. can fake anything in his studios—all he needs is some authentic information for his scriptwriters and set designers. So, in that sense, we're all acting as eye-witnesses, quite apart from the cameras. If they won't let us shoot a riot in Bethnal Green then we can reconstruct it in the States, and probably make it a darned sight more realistic."

Clive found himself suppressing a surge of irritation. He felt that Beigal, although one of E.L.'s executive producers and a competent cameraman, was being rather too smug and facile in the face of a genuine problem of policy. Why bother to do any film reporting at all, he thought; why not go back to New York, all of us, and reconstruct the entire catastrophe in a film studio? Who could tell the difference?

He slapped his hand on the table and said: "Let's get one thing straight. We're attempting to record a pretty dramatic segment of history. Fiction and faking are out. This has got to be the real thing."

"Agreed." That was Noelle.

"I've already prepared a tentative outline," Clive went on, referring to a pocket diary. "There are two parallel conflicts involved. One is the medical world versus the virus. The other is the Establishment versus the people. Both subjects can be subdivided into independent categories, though we may not get COI permission in all cases. I'm referring in particular to film sequences taken in underground shelters and IVRO laboratories."

"Danninger has already applied a veto there," Noelle pointed out. "But COI already has its own film units operating underground, and he said we might be able to have access to some of their film footage under a licensing agreement with Telerama."

"That means we'll have to work above ground for the present—street scenes, hospitals, evacuation zones and crematoria, following up with the industrial angle—empty factories, picket lines, food queues at street kitchens, the rationing set-up generally. Then we might cover the police and security services, and the information channels such as the press, and radio and TV."

"Okay," Beigal assented. "The important thing is to get permits—as many permits as possible so we can go as many places as we can. We pay lip service to censorship, but we don't have to worry."

"Why not?" Clive demanded.

By way of reply Beigal put one hand into an inner pocket of his coat and withdrew a tiny cine camera only a little larger than the average cigarette lighter.

"Japanese," he said. "It takes a special microfilm and uses an anamorphic lens, so you get four runs on a film. That's a total of ten minutes' movie time for each film."

"Ingenious," Clive commented, taking the camera from the other man. It was a precision-built instrument with a self-contained light cell controlling the lens iris, while the lens itself was recessed unobtrusively into the body of the camera.

Noelle said: "We have two of them and plenty of film. They were smuggled in, of course, otherwise they'd have been confiscated. They're too spy-angled to beat the security barrier."

"What's the point?" Clive asked.

"They're our second line of attack. We'll be using the standard sixteen-millimetre cameras in the proper way with official permits, but we can double up on the Japanese cameras for controversial shots. And there will be other things we'll need to shoot undercover and in a great hurry, either because we can't get the standard equipment set up in time, or because it's against the rules. That's where the miniatures will be useful. You can conceal them in the palm of your hand, and shoot between the fingers."

Clive nodded his appreciation of the device. "Could be dangerous, though," he added.

"Only if we get caught," the girl said. "Beigal and Ross will have one of the miniatures between them, and you and I will share the other." She opened her handbag and produced another miniature camera, which she handed to him. "It would be safer in your pocket, Clive. Handbags can easily get lost."

"All right," he agreed, slipping the midget camera into the inside pocket of his coat.

At last we're in business, he thought, whether Danninger's office decides to play ball or not.

The next day, while Noelle went to see Danninger at the Information Centre, Clive made a circular tour of London in his car, referring to a map on which he had marked a number of key points for possible location shooting. Even in daytime London seemed a deserted city. He saw only five cars and one bus in the whole length of Oxford Street, where, in pre-virus days, the choked traffic had crawled in convoy from one signal to the next. Pedestrians were few in number, and most of them were wearing virus filters over the nose and mouth. Many of the big stores were closed, presumably due to shortage of staff or possibly the imposition of even more stringent anti-crowd regulations by the local authority.

Hyde Park, site of one of the first of the underground shelters, had acquired a distinctly military aspect. Driving leisurely by, Clive saw barbed wire fencing patrolled by armed troops, and inside the wire were Nissen huts and armoured cars. At the southern side of the park, near Knightsbridge, two tanks stood squatly on their caterpillar tracks, guns facing outwards across the wide road junction.

He drove on down Piccadilly, noting similar evidence of military installations and equipment in Green Park on the right of the road. Two white ambulances overtook him at high speed in quick succession, no doubt rushing virus cases to the nearest evacuation centre.

At Holborn he began to make his way towards the northern suburbs of London, and now the atmosphere began to change in a subtle manner. Although traffic density, such as it was, began to decrease, there were more people about, mainly men who, unlike the hurrying, furtive pedestrians of central London, walked idly in groups or loafed at street corners. For the first time he saw the newly recruited security militia—two young men in black battledress with peaked caps, walking purposefully together along the edge of the pavement. He observed their black leather belts with revolvers slung in holsters and noted their solid, slightly arrogant manner. He saw, too, the cold resentment in the eyes of the idling men.

A dual-carriageway through a factory area; solemn-faced pickets holding placards—*On strike for the right to survive—All we ask is an equal chance to live—Protection for all or none*, and so on. Clive's lips framed a thin smile of irony: the basic law of nature still applied. Two black police cars stood by, watching and waiting. Factories with smashed windows, and one gutted by fire—more militia patrols, the heavy steel buckles on their leather belts gleaming in the afternoon sunshine—barbed wire surrounding a food canning plant, with an armoured car stationed in the forecourt. A shopping centre, dead and desolate—more pickets and more placards—and then, passing swiftly by, a skirmishing fight between strikers and police and black-uniformed security men outside a frozen food warehouse. A mile further on... a small factory engulfed in fire, attended by bright red fire engines and salvage tenders and hoses squirting thin plunging jets of fierce water into the smoke and flame.

A kind of insurrection, Clive thought, accelerating into an off-limit country road. At least, this was how it would begin, with demonstrations, strikes, riots and sabotage, and the quick build up of organised resistance to authority. And the violence, of course—the inevitable violence. And in the course of time a leader would emerge and the rioters would become insurgents, and if they gained ground they would set up a revolutionary government.

But it couldn't happen in England, he told himself. The forces of law and order were too powerful, and, in any case, there was no reason to suppose that the present disaffection was politically motivated. It was simply a by-product of desperation expressing itself in the form of civil disobedience, and it would fade with the virus in the course of time.

He stopped the car to check his map, then drove on in the direction of Enfield, presently turning off the main road to proceed east between tall hedges. Abruptly he swung round a bend to find himself facing a striped road barrier manned by two security guards. Beyond the barrier was a field that had been bulldozered and strewn with gravel, and further back still lay an encampment of prefabricated huts and canvas marquees. At the centre of the site stood a long, low brick building with a tall chimney from which black smoke curled lazily. On the gravel forecourt a dozen or more white ambulances were parked, and as he stopped the car he could see ambulance men carrying plastic-enclosed stretchers towards a big grey hut labelled *Intake*.

One of the security men approached him leisurely, thumbs hooked in the leather gun-carrying belt round his waist.

"Sorry, sir, but you're not allowed in here without a written permit."

Clive produced a card signed by Danninger of COI, which simply stated that he was an executive of a film unit authorised to visit certain specified sites for the purpose of making documentary film records, subject to additional written authorisation bearing an official COI seal. At this stage, of course, he had no supplementary permit; Noelle was at that moment negotiating it with Danninger. Nevertheless the guard seemed mollified and vaguely impressed.

"Just a preliminary look round," Clive explained. "I'll probably be back in a day or two with cameras and equipment and a supplementary permit."

The guard nodded. "Very well, sir. But I can't let you in now, you understand."

"Quite."

A bell jangled shrilly behind him. In the car mirror he saw a white ambulance immediately to the rear, so he engaged first gear, let in the clutch and pulled the car over to one side of the road. The guard raised the barrier to allow the ambulance to enter the site, and before he had time to lower it again two more ambulances arrived to discharge their load of AB virus cases.

"Keeping busy," Clive remarked when the guard returned.

"Busy enough. It'll get worse before it gets better."

Clive began to reverse and turn the car. "See you again soon," he called. The guard waved one hand in a casual manner.

Clive retraced the route back into town. Just a quick look round, he told himself. Everything seems to be under control, but these are early days yet, and somehow the country seems to be in a state of precarious balance, with security poised against the people while the real enemy, the Hueste virus, carries on its grim work without opposition.

It's all a question of balance, he reiterated silently in his mind. Poise and balance. If they can be preserved then the nation will emerge from the crisis without too many scars.

Driving through Palmers Green on the way back he saw the blue sky ahead light up in transient incandescence. A moment later came the shuddering blast of a tremendous explosion. The car swerved and almost ran off the road, but he gripped the wheel firmly and swung it against the thrust of the blast. The sky darkened with ascending smoke, but he by-passed the site of the explosion and did not bother to investigate. More sabotage, he thought—perhaps a factory blown up, or even an underground shelter. In the end it's all futile. Why can't they live and let live... or, for that matter, die and let die.

He squeezed the accelerator and hurried back to his flat in Queens Gate and Noelle.

CHAPTER ELEVEN

URING THE FIRST TWO WEEKS OF ACTIVITY THE TELERAMA
film unit shot an immense amount of footage, both in black
and white and colour. Beigal and Ross proved to be quick and
competent at their jobs, with a keen sense of news and a sharp eye
for effective visual presentation, unusual angles and powerful close-
ups. Beigal invariably thought in terms of close-ups, the bigger the
better, for he was essentially a television man and he knew how to
make the most of the small grey screen.

A great deal of film was initially in the nature of background
material, but as time went on and scenes became more specialised,
much of the material became macabre and rather horrific. They
spent an entire afternoon, for instance, in an unnamed evacuation
centre and crematorium in the fringe suburbia of South London,
where a special cold store covering an area of about a thousand
square yards had been built to cope with the overflow of dead
bodies awaiting final disposal in the furnaces. The corpses, some
twenty thousand of them, were stacked side by side on tiered shelv-
ing, and an electrically powered conveyor belt had been installed
to mechanise and facilitate transport into the ovens. Even so, the
capacity of the crematorium, working day and night, was severely
overloaded, and plans were in hand to build an extension to the
cold store.

The administrative office attached to the evacuation centre
employed electronic data processing equipment to cope with the
vast quantity of documentation required. Relevant details of every
AB fatality case were recorded on punched cards and transmitted

over underground telecommunication cables to a statistical office in Whitehall.

Clive found himself suitably impressed with the evacuation centre, which operated with all the clean efficiency of a modern factory. After the first shock of finding oneself in a warehouse of death, with still grey bodies stacked on all sides like mass produced commodities, one began to appreciate the foresight and shrewd planning behind it all. The Government had assessed only too accurately the fantastic extent of the problem, and had made adequate preparations.

They shot enough film to make a couple of full length movies, knowing that much of it would be cut and vetoed by the COI censor, but doubled up on the miniature Japanese cameras for the more dramatic scenes in order to make sure that the censor would not have the final say. Noelle retired early in the proceedings; she went back to the car to wait. Despite her superficially businesslike air she was forced to admit that the crematorium sequence was just a little too gruesome for her personal taste. Clive, Beigal and Ross carried on in a sombre fashion, saying little, but concentrating on lighting and camera angles.

Later, Clive tape-recorded an interview with the director of the evacuation centre, who talked guardedly of his work and expressed the view that the peak of the virus death roll would be reached in about a month, and after that the pressure would begin to relax.

The COI processed the film, checking each reel off against official permits, and as anticipated cut out a considerable number of sequences which, they considered, were not in the public interest. However, the micro-miniature anamorphic shots taken by the Japanese cameras would adequately fill the gaps. So far as Clive was concerned, posterity could best decide what was in the public interest.

They were also fortunate enough to film a pitched battle between the military, aided by the police and the new security force, and a well organised gang of some fifty men who had taken possession of a store in the East End of London, presumably to steal and stockpile food and alcoholic drinks.

The raid had begun in a small way during the night and had been discovered by the police. Within two hours both sides had been substantially reinforced and effectively armed.

There was no possibility of using the standard camera equipment, for this was one of those sudden off-the-cuff events for which prior filming permission could not be obtained from COI. Clive used one of the miniature cameras, and Beigal the other, splitting up into two groups to cover the scene from opposite angles.

The store was a three-storey corner building consisting of a licensed self-service shop at ground level, a stockroom above, and offices of a small hire-purchase investment company at the top. The gang were in occupation of all three levels, defending themselves with revolvers and automatic weapons, probably Sten guns. The military and security forces had lined up a number of heavy trucks along the opposite side of the road and were using them as screens. In addition, two armoured cars had positioned themselves at the road junction.

It was around eleven o'clock in the morning, and the state of siege was already some six hours old. Spectators—and there were more than a thousand of them, Clive estimated—were standing well back, outside of the immediate line of fire. The shooting was sporadic from both sides, as if all concerned were waiting for a sensational event to take place.

The police had already used tear gas, but to no avail. The raiders had equipped themselves with goggles and antivirus masks, and with the aid of these accessories seemed to be relatively undisturbed by the gas. They had responded by lobbing two plastic hand grenades out of a high window. Result, no deaths—but five casualties among the security forces.

The situation seemed to be static at present, so Clive took some establishing shots from different angles, moving forward to a more advantageous position at the advance fringe of the crowd. Noelle, clinging to his arm, followed behind.

Gunfire crackled intermittently, and then the armoured cars opened up with cannons. Bricks tumbled and fell noisily in a shower of debris. More hand grenades and more casualties.

The military brought up a flame thrower and trained it on the building. Liquid fire spurted in a thin jet, splashing incandescently over the walls, seeking the shattered windows. Sten guns chattered, and the flame thrower stopped abruptly. But smoke billowed from the windows of the stricken building; flames surged and gained a hold.

More tear gas shells, and more bursts from Sten guns—and then, incredibly, reinforcements arrived in support of the raiders. Half a dozen trucks and vans, protected with shining steel plate, drove towards the road junction, then turned, straddling the exit roads. The deeper roar of Bren guns filled the air. Smoke bombs exploded and burned, breathing dense fog into the turbulent atmosphere.

Clive kept moving, using the miniature camera. When the spool was finished, he dived into a shop doorway to replace it with a fresh magazine. This was more than just a well planned burglary—it was a highly organised commando raid with all the makings of a miniature civil war.

Noelle, rather pale and anxious, said: "Clive, do you think it's wise to stay here?"

"Maybe not, but I feel we ought to stay because this is a fore-taste of what's to come. The origins may be more important than the aftermath, taking the long view. If we can get some of it on record…"

"I can't help feeling—well, uneasy. I never guessed things would reach this extreme."

"This is organised insurrection in its early stages," he said.

The smoke was spreading in a dense grey cloud that obscured vision and made photography difficult. Something exploded with a brilliant orange flash, but it was impossible to determine what had happened. Now there were shouts and the sound of running feet—more bursts of firing from automatic weapons, and then, remotely, but growing louder, a metallic grinding and rattling accompanied by the drone of a diesel engine. Suddenly out of the fog loomed a tank.

Clive shot more cine film, then, taking Noelle's arm, backed away. "Things are hotting up a bit," he murmured. "I think we'd better stick to longshots."

The tank turned in a narrow circle and lumbered towards the front of the building under siege. Bullets sparked as they ricocheted from its steel plating. Came the grinding crash of powered impact. Bricks shattered and tumbled. The tank reversed, then came on again, widening the gap in the wall. Now figures were moving across the road through the haze, and suddenly the flame thrower was active again, splashing fire into the gaping cavity. Screams pierced the troubled air, and the firing became more insistent.

A moment later a solid phalanx of men streamed from the wrecked building, around the tank, climbing on to it. Hand grenades flashed and roared. Now there was hand-to-hand fighting and continuous shooting, with the Bren guns keeping up a relentless background thunder, and the flame thrower began to sweep wildly, jetting fluid fire upon men like a hosepipe. The phalanx grew and extended. Abruptly the flame thrower went out, and a moment later orange fire belched through the slit windows of the tank. The smoke-laden air grew heavy with the sweet pungent smell of roasting flesh.

Clive looked around. The spectators were retreating hurriedly from the scene of battle; it was no longer entertainment, but a personal threat to life itself, where even the casual observer might be destroyed.

The fight was spreading rapidly now that the raiders had broken free. Dark figures were running and pursuing each other along the street. Clive took the final shots, finishing the spool of film in the camera, and then decided that it was time to contract out of the proceedings. Attack and counter-attack were becoming too close for comfort.

Pocketing the camera, he escorted Noelle to the side street where his car was parked, and drove off without delay. After the smoke bombs had exploded he had seen nothing more of Beigal and Ross, but presumably they would pull out too at the right moment, if they had not already done so. Noelle sat beside him as if dazed, staring blankly through the windscreen as he raced the car towards the West End and Kensington.

"Is it a revolution?" she asked presently.

"Sort of," he admitted. "Whatever it is, the Government is apparently taking it seriously. When a burglary ends up in a military operation…"

"But where did they get their weapons from—I mean the raiders? Guns, grenades, armoured trucks…"

"Raids on army camps, defection of army personnel—the usual manoeuvres of an underground movement. These boys are keen, make no mistake about it. Today was just a trial of strength. We don't know who won—probably never will. The newspapers and radio will present a distorted security-angled view of the news."

She sighed despondently. "So what happens next?"

"Your guess is as good as mine," he said, spinning the car round a corner. "Trouble, I think. Real trouble. But speaking personally, I'm in favour of a drink."

"Several drinks. We both need something to wash away the smell of gunsmoke."

Later, back at the flat, they had their drinks. Noelle snuggled herself into his arms. "I love you, Clive," she whispered, "for ever and ever."

"Amen," he added laconically, then kissed her.

"I wish," she said, "that this damned virus business was all over. I wish we could feel secure."

"I wish we were both BAX types," he countered. "Then we'd have nothing to worry about."

"Perhaps we are. Maybe it could have happened without our noticing it."

"Not since the last blood test. If there's one thing I'd notice, it would be a temperature."

She regarded him pensively. "Yes, you're right, Clive. I suppose it's inevitable, isn't it?"

"What's inevitable?"

"The virus. Sooner or later it's going to catch up with you and me."

"Yes," he agreed, "as inevitable as death, but normal people don't worry about the inevitability of death. The virus offers better odds. We may both catch the BA type."

"Or the AB."

"Or one of each."

She grimaced. "That would be the cruellest thing of all. I think I need another drink."

He refilled the glasses.

A consignment of arms, comprising automatic weapons, rifles with telescopic sights, ammunition, tear gas bombs and plastic hand grenades, arrived one night at the deep shelter in Zone M45. Pauline was awakened around three a.m. by sounds of movement along the corridor and staccato voices issuing instructions. Momentarily alarmed, and then curious, she got out of bed, slipped on a dressing gown and went to investigate.

Staff troops were carrying wooden crates stamped with the letters W.D. and a broad-arrow to a small storeroom adjoining the clinic. Captain Villier appeared, looking pale and fatigued, his brown hair awry and his moustache drooping in dejection.

"I'm sorry if my men disturbed you, Dr. Brant," he said. "We were rather caught out by the War Office."

"What's happening?" she enquired.

"We're setting up an armoury. Apparently there's some danger of attack, and we've been authorised to use any measure to defend the centre."

"Attack?" she queried. "You mean—by strikers?"

"Strikers and others. The Liverpool contingent is headed by a man called Riley who's had I.R.A. experience of sabotage and guerilla tactics."

"But what do they hope to gain by it?"

"Food, for one thing. They know the underground shelters have food stocks to last for several months, and there really is a serious shortage of food on the surface. Apart from that they've developed a political hatred for what they call 'the privileged fascists'—that is, the people in the shelters. So we've been supplied with arms and ammunition, just in case of trouble."

She eyed him thoughtfully, pulling the cord of her dressing gown tighter. "I've heard of some attacks on shelters, but they were more in the nature of mob violence, with no particular leadership."

"Well, the leadership seems to be emerging and the violence is being systematised. They've acquired weapons and they're ruthless enough to be dangerous."

More soldiers passed by, carrying wooden boxes of hand grenades. "I can't see how rioting is going to help the fight against the virus," she said.

"It isn't. The movement is evolving into an uprising against the Government—against authority in general. There's a feeling that the Government has acted in an unfair and arbitrary way."

"I suppose that's true, up to a point."

"Let's face it, Pauline, there was no other possible course of action. The irony is that the so-called revolutionaries themselves would have done exactly the same if they'd been in power. Every government, whatever its colour or creed, has the duty to safeguard its assets in terms of scientific, administrative and executive personnel. They're doing it all over the world."

"They didn't do it in Japan," she said, "at least, not while I was there."

"They were probably taken by surprise at first. I'd be prepared to bet that within a few weeks of the start of the epidemic several hundred deep shelters had been built on a crash priority basis for the Japanese top brass."

She sighed. "Could be, I suppose. The trouble is we don't really know what's going on overseas at all."

"The Foreign Office knows, and occasionally there are leaks. Most countries in Europe are already in a state of virtual civil war. There's martial law in France and Western Germany, and states of emergency all over the place. Conditions were never so right for complete anarchy."

"Is there anything one can do about it?"

Villier stroked his cheek forlornly. "Find a vaccine for the virus. Then we could close down the isolation centres and put an end to rationing. That would knock the bottom out of the insurrection."

"And in the absence of a vaccine…?"

"Just hold out until the virus is past. The important thing for us is to maintain strong defences and keep the enemy out."

"You make it sound as if we were at war," she said, with a wry smile.

He patted a box of hand grenades as the soldiers carried it past. "That's exactly what we are, Dr. Brant. A particularly nasty war concerned with class and privilege, and for that reason it will be fought ruthlessly."

She accepted his statement with a certain amount of reserve and went back to bed, but for the remainder of the night she slept only fitfully and was glad, when morning came, to get up and make coffee.

After two weeks at a recruiting centre near Barnet in North London, Dr. Vincent finally contracted Hueste virus. At the first shivery symptoms of rising temperature he took a sample of his own blood and made a routine test in the established manner. He was immensely relieved when, some three hours later, he was able to confirm that the virus in his blood was of the harmless BA type.

Nevertheless, it had to be reported, and he would need to spend the best part of two weeks in a quarantine hospital because he was now acting as an AB carrier and had probably infected a number of people with whom he had come into contact in the past few hours.

He telephoned Dr. Youde over a scrambled security telephone circuit, and then attempted to call Zone M45 in Liverpool, but as always the available lines were booked for hours ahead on a priority basis. Only once had he ever succeeded in establishing telephone contact with the Newsham Park centre, and even then he had been unable to speak to Pauline, although he had had news of her from a Captain Villier, who had reported her as being in good health and good spirits.

He then arranged for his own admission to hospital, and settled down to wait for the ambulance to arrive.

I'm glad to be out of it, he thought, smoking a cigarette. I don't like this security militia recruitment job, and I don't care much for the quality of many of the BAX-type candidates. It was all right at the beginning, in the early days, before the first of the trained militia began to patrol the cities and towns. The applicants had generally been adult and fairly responsible types of men, many of them strikers who had abandoned loyalty to their unions because they had not wanted to strike, and had chosen the militia as an alternative form of employment.

But very soon, as it became generally known that men in the militia force enjoyed good pay with extra rations, wore attractive black uniforms and were issued with revolvers, the type of potential recruit had changed. Now they were tough, cold-eyed young men, some hardly out of their teens, many of them illiterate and inarticulate, but none the less arrogant for all that, usually dressed flamboyantly and fussy about their coiffured hair styles. There was always a leavening of mature men, of course, but the proportion was decreasing.

The disturbing thing was that nearly all candidates were being accepted and trained for the militia, discrimination only being exercised against those regarded as too mentally retarded to be capable of assimilating the training course, or suffering from some physical handicap or infirmity. Checking on the confidential files, Dr. Vincent had discovered that previous jail or Borstal sentences had not, in certain cases, disbarred the recruit, and one successful candidate had served a long prison term for rape. They all had one thing in common however, the only essential qualification: they were BAX-types and were consequently immune from further infection.

I wonder, he thought, as he watched the ambulance arriving in the gravel driveway of the recruiting centre, I wonder whether it will still be the same world when I'm released from quarantine in two weeks' time.

He finished packing the small suitcase and made his way down to the main entrance to meet the ambulance men.

CHAPTER TWELVE

T HE BATTLE OF THE EAST END STORE WAS REPORTED IN ONLY the briefest terms in the newspapers, and ignored completely by the radio and television news services. Typically, the *Daily Monitor* gave it two column inches at the bottom of page two. The story began: *Police and security forces yesterday thwarted an attempt by an organised gang to steal rationed provisions from a self-service store in Bethnal Green, London. Tear gas was used to expel the raiders. A number of arrests were made.* The remainder of the report added nothing of factual significance, and no reference was made to the use of arms, smoke bombs, the tank and the flame thrower.

Nevertheless, the raid seemed to act as a trigger, setting off a chain reaction that broke out almost immediately in sporadic raids of a similar type all over the country. It was as if an extensive underground communication network were in existence, co-ordinating a nationwide programme of violent subversion. Shops and warehouses were broken into and robbed by commando tactics, disorganising the rationing system in many areas and strengthening the Black Market, where bread already cost eight shillings a loaf and a tin of corned beef left little change out of one pound sterling.

Attacks on the deep shelters increased in number and ferocity, and it was in this direction that ruthlessly applied violence reached a new peak of horror. It was as if the rebels had decided in advance that the survival groups in the antivirus shelters were under sentence of death. Breaking open an underground shelter was like digging up an ant-hill, and a standardised technique began to emerge. First the main entrance and airlock would be breached with gelignite and improvised explosives, and smoke bombs and tear gas bombs would be hurled through the gap to paralyse the defenders. Finally immense quantities of petrol and paraffin would be pumped into the shelter and ignited. Survivors who were lucky enough to escape were shot down indiscriminately because they were members of a privileged and protected class.

The police and security forces were by no means inactive, and many vicious battles were fought between the rebels and the guardians of authority, but as each day went by the defenders tended more and more, obviously acting under orders, to concentrate on protecting the centres of administration—the underground shelters where Government officials and local authorities were installed.

But although the insurrection seemed to erupt almost simultaneously throughout the country, it soon became apparent that the insurgents were operating independently in localised groups, though undoubtedly in communication with each other and directed by a central command.

Rebel radio stations jammed the ether, interfering with BBC transmissions and broadcasting on adjacent wavelengths. *Essex Freedom Radio calling*, said one voice. *The county urges all workers and common people to support the efforts of the rehabilitation group to establish a new democratic authority. We proclaim a new executive council for Essex, and we call on all free citizens of Essex to join us in this campaign against fascist privilege and protection.*

Clive, switching on the radio one evening and tuning round the dial, heard an eloquent voice announcing with intense fervour: *The Government of the United Kingdom has gone underground to escape the virus. How can we who have been left behind to face the worst epidemic in human history ever again accept the authority of those who chose to save themselves and their kind in the most cowardly and irresponsible way? And in the course of time, when the virus has passed over, are we who are left going to submit passively to the cringing executives from underground as they crawl back to the surface to take up their authority where they left off? In the sacred name of the dead and the dying, the millions who have had to surrender their lives to the incinerators because they were denied privilege and protection, we must reject the authority of the opportunists. They abdicated from life as it is, and so they have forfeited the right to re-establish life as it was before the crisis. They have committed suicide.*

On the short-wave bands a multitude of low-powered transmitters chattered incessantly, conveying messages to the police, military, security forces, rebels and insurgent groups. Clive was able to tune in to a number of distorted and incoherent transmissions, and made tape recordings of some of the garbled dialogue.

Hampstead Blue to sub-units. Assemble Roxburgh. Close all entrant roads.

K-group, K-group—much crackling and background static—*siege at Paddington twenty-four. Second wave assemble Cronin Place.*

… and sending fifty men with Stens and grenades within the half-hour.

Unit Five to Black Leader. Have taken over Onyx Hotel as temporary HQ. Please send four armed trucks to block access roads. Security expected to close in.

Bishopsgate Control to all patrols. Proceed Monument area for anti-riot tactics. Four armoured cars and two tanks following.

He switched off the set with a grimace of disgust. Noelle, straight out of the bath and wrapped in a green dressing gown, was combing her long blonde hair in front of the ornate mirror above the fireplace.

"What a mess," she observed.

Clive raised an eyebrow. "The state of society or your hair?"

"Both."

"Your hair is fine," he remarked. "The state of the nation is not so good."

"There isn't a darned thing we can do about it, Clive."

"I guess not," he said thoughtfully. "Funny thing about revolutionary movements—one never quite understands just how they originate, but once they start they spread like a forest fire."

"There are always plenty of people willing to agitate and seize power."

"Maybe—but what do they propose to do with power once they've seized it?"

She smiled at her reflection in the mirror. Very attractive, she thought, and almost beautiful. In another five years, with full maturity and poise...

"They probably don't know, darling," she replied. "One never does. The whole thing is a kind of shot in the dark, given the right conditions and opportunity." A pause, then: "Who's winning?"

"Hard to say. I think the Government and security have things under control, but the rebels seem to have the initiative. They keep striking here and there, unexpectedly, and the police and security forces are obliged to chase round after the event, taking corrective and punitive action."

She nodded into the mirror in a casual fashion, finished combing her hair and went into the adjacent bedroom to dress. Clive poured himself a drink and stood by the window for a while, staring out at the quiet tree-lined road, peaceful and timeless in the fading afternoon sunlight. Beigal and Ross had gone off to make a film survey of road traffic, such as there was, and to find out which transport services were still continuing to operate on the major countrywide highways. Presumably they would also shoot film of any incidents they encountered en route to illustrate the build up of the insurrection.

Suddenly the air screamed and vibrated with the swooping noise of fast moving jet aircraft. Glancing upwards he saw three jet fighter planes hurtling above the rooftops in the direction of the West End. The noise faded and half a minute ticked quietly by—then came the concussions. A series of distant explosions rattled the window frame. He stared at the clouded blue sky above the rooftops opposite, but there was nothing to indicate aerial bombing. At a rough estimate the explosions had occurred in the vicinity of Hyde Park, or in the park itself, and the bombs were more likely to have been of the anti-personnel type rather than high explosive.

In a disturbed, restless mood, he went into the bedroom. Noelle was zipping up a dark green dress which made her look immensely sophisticated and extremely desirable. "What was all the noise about, Clive?" she asked, glancing briefly at him.

"Bombing of some kind. We ought to go up west. There may be something big going on."

"All right. Danninger isn't likely to approve, though."

"What Danninger doesn't know, he won't grieve over. We'll take the Japanese camera."

"I'll be with you in three minutes."

Clive nodded. "I'll be starting the car."

The Hyde Park incident appeared to be all over by the time they reached the end of Knightsbridge. Black-uniformed security men swarmed everywhere, waving the sparse traffic on and not allowing anyone to stop. Eight ambulances were lined up in Park Lane, and a military patrol with fixed bayonets marched along the other side of the road. A peculiar dry smell of dust and burning hung in the air, but there was no immediate sign of fire or bomb damage.

Clive drove on down Piccadilly until he reached the Astoria Hotel, where he pulled into the underground car park. As he and Noelle walked round to the main entrance of the hotel the crackle of remote gunfire trembled in the air. Mr. Beigal and Mr. Ross were still out, the receptionist said, but if they cared to wait...

The hotel lounge had been divided into sections by hardboard partitions painted cream and pale blue. The purpose was, Clive supposed, to provide small compartments of comparative isolation offering a certain degree of protection, even if only psychological, against the virus, and the device obviously overcame, to some extent, the regulation prohibiting public assembly. Assembly was still possible in theory, but the partitions broke up the mass into small individual groups, which was presumably permissible.

It was too early for a drink, so Clive ordered tea. The waiter wore a white virus filter across his face and seemed nervous and preoccupied.

"Has there been some military activity round here?" Clive asked.

The waiter's voice was muffled behind the gauze mask. "I understand there was a mass attack on the army camp in Hyde Park. About a thousand rebels broke into the armoury to steal weapons."

"Did they open the deep shelters?"

"I don't know, sir. I think they were trying to do something like that when the fighter planes came over and dropped anti-personnel mines. I hear there's been a great number of casualties."

"We heard gunfire as we came in."

The waiter nodded. "There's fighting going on around Grosvenor Square. The Government are sending in tanks, I believe. I hope they don't come in this direction—the rebels, I mean—otherwise your tea is likely to be delayed or interrupted, sir."

"We'll take a chance on it," Clive said.

But the time passed peacefully enough. In the spacious lounge of the Astoria the outside world was little more than an abstraction, and if there was gunfire in Mayfair, it failed to penetrate the solid walls of the hotel. Tea was duly served, and they had almost finished it when Beigal and Ross arrived. Clive saw them entering the foyer, making straight for the elevator which led to their rooms on the second floor. Excusing himself to Noelle, he left the table and intercepted them.

Both men looked tired, dirty and dishevelled, and there were bloodstains on Ross's grey jacket.

"Hello, Clive," Beigal said in a toneless, matter-of-fact way. He nodded towards Ross. "Dave's hurt. Caught a stray bullet while we were taking pictures just now in Grosvenor Square."

"I thought you were supposed to be covering the A1 and the M1 for traffic movements," Clive said.

"That didn't take long. There isn't any traffic movement that you could notice, apart from military trucks and armoured cars. County boundaries are blocked. You've got to have the equivalent of a passport to travel from Hertfordshire to Middlesex. We got back early and saw trouble in Hyde Park. We staked out with the Japanese camera and then the bombers came over, and the army counter-attacked and drove the rebels back into Mayfair. Then Dave caught his packet."

"It's all right," Ross said, smiling in a sickly fashion. "Just a shoulder wound, but the bullet's still in there so we'll need to get a doctor, if that's possible."

"I'll fix it," Clive said. "Better go on up to your room and rest."

"No dice," Beigal said. There was a strange urgency in his voice. "We're going up there to pack. This place is going to get mighty unhealthy any time at all."

"Why?"

"Well, Dave and I estimate there's about a couple of thousand rebels centred on Grosvenor Square. They're well armed, and reinforcements are pouring in all the time. They've got radio cars and armoured cars and maybe a few tanks. They're moving south and the security men think they're likely to set up a defence line at Piccadilly, with Green Park ahead of them because it would be easy to defend. That means they might take over hotels as bases and headquarters."

"Sounds a bit ambitious to me," Clive commented.

"Don't underestimate them. They're tough and active."

"What about Dave? Can he hold out for a while?"

Ross nodded. "I can manage, I guess. The bleeding has stopped."

"All right. Pack up your stuff and we'll all go back to my flat. At least there's no civil war in Kensington."

"Not yet," Beigal said sardonically.

Clive went back to Noelle, who was still eating her tiny sandwiches. Briefly he explained the position to her.

"Poor Dave," she remarked, pouring out more tea.

"I think he's overwrought, and Beigal is more than a little neurotic about things. All the same, it might be a good idea for all of us to go back to my flat."

She nodded. "Retreat and consolidate. I never imagined Mayfair would become a battlefield. Which side are we on, Clive?"

"We're on our own side, of course. The rest is a matter of expediency."

"You mean—we're always on the winning side."

"I think it's the best place to be, honey. Let's face it—nobody is being honest any more. Even genuine human grief and resentment are being exploited for political ends. Taking sides is pointless because one side is just as corrupt as the other in the long term."

Her expression became sombre and resigned. "We, then—let's be as neutral as hell."

"Hell may not be very neutral at all," he remarked, with a wry grin. "The only rational policy is to avoid being forced into having to make a choice—to avoid the mainstream of action and continue to play the part of an objective observer."

"Now you scare me," she admitted. "Don't you think we ought to go as soon as possible?"

A latent inarticulate fear pricked his spine momentarily. Crazy, he thought—insane, all of us. Here we are in the middle of a virus epidemic, perhaps the worst killer plague in all history, and suddenly the issues involved are political, and life and death are no longer matters of whether one contracts AB or BA type virus, but depend on one's political affiliations.

He stood up slowly, almost leisurely. "I suppose we ought to wait for Beigal and Ross, but they're packing and they may be some time yet. Ross is wounded, and that will slow him down. He'll need some pretty urgent medical treatment."

"Let's go, anyway, Clive," she said anxiously.

He nodded his agreement. "I'll leave a message for them to follow on."

They walked towards the foyer and the reception desk of the hotel, but never quite made it. The swing door burst open suddenly, admitting a column of shabby, grimy men carrying guns and automatic weapons—ten, twenty, thirty of them, and still they kept coming in.

A bearded man in faded khaki battledress, wearing a red armband and a black beret, seemed to be in command. He waved a Sten gun towards Clive and the girl and the dozen or so other people in the hotel lounge.

"Stay put and you won't get hurt," he ordered.

More men poured into the lounge, variously attired in suits, overalls, denims, and some in shirt sleeves, but they were all wearing red armbands, presumably the insignia of the insurgents.

A squat, pudding-faced man with bloodshot eyes came up to Clive, waving a revolver. "All right, mate—turn out all your pockets."

"I'm not armed," Clive stated calmly, "and I'm not hostile. I'm a member of an American television news unit."

"Shut your bleedin' trap and do as I say."

"Let me speak to your leader."

The arm holding the revolver swung in a swift wide arc. The barrel struck Clive across the jaw, ripping the flesh of his cheek. All his teeth began to ache simultaneously. Distantly he heard Noelle scream.

It was at that precise instant of time that Clive touched bottom and found a temporary orientation. He was no longer neutral and no longer inclined towards expediency. Reacting instinctively, he swung a hard curving fist at the fat pallid face confronting him, and had the immense satisfaction of feeling his bare knuckles plunging into flabby flesh and impacting against bone. The other man spun round and crashed to the floor, but a fraction of a second later half a dozen others had taken his place.

Like a hydra, he thought—chop off its head and it multiplies. Somebody was swinging a reversed rifle at him. He dodged it successfully, but a moment later it swung again, and this time it caught him squarely on the side of the head. The hotel lounge exploded into momentary incandescence, then dissolved into a timeless night.

*

Consciousness brought an agonising headache and a stiff soreness in the right side of his face. He found himself staring upwards at a bare whitewashed ceiling with a naked electric lamp hanging from purple flex. The ground was cold and hard to his back, and presently he realised that he was lying on bare concrete.

The room was big and ugly—a stark cellar with a cold furnace at one end and a slag heap of coke at the other. As he pushed himself into a sitting position he realised that he was not alone, but was one of about a dozen men sitting against the walls or lying on the floor. To the right was a green-painted door, and leaning against the door was an unshaven young man wearing a beret well back on his dark tangled hair, and the inevitable red armband over a ragged white shirt sleeve. He was smoking a cigarette in a bored fashion, and supporting a Sten gun under his right arm.

Memory returned in painful fragments. His movements as he achieved a sitting position attracted the momentary glance of the guard. There was little cause for reassurance in those cold, weary eyes and the hint of arrogance in the narrow curve of the lips twisted round the cigarette.

Clive looked around cautiously, striving to marshal his thoughts and memories into a coherent pattern. The other men, a motley assembly of the affluent middle-aged, were sour and apathetic, sitting and reclining without apparent movement, like statues. Only the guard was smoking, which seemed odd at first until Clive fumbled in his pocket for cigarettes, to discover that it had been emptied. Further investigation showed that all his pockets had been looted; they had taken his cigarettes and lighter, wallet, private papers from the inside pocket, keys and loose change, and worst of all, the miniature Japanese camera.

He accepted the fact without dismay, suppressing an angry feeling of personal loss. It was always the same in time of war—and this was certainly war: to the victor went the spoils. He found himself worrying about Noelle, as, no doubt, the other men in the cellar were worrying about their women. It seemed likely that all the women were imprisoned elsewhere under guard, but it was only too easy to imagine a more horrific fate.

Looking around him more carefully he observed that most of the other men were the worse for wear. Their white shirts bore bloodstains, and on their sombre faces were marks of violence. Carefully he explored his own face with hesitant fingers, outlining the three-inch splash of hard enamel on his right cheek that was dried blood. Meanwhile he studied the guard more closely. A youngish man, probably under thirty, dirty and slovenly, but well aware that he was top dog with his Sten gun, and enjoying the situation in a blasé fashion.

He'll shoot if necessary, Clive thought, and perhaps shoot to kill. He's one of those—the gangsters that crawl from under their stones when law and order break down. He knows he's got the measure of us here and now, but his power is in the gun. It lends him the authority to kill, and by the same jungle authority we, too, have the right to kill. When you revert to the law of power and force, only the fittest survive.

For a while he inspected the guard in a remote, objective way: the pinched face with its high cheek bones and dark stubble of embryo beard, the brown eyes and the careless hair, the dry lips holding the almost burnt-out cigarette; and the baggy grey slacks and the stained shirt, with the sleeves rolled up; and the black Sten gun with its magazine projecting squarely at right angles to the barrel, old but well oiled and shining—the ultimate authority.

No point in remaining idle, Clive decided. Inaction merely strengthened the hand of the enemy. Even against an automatic weapon a dozen determined men had a reasonable chance of reversing the situation... but somebody had to take the initiative, and there seemed to be negligible spirit or enterprise among the other prisoners.

He made up his mind abruptly, and began to drag himself across the floor towards his nearest fellow prisoner, a flabby, semi-bald man who was leaning back against the brick wall with an air of melancholy patience.

The shot exploded and reverberated in the cellar, the bullet ricocheted around the walls. Splinters of brick and whitewash fell on to his head. A wisp of smoke curled from the muzzle of the Sten gun, and the guard's lips were drawn back into a wide sneering smile.

"Next time you move you get it right between the eyes, pal, and no kidding," he said. "This ain't no bloody convalescent home. No exercise allowed and no talking. Get it?"

Sullen silence all round, and even resentful stares from other prisoners directed at Clive—that he should dare to jeopardise their lives by moving!

Slowly Clive edged himself to the wall and leaned against it, eyeing the guard steadily but without defiance. At least the balance of power had been tested, and he could expect no support from the other prisoners—at least, not while the Sten gun remained in control of the situation. At the same time, he realised that the guard had limits to his toughness and ruthlessness: the bullet had been fired deliberately into the brick wall, and it was clear that the weapon was intended to deter rather than to destroy, although it was difficult to decide whether, if it came to the point, it would be used for murder. Much depended on the common humanity of the guard and the degree of provocation, but if the guard possessed any humanity at all, then that was a weakness which could be exploited.

Perhaps, if it came to the point, I could be more coldly inhuman than him, Clive thought, and that might cancel out the advantage of the weapon.

He waited for half an hour or more, just sitting quietly and recouping his energy. The guard's boredom increased perceptibly until suddenly the green door opened and somebody unseen, presumably another of the rebels, thrust a tumbler almost full of amber liquid into his hands. The door closed again and the guard, still holding the Sten gun beneath his arm, quenched his thirst on what appeared to be a large quantity of whisky undoubtedly looted from the hotel bar. After that he seemed less bored.

Another quarter of an hour went by. The guard had half finished his drink, which would at least help to slow down his reactions, Clive told himself. Now he took out a cigarette and lit it, never relinquishing his grip on the Sten gun for an instant.

As if on cue, Clive said: "I could do with a smoke myself, mate."

The guard stared at him coldly but said nothing.

"In this hotel there must be hundreds of packets of cigarettes," Clive went on. "Maybe enough to allow us all to chain smoke for a week or two. How about it?"

"Belt up," said the guard brusquely.

With a painful effort Clive pushed himself to his feet, holding the wall for support. The Sten gun, as anticipated, swung into readiness, the muzzle pointing straight towards him.

"Take it easy with that thing," Clive said amiably. "I'm not the enemy."

The guard scowled, and the gun remained steady and menacing. "You're all enemies so far as we're concerned. Them's my orders."

"No point in shooting me," Clive went on. "All I want is a cigarette. Somebody's taken mine." Already the rattle of remote gunfire could be heard beyond the cellar.

"Bit of a smart dick, aren't you?" the guard said. Nevertheless, he took a packet of cigarettes from his trouser pocket and held it out grudgingly.

"Come and get one, then."

Aware of the fact that every man in the room was eyeing him with curiosity and suspicion, Clive walked slowly forward, but although he affected nonchalance he did not trust the guard, and expected violence.

He was three feet away, reaching out for the cigarettes, when the guard moved as anticipated. The cigarettes were allowed to fall to the floor. Clive, looking down, was on the point of stooping to pick them up when he noticed the preparatory flexing of the guard's right foot. He straightened up instantly, seeing the other man's intention defined clearly in his expression. For an electric moment they faced each other, silent, motionless.

"Pick 'em up," ordered the guard.

Clive smiled grimly. "Pick them up yourself, brave boy. I'm handy with my feet myself when it comes to the point."

By way of answer the guard clasped the Sten gun firmly with both hands, swinging it upwards in a swift, vicious arc. Clive dodged, but even so the steel barrel missed his face by less than an inch. At least it proved one thing: despite his orders the other man was not willing to commit murder in cold blood—at least, not until a desperate struggle for survival made it imperative, and then the bullets would start flying.

The gun was still swinging and the guard was slightly off balance. In that fractional instant Clive weighed up his adversary. He was tough, admittedly, but probably lacking in combat experience—too young to have seen active service during the war and untrained in the primitive but scientifically devised skills of unarmed defence. A thug—no more, no less—once he had been deprived of his gun.

In the same fractional instant of suspended time Clive's mind flashed back to the hard, relentless Commando training and the occasions in Malaya when it had been put into effective use against the Japanese. Then, acting on conditioned reflexes, he helped the swinging gun on its way with the edge of his hand. A moment later he used his knee to good effect, and as the other man doubled up with a gasp of pain, brought his shoe down with all the force he could muster on the guard's foot, crushing the instep.

The guard hit the floor as if slung from a catapult. Clive promptly knelt on his mouth to stifle the outraged howl. He reached for the Sten gun which had clattered to the ground and took command of the situation.

The transformation in the other prisoners had to be seen to be believed. Suddenly they were scrambling to their feet, possessed of unexpected energy and enthusiasm, shouting their aggressive approval now that the guard had been overcome. *"That's the stuff— damn good show—kill the bastard, he'd have killed us..."*

"Hold it!" Clive shouted, gripping the gun firmly.

They hesitated. He stood up, leaving the crippled guard free to curse and moan, and eyed the circle of eager men with bleak contempt.

"Let's get one thing straight," he went on. "There'll be no killing unless it's absolutely necessary in self-defence. We're not out of trouble yet by a long way. All we've gained so far is freedom to move around in this cellar. Taking over the rest of the hotel and rescuing the women is quite a different proposition."

"We've got a gun," a man said. "We can shoot them down and ask questions afterwards."

"*I've* got a gun," Clive stated factually. "But they've got lots of guns. The odds are too long for my liking."

The guard was beginning to howl again, so Clive collected some handkerchiefs from the other men and gagged him. He removed the red armband and studied it thoughtfully. Here in embryo was a possible plan of action. There were so many of them—the insurgents—that they could not possibly know each other personally, not on a mass basis. Any man looking shabby enough and wearing a red armband could reasonably pass as one of the two-thousand rebels trapped in the Mayfair area, and the Sten gun in itself would certainly be accepted as a badge of office. It offered a slender hope— but, nevertheless, a hope.

He slipped off his coat and placed the armband round the sleeve of his bloodstained shirt. "I'm going to make a quick reconnaissance," he said. "If it's at all possible I'll bring back weapons—guns, knives, anything."

"How do we know you'll come back at all?" asked a pouchy, red-faced man in evening dress.

"Just keep your fingers crossed. If I can stay alive and not get caught I'll be back as soon as I can—maybe in ten minutes or so."

The red-faced man pouted. "What I mean is—how do we know you won't scarper and leave us all in the jug down here?"

Clive raised his eyebrows sardonically. "You don't know at all, friend. You'll just have to take me on trust. I'm the one with the gun, remember, and I got it while you lot were sitting on your backsides playing yes-men to the guard."

He scanned his audience with a sour twist of his lips. "I think that gives me what you might call privilege. Let's face it—without weapons we don't stand a chance against the cutthroat mob upstairs. Even if we're armed we'll need to operate as a team so that some of us at least will get through. Our chances are slender enough, but we can't even begin to make plans until we know what the situation is outside and where they're holding the women."

He nudged the guard with his foot. "Keep an eye on him. I don't think he'll give trouble. He's got a fallen arch that will keep him horizontal for a long time to come."

As an afterthought he removed the guard's wristwatch, which had probably been stolen from a prisoner, anyway, and put it on his own wrist. "Just so I can check the time," he explained. "Give me fifteen minutes. If I'm not back by then you can assume I've been trapped or shot dead and you'll have to start making new plans."

He nodded towards the guard. "You can use him as a hostage, though I doubt if it will count for much."

"All right," said the red-faced man hesitantly. "We'll have to trust you, I suppose. Fifteen minutes, you said."

"That's right."

"Well, best of luck, anyway."

Clive waved one hand in acknowledgement. "Thanks. I'll be seeing you soon, if all goes well."

Slowly he opened the green door and went out into the passage.

CHAPTER THIRTEEN

AT THE END OF THE SHORT PASSAGE WAS A FLIGHT OF STONE steps, and now the sounds of gunfire were louder and more insistent. He climbed the steps slowly, holding the Sten gun with assumed carelessness but keeping it ready for use at an instant's notice. At the top of the steps was an austere vestibule with a number of doors, two of which bore plaques announcing *Ladies* and *Gentlemen*, and the others *Private*. The air was heavy with a greasy smell of cooking mingled with acrid gunsmoke and the more subtle odour of coffee.

Here there was carpet on the floor. Another flight of stairs, also carpeted, obviously led up to the ground floor of the hotel.

He paused for a moment to consider his next move, and decided to go into the men's lavatory. There, in a mirror, he examined in suppressed horror the apparition that stared at him from the other side of the glass. The gash across his left cheek was serious enough to warrant stitching, but the blood had hardened into a strip of dark brown paint. The right side of his chin was grazed, and there were bruises on his forehead, already swollen and discoloured.

The effort of washing with soap and water was futile, for the wound on his cheek opened up again and blood began to run sluggishly down the side of his face. He tore a fragment from his handkerchief and pressed it against the wound to absorb the blood and aid coagulation. In a few minutes the bleeding stopped.

He was about to pick up the Sten gun and continue his mission when the door of the washroom opened and three of the insurgent rebels came in. Through the mirror he saw them eyeing him curiously as they walked towards the urinals. All three seemed slightly drunk and unsteady.

Presently one of them waddled over to him and peered at his wounded cheek. "Jeeze, mate," he exclaimed, "they copped you one all right."

"Stray bullet," Clive said quietly. "It's only a flesh wound."

The other man slapped his shoulder and chuckled. "That's the stuff, mate. Don't let 'em get you down. We can shoot better than them, that's what I always says, come to the point."

"Sure thing," Clive remarked, picking up the gun. "When it comes to shooting, we've got the edge."

The man went back to his comrades, while Clive left the wash-room and cautiously ascended the stairs leading to the ground floor. The staircase emerged to the rear of the entrance hall with the lounge on the right, reception desk to the left, and the double glass door fronting the main road straight ahead.

The door had been barricaded with massive furniture behind which four men armed with Sten guns mounted weary-eyed guard. Clive glanced briefly into the hotel lounge; here again the furniture had been upended and stacked by the windows overlooking the road, and each window had its vigilant guards. The glass in the windows had been shattered, and the walls of the room were peppered with bullet holes—a souvenir of the night's fighting. Outside was the cold, blue-grey light of early morning, but the road seemed relatively quiet apart from the occasional spasmodic chatter of automatic weapons which, oddly enough, seemed to come from above.

At the other side of the room, away from the windows, the rebels had set up a combined canteen and bar on trestle tables. Two haggard waiters, their uniforms faded and crumpled after a long night of enforced toil, were keeping supplies of snacks and sandwiches, coffee and drinks moving across the table. About a dozen men were grouped round the improvised bar, sipping coffee and eating whatever food was available, but a few diehards were still knocking back whisky and gin, making the most of their opportunity before the inevitable counter-attack started.

Clive was about to walk on and make his way to the upper floors of the hotel when he saw a strange confusion of white sheets on the floor at the far end of the lounge, and it came to him that under the sheets were bodies. For a moment he debated whether to waste a few minutes in the lounge on the pretext of having a drink in order to find out more about the casualties under the sheets, but decided against it. They were probably rebels who had been killed in the fighting, and, anyway, there was no time to waste on the dead—it was the living, in particular Noelle, that mattered.

Unchallenged he climbed the carpeted stairs to the first floor, and here was a wide corridor slotted with doors. A guard, in shirt sleeves and armed with a revolver, leaned against the wall half-way along the corridor, smoking a cigarette—a young man with tousled red hair and an embryonic beard. He watched Clive speculatively but without suspicion as he walked towards him.

"Seen Henderson around?" Clive asked, using the first reasonable question that leapt into his mind.

"Who's Henderson?"

"Tall bloke with glasses—Yorkshire accent."

"Don't know him," said the guard, spitting the cigarette butt to the floor and grinding it under his heel. He eyed Clive shrewdly. "You're not one of our mob."

"No. I got winged…" He touched his wounded cheek, leaving the rest unsaid. "There was a great deal of confusion, and Henderson and me got separated."

"Which is your mob?"

Clive thought quickly. The answer had to be pat and plausible. "Bloke called Smith. West London…"

"You mean the Bayswater crowd—number eleven unit."

"That's right."

The guard snatched the revolver from its holster and pointed it at Clive. "You're a bleedin' liar, mate. Bayswater's number eight and its leader is Delancey. Anyway, I've seen you before. You was one of those bloody pansy civvies we chopped up when we took over the hotel." His eyes focused upon the red armband which Clive was wearing. "You're a bloody spy, that's what you are. Gregg'll be interested in you…"

He got no further. Clive hit him in the stomach, then, as he doubled up, chopped him down with a hard blow to the back of the neck. He picked up the revolver and slipped it in his trouser pocket.

There was no time to waste. Tentatively he tried the nearest door, but it was locked. He went on to the next door in the corridor; it, too, was locked, but the key was on the outside. Carefully he opened the door and looked in.

Three women stared at him in helpless fear. Two of them were standing by the window and the other was sitting on a chair near a dressing table in what was a typical bed-sitter hotel room. He thought he recognised them vaguely as some of the women who had been with their men in the hotel lounge when the rebels had broken in.

"Don't worry," he reassured them quietly. "I'm on your side. Above all, don't make a sound."

He went back into the corridor and dragged the body of the unconscious guard into the room, locking the door behind him.

"Where are the other women?" he asked.

One of them, whose eyes were red-rimmed from tears and sleeplessness, said: "We don't know. They split us up into groups. Some of the younger ones they took upstairs."

He surveyed the three of them sombrely. They were all middle-aged and overweight and one wore glasses. He began to appreciate the terrifying basis of the segregation. Cold anger sparkled in his brain like a frozen point of incandescence.

"Where's the bathroom?" he asked.

They indicated a door. He dragged the guard over to it.

"If you hear any strange noises, pay no attention," he told the women. "I've got to beat some information out of this character. If anyone tries to get into the room, let me know at once." He tapped the Sten gun significantly. "We can hold them at bay for a while."

They nodded in silence and apprehension. He opened the bathroom door and pushed his prisoner inside, then bolted the door from the inside. The lino on the floor was black, and the tiled walls and bathroom fittings were pastel green.

With some difficulty he heaved the other man into the bath and turned on the cold water tap.

"Brother," he murmured, as the guard began to stir, "I ought to beat you up the same as you and your kind beat me up, but drowning is cleaner. You can talk or inhale water, whichever you choose—it's up to you."

He stood back for a while, watching the water level rise, until presently the guard opened his eyes, and then he set to work.

Some fifteen minutes later Clive emerged from the bathroom looking pale and weary, his shirt and slacks splashed with water.

"He's all yours," he said to the women. "He's in pretty bad shape and he won't put up a fight. Keep him in the bath to cool off and if he tries to get out push his head under water for a while. That way you won't have any trouble."

"But what's going to happen to us?" one of the women asked.

"You'll all be rescued," Clive promised. "It will take time, but so long as you stay in this room and keep the door locked, nothing can happen. You'll just have to be patient."

"Where's my husband?" a woman demanded, and the question was taken up by the others.

"All the men are in the cellar," he explained. "They're quite safe, and it's only a matter of time before they're released."

He left the room, waiting only to hear the sound of the key being turned inside the door, and then made his way along the corridor.

There was a cold blackness in his mind and venom in his heart. The guard had talked willingly enough once he had realised fully his vulnerable position, although it had taken half a lungful of water followed by ten minutes of choking and spluttering and near-unconsciousness to soften him up. This was no mere spontaneous adventure, he had said in effect. It was the first stage of a co-ordinated revolution, and similar attacks were being made at this very moment in every major town of Britain. The rebels were well armed and adequately equipped for the operation, and there was considerable support from defecting Army and Air Force personnel. There was even a possibility that aircraft might be available for rebel use as the insurrection gathered momentum.

So far as London was concerned, the occupation of the Mayfair zone had been planned as the focal point in anticipation of a major counter-attack by government security forces. During the day it was expected that a ring of steel would surround Mayfair, and on a signal tanks and guns and flame throwers would close in to crush the heart of the revolution. But in the meantime an outer ring of steel was assembling in the nearer suburbs of London, comprising more than twenty-thousand armed rebels with trucks and vehicles of all kinds, armoured with steel plate and equipped with Bren guns and mortars, and this outer ring was destined to contract upon the inner security ring in a sandwich pincer movement, cutting off communications, supplies and reinforcements.

Who was the head man? Clive had asked—the organising genius behind the whole thing? There wasn't a single man, the guard had explained, between bouts of coughing and spluttering and vomiting. There was an unnamed operations committee. The members were known by code names such as Mephisto, Plato, Apollo, and so on, but behind the committee was someone else, a big name, somebody in governmental circles with an established political record, who would be ready to emerge as leader of the new republic when the revolution was won.

As to insurrectionist policy—well, it was simple enough. Everyone now knew that the top administration and executive authority of the nation were buried underground in the virus shelters. They were sitting targets, practically defenceless, just waiting to be eliminated by deliberate acts of sabotage. It was an inflexible rule to take no prisoners; the Establishment had to be destroyed completely, not put behind barbed wire.

And as for the ordinary uncommitted civil population, those who were neither rebels nor virus refugees, they were to be regarded as potentially hostile, for the majority would certainly support the conventional forces of established law and order. The recommended procedure here was one of intimidation, to enforce obedience through fear until the insurgent government had been brought to power, when the public in general could be expected to fall into line. No unnecessary violence, the orders said, but all essential steps should be taken to ensure absolute non-intervention on the part of the non-insurgent civil population.

Clive wanted to know what had happened to the women, and at this point the guard became evasive. They were simply to be isolated and held as prisoners in locked rooms, he explained, but you knew how it was with fighting men, especially when they'd occupied a hotel and filled their guts with alcohol. After all, you couldn't expect much chivalry in war. He, personally, had had nothing to do with the women at all, but he knew they had been dispersed among the various rooms on the upper floors of the hotel. He couldn't answer for what the other rebels might have done in their drunken way throughout the night.

Yes, he remembered the blonde American girl, but only vaguely. He had no idea what had happened to her after she had been taken from the hotel lounge. One had to be philosophical about such things…

Displaying his own variety of militant philosophy, Clive had pushed the guard's head under the water again if only to prove that you couldn't necessarily intimidate all of the people all of the time, and then he had abandoned him to the three middle-aged women, who would no doubt exploit the advantage in their own way.

He reached the staircase at the end of the corridor—and at the same instant the thunder of heavy cannon fire shook the hotel. Somewhere in the building brickwork tumbled with a tumultuous crash, and there were shouts and screams and the swift chatter of Bren guns. Smoke floated pungently in the noisy air.

Slowly he ascended the stairs to the next floor.

Almost by accident he came upon the adjacent rooms occupied by Beigal and Ross, and it was with a profound shock that he realised that he had completely forgotten their existence since he had spoken to them on the previous evening when they had returned to the hotel. They had not been among the prisoners in the cellar, and it seemed possible that they might have escaped in some way before the rebels had gained possession of the upper storeys of the building. Nevertheless, it was with a certain prickly sensation of apprehension that he opened the door of Beigal's room and peered inside.

Beigal was lying on the floor, face down, and there was dried blood in his matted hair and a vast crimson stain on the fawn carpet. Clive examined him cursorily, suppressing a wave of sickness that threatened to unsettle his stomach. The body was cold and the pockets of the coat and trousers had been emptied of all personal possessions. Perhaps Beigal had put up a fight; if so, it had been his final fight.

In the next room there was no sign of Ross at all, but he saw indications of a violent struggle and the window had been completely smashed. Crossing the room and looking out and down through the jagged gaping hole in the glass, he saw a twisted body that might have been Dave Ross impaled on the railings surrounding the rear basement area of the hotel two storeys below.

He left the room, closing the door quietly behind him, and paused for a moment to think. The noise of shooting seemed to be building up to a crescendo, and every minute or so came the deeper, heavier concussion of mortar fire. Four rebels carrying Sten guns rushed suddenly along the corridor, ignoring him, and went into a room further down. The crisis seemed to be building up; probably security forces were counter-attacking, and there would be tanks and field artillery in Green Park. He continued his exploration in an uneasy frame of mind, afraid of what he might discover in the other rooms of the corridor.

He encountered three locked doors in a row, each with a key on the outside, and in each was a young woman, one naked and two partly clothed, bearing the marks and bruises of assault, the horrors of the night only too apparent in their stark terrified faces.

"Better stay where you are for now," he told each of them in turn. "You'll be safer here. There's vicious fighting in progress."

He went on, and came to another locked room, and here he found Noelle. She was lying diagonally across a bed, stripped of her clothing, her eyes staring blindly towards the window. He examined her in a remote, almost dispassionate frame of mind. Her hands had been tied together behind her head with one of her nylon stockings, and this had been secured round her neck so that she could well have been strangled in the struggle to free herself, but in addition there were numerous scratches and purple bruises on her body, and blood was still oozing from a knife slash across one breast. Gently he touched her cheek, noting with complete resignation the coolness of her flesh, then he drew the bloodstained sheet across her.

He said good-bye, silently, in his own way, and left the room, locking the door behind him and pocketing the key. There was a cold hard knot in the substance of his brain and a strange scintillation in his mind that replaced thought. No need to think, only to respond to an attitude. It was as if all feeling and emotion had been drained from him so that he was no longer a human being, but rather an automaton carrying out a programmed sequence of activity.

The gunfire was now an abstract rhythm triggering the movements of his body as he walked slowly, almost leisurely, along the corridor. There was no hurry, for the future had been erased and time had come to a stop, and it was necessary to find a new orientation in a strange, vicious world. For the present it was impossible to appreciate the enormity of what had happened; one viewed events through a thick glass window, and even Noelle seemed as insubstantial as a dream half forgotten in the way that one forgets dreams.

His feet led him instinctively to the room where the four rebels had rushed with their weapons. He opened the door without ceremony, fingering the strap of the Sten gun over his shoulder, and looked around with no great interest. They were squatting by a broken window, firing short bursts into the street below. One of them glanced back towards him and shouted: "Come on, mate—the bastards are gaining ground." He was a young man, probably in his early twenties, with dark wavy hair and a fresh complexion.

Clive's brain began to tick over in a sluggish manner. It could be you, he thought. It could be any one of you—or perhaps all of you. You're all guilty, each of you. I am my own judge and jury and I find you guilty.

Without premeditation or deliberation he unslung the Sten gun and clicked the safety catch. What he was about to do was logical and inevitable—part of the pattern of fate. There was no reason to have any feeling about it whatever, even if one were capable of feeling.

He pulled the trigger of the Sten gun. Bullets spurted for nearly five seconds, until the magazine was empty.

Calmly he went to the window, stepping over the dead bodies, and looked out on Piccadilly. Heavy tanks were crawling in convoy along the road and Green Park was swarming with troops and black uniformed security men digging in machine-gun nests, and firing mortars and bazookas. Further along the road, towards Hyde Park Corner, a dense grey smokescreen had been laid, so that visibility was nil. As he watched, smoke bombs exploded outside the Astoria.

A wave of men wearing respirators began to surge forward from the park.

He shrugged. Still no feeling or reaction. Methodically he picked up the four Sten guns from the floor, noting without great interest the splashes of blood on the hot barrels, already hardening into dark matt enamel. Somewhere deep in his mind was the realisation that the guns were needed, that he had made a promise to a number of men in a bleak whitewashed cellar, and that they were waiting for him to return. He set off on the return journey to the basement.

I'm late, he told himself, but better late than never.

He never quite made it. On the final staircase leading down to the entrance hall he ran into a hand-to-hand battle. Tear gas stung his eyes and a hand grenade exploded just outside the double door, hurling shards of glass across the foyer. Tracer bullets from a Bren gun swept across the entrance in a lethal stream. Among the smoke and confusion he saw troops advancing through the wrecked doorway and clambering over the furniture barricade—only to be shot down by rebels waiting in the smoke-filled hall. But still they came on in overwhelming numbers, and bayonets flashed in the obscured daylight.

Clive let the Sten guns slide from his shoulder and sat down on a stair to think, although he found himself capable of only the most elementary kind of thought. The cellar was clearly inaccessible. The risk in reaching the lower steps without being shot or bayoneted seemed greater than the benefits to be gained by carrying four Sten guns to the men waiting below. In any case, it was beginning to look as if the battle was already decided. The security forces were in possession of the entrance hall and were now fighting in the lounge.

He stood up again as he heard footsteps rushing down the staircase from above. Reinforcements were obviously arriving from the upper floors, and he had no wish to be trapped between the two opposing forces. He abandoned the Sten guns, remembering that he still had the revolver in his pocket, and descended into the smoke, taking up a position by the reception booth where he was partly screened from the lounge and staircase by the tumbled furniture.

A score of rebels came down the stairs in a solid mass and at the same time another wave of security troops flooded the barricade. He moved back behind the reception counter, stooping down and peering over the top. The shooting became almost continuous, like the raucous noise of a road drill going on and on incessantly. The rebels on the staircase were trapped, unable to advance into the hall. Some of them began to retreat up the stairs towards the first storey.

Two hand grenades flashed and exploded, showering splinters of metal in every direction. The wood of the reception counter split open as the shrapnel ploughed through it, and something sharp and painful plunged deep into Clive's shoulder with tremendous impact. He crawled backwards into the shadows, his eyes streaming from the tear gas, no longer anxious to follow the progress of the battle, but content to find a place of comparative security until the issue had been decided.

Minutes later, as the firing seemed to die down, the walls of the foyer became effulgent with a flickering orange glow. Anxiously he peered over the top of the counter to see a flame thrower in action, spraying the staircase with liquid fire. In an instant the stairs were ablaze with angry tongues of flame licking upwards towards the rebel rearguard on the upper floor. The shooting recommenced sporadically, but the battle was already over. Troops and black uniformed militia were busy clearing the furniture barricade from the main door.

He waited for some five minutes, watching the fire take hold of the staircase. They were escorting prisoners out now, arms raised high above their heads, while from above, beyond the leaping flames, came frantic shouts of surrender.

A moment later the troops were dragging a hosepipe through the doorway, and then a powerful jet of water was attacking the flames, hissing and raising white clouds of steam that filled the foyer with a moist, suffocating fog. Soon, when the fire was extinguished and the remaining rebels were descending the charred stairs with arms upraised, he came from behind the reception counter and went into the hall.

In an instant a steel bayonet was pointing at his stomach. A young cold-eyed soldier said: "Get your arms up."

"It's all right," Clive explained in a toneless voice. "I'm not one of them. I was their prisoner. I managed to escape."

"Like hell you did."

Another soldier had come behind him and was patting his clothing. Within a second he had discovered the revolver.

"With a bloody red armband and a gun in your pocket," said the first soldier. "Get moving." The bayonet waved towards the hotel entrance. "And get your arms in the air."

Clive raised his arms reluctantly. "There are civilian prisoners in the cellars and women locked in rooms upstairs…" he began.

"Shut your trap and get moving," the security man ordered.

"I'm not a rebel," Clive insisted. "I've already shot four of them. I put on the armband so they wouldn't know…"

The bayonet dropped fractionally and lunged forward, biting

like a hot iron through the thick muscle of his thigh. Hot blood trickled down his leg.

"Get moving," the soldier repeated, "or would you like it in the guts?"

Clive surrendered the argument. If only he had had sense enough to remove the armband and ditch the gun—but it was easy to be wise after the event. It didn't really matter, anyway. Nothing mattered any more; the entire foundation of his life had collapsed and the future was a blank enigma. I'm like a blind man, he thought, feeling my way in the dark, and I have no allegiance, but I despise them all and there is nothing to choose between them. Rather the virus than this. If Noelle had died of the virus it wouldn't have been so bad. At least I could have produced tears and regrets in place of this cold numbness. I could destroy them all, whatever their politics and creeds, and feel no remorse—feel nothing.

He allowed himself to be pushed out of the door of the hotel into the street, where he was immediately seized by two militia-men and dragged to an enormous truck resembling a furniture van. Impelled by a bayonet prodding his back he climbed the tailboard of the vehicle to find himself squeezed among fifty or more other prisoners, some seriously injured, others badly burned, standing, kneeling, sitting and lying on the cold iron floor. All wore armbands.

Within the next few minutes a dozen more prisoners were forced into the already overcrowded truck, and then the back was thrown up and bolted into place. A few seconds later the vehicle moved off with an abrupt surge of acceleration. Clive, near the back, considered the possibility of jumping clear, but it was no more than a thought. Following closely behind the truck was a small jeep-like vehicle with two militiamen in the rear, each holding a sub-machine-gun at the ready. The only possible escape route was effectively closed.

The truck sped on, but not for long. The prison camp was established in a vast field in Regent's Park, just north of London's West End.

The perimeter of the camp consisted of coiled barbed wire piled up to a height of eight feet or more. Several trucks were disgorging their human freight, and the prisoners were being hustled with kicks and blows to a narrow gap in the wire which formed the entrance to the camp.

Here six ridge tents in a twin row formed temporary offices for the security staff. Beyond, hugging the southern perimeter of the wire, four sandbagged machine-gun nests kept the field under grim surveillance.

At the head of the queue, to the rear of the tents, he saw that the prisoners were being searched and interrogated by militia officers. Personal belongings were thrown on to a big trestle table, where they were scooped into canvas bags which were then labelled and thrown into crates. Progression was slow, but after some three quarters of an hour he reached the head of the queue and found himself facing an officer in black uniform seated at the other side of the table, while two guards searched him and turned out his pockets. They were, of course, empty, apart from one soiled handkerchief splashed with old blood. Then one of the guards ripped the red armband away in a single powerful tug that nearly dislocated his shoulder.

"Just answer my questions," said the officer curtly. He took a white card from a box and began to write on it with a ball pen.

"Name?"

"Clive Brant."

"Address?"

The questions followed tonelessly, parrot-fashion. Clive recited his address, age, religion, job (television executive—but it did not even produce a raised eyebrow). Finally he was asked for the name and address of his next of kin.

"Just in case you should die, sudden like," the officer added in a matter-of-fact voice.

A phantom image of Noelle as he had last seen her formed transiently in his mind, but Noelle was already out of the picture, and already his mind was recovering from the shock of the past few hours to take account of the need for expediency. With odd reluctance he said:

"My next of kin is my wife, Dr. Pauline Brant. She's a doctor on the staff of the International Virus Research Organisation. I believe she's in Liverpool, but you can always trace her through IVRO."

The officer put down his pen and eyed him disparagingly. "Is that so? Do you suppose she knows she's married to an assassin?"

Clive restrained a surge of anger. "I'm not one of the rebels," he stated. "I was taken prisoner in the Astoria Hotel. I managed to overpower the guard. Why do you suppose I've got nothing on me apart from a bloodstained handkerchief—not even a jacket?"

"Why, indeed?"

"They robbed me. They beat me up and took everything—my wallet, passport, camera, cigarettes—the lot."

"Bad luck," the officer said. He seemed bored. "We've got plenty of other blokes like you. They try to save their skins by changing sides. So far as I'm concerned you're an insurgent, and my guess is your wife will be slung out of IVRO within twenty-four hours—that is, if she *does* work for IVRO. She'd be a bad security risk with you for a husband."

The supercilious insolence of the other man's voice finally broke through the non-reactive defence barrier of Clive's mind. He found himself immensely irritated and not caring very much what happened to him. On a sudden irresistible impulse he plunged his bunched fist into the pallid mocking face, and had the transient satisfaction of seeing the officer in his chair topple over backwards to strike the ground with a sickening thud.

But his triumph was short-lived. Something hard struck the back of his head with incredible impact. The world flashed into incandescence and spun crazily for a millionth of a second. He saw blue sky above with an immense white cloud crawling amoeba-like across it, then the faces of three young security militia vertically above, and a swinging rifle butt that hissed as it curved through the air.

There was no way of avoiding the blow. His mind clicked into apathetic resignation an instant before the consciousness was beaten out of his brain.

It was beginning to rain. The white cloud had spread across the blue sky, thickening and darkening and descending upon the shadowed ground. The raindrops were heavy and tepid, but cooling on the painful heat of his face. Thunder seemed to rumble continuously in the air, but presently it came to him that the noise was not thunder, but gunfire. The rain splashed more insistently, but still the intolerable pain persisted in his head.

A burly red-faced man in a faded boiler suit was looking down at him. His eyes were sullen and heavy with fatigue, but there was a reserved kindliness in his defeated expression.

"You all right, son?" he enquired.

Clive made no reply, but looked around him. He was in the same field, lying flat on the grass, surrounded by countless other men, some sitting or standing, others lying down. He caught a distant glimpse of the barbed wire, then closed his eyes again as the headache pounded his skull.

"Lucky they didn't kill you," the other man went on. "That was some chance you took. Could've laughed me head off when you poked that putty-faced bastard on the conk, but they got their own back, mate. Gave you a fair working over. You feel all right?"

Clive grimaced and attempted to sit up, but was unable to sustain the effort. A moment later the other man was kneeling beside him, supporting his shoulders and easing him into a sitting position.

"Franklin's the name," the other man went on, "but mostly they calls me Frankie." He glanced at the leaden sky. "Would have to damn well rain, just to make things worse."

Clive found the wet sprinkling of rainwater on his face quite pleasant, and it acted as a mild antidote to the headache. He still could not find energy enough to say anything, however, and was content to sit quite still, slowly regaining his strength, while the plump, rather elderly man named Frankie prattled on in an amiable way. In the background the gunfire seemed louder and more persistent.

"Keep piling them in here," Frankie continued. "Two hours or more since they done you. Reckon they've got some two thousand men in this field, mostly from the West End do."

He cocked his head to one side and put a hand to his ear. "Hear all that shooting? That's our outer ring boys coming in from up Hampstead way. They can't be more than a mile off. We ought to be free again before dark. Some of us is talking about breaking out, anyway. They got the machine-guns, but we got the numbers. They can't hold us here for long without food or water or shelter."

Clive attempted to stand up, and with the help of Frankie succeeded in balancing shakily on his own two feet. Now he was able to take a more comprehensive view of his environment. The other man's estimate of two thousand prisoners was about right, he decided. The men were herded into some two thirds of the area of the field, while the remaining third containing the tents and machine-gun nests of the militia. In addition, guards patrolled the camp on the other side of the barbed wire.

Outside the prisoners' enclosure, he observed that two trucks with searchlights mounted on elevated platforms were moving into position, which suggested that the militia were thinking in terms of an all night session. It was easy enough for Frankie to talk about breaking out, but even under the cover of darkness it would be a hazardous operation, what with the wire, the searchlights and the machine guns. A determined exodus might well become a suicidal massacre.

"You feeling better now?" Frankie enquired.

Clive nodded. "What's the time?"

"Don't know exactly. Early afternoon, I'd say. I wish this bloody rain would stop."

In all directions the sky was swollen with grey cloud. Clive surveyed it briefly, then inspected his own shirt and slacks, already soaking wet and shapeless. Most of the prisoners had taken to standing up and walking about because the ground was now saturated.

Two more trucks arrived at the camp entrance, unloading further batches of prisoners. The officer at the trestle table had moved into the shelter of one of the tents, he noticed. The prisoners queued in the rain, went into the tent one by one, and were then escorted by militia guards in groups of three or four at a time to the inner enclosure.

Accompanied by Frankie, Clive began to circulate among the other prisoners, listening to snatches of talk and occasionally engaging in terse conversation. He learned that the rebel attack from the so-called outer ring had started well and was gaining impetus; on the other hand there was little effective rebel opposition left in the Mayfair area. It was rumoured that the insurgents had seized the television transmitting station at Crystal Palace and had put it off the air until they could gain full control of studio facilities. Underground stations had been taken over, but no trains were running; nevertheless they formed excellent bomb-proof headquarters for insurgent units. And as the rebels advanced, deep virus shelters in each district were being eliminated systematically, step-by-step.

Although there was despondency among the prisoners, aggravated by the rain, Clive found no evidence of pessimism. One man said: "All we've got to do is sit tight and wait"—he was standing, and the rain was running down his face in tiny rivulets—"and the lads'll have us out of here in no time at all. Wouldn't be much point in defending an open park, would there? Those black rats'll be off like a flash as soon as our men get within shooting distance." And that summarised the general feeling in the prison camp—an air of hopeful and occasionally tense expectancy.

Clive identified himself only superficially with the rebels. For the moment he was waiting, as they were, for release. He found himself utterly without allegiance to either side, for the militia were no better than the insurgents, if no worse. Whenever his thoughts reverted to Noelle as he had last seen her, he suppressed them ruthlessly. The past was irreversible, and the present demanded a cold heart and a calculating brain devoid of sentiment.

About two hours later, after a lull in the distant gunfire, shooting broke out close at hand. Excitement burst spontaneously among the prisoners—the rebels were in the park already and it could only be a matter of minutes before they had taken the prison camp and torn down the barbed wire fence.

But the few minutes dragged on into an hour. Clive, followed inevitably by Frankie, pushed his way to the perimeter wire to make a personal assessment of the situation, but there was nothing to be seen apart from the inevitable militia guard straddling a motor-cycle with a sub-machine-gun bolted to the handlebar. Beyond a row of trees about a quarter of a mile away orange flashes of light pierced a hanging smoke haze. The rain had eased and the sky, though still uniformly grey, seemed brighter.

"They may not come this way at all," Clive pointed out.

"What do you mean?" Frankie asked.

"Well, they're fighting a spearhead operation. They're bound to spend some time consolidating and preparing their positions for the next attack, and it may not be here. Their main job is to smash the enemy opposition rather than go round rescuing prisoners."

"Us two thousand in here could make a lot of difference."

"Provided they've got arms and ammunition for us."

"Don't you worry about that. They've got arms enough—all they want is men to use them."

"You may be right at that," Clive conceded.

The first signs that the rebels were in fact breaking through came when the militia guarding the camp started to load equipment and boxes from the tents on to trucks. In an instant a whisper had circulated among the two thousand prisoners—*They're pulling out—we've won.* The men began to press forward against the wire, pulling at the barbed strands in elation and confidence, but the machine-gun nests were still manned and the guards beyond the wire sat stony-faced astride their motor-cycles.

"Why don't we break out now," Frankie said eagerly. "We've got them on the run good and proper."

"I'm not so sure," Clive murmured, aware of a squirming uneasiness in his mind. The withdrawal of the militia seemed too orderly and methodical, and because of that he was suddenly afraid. They were being coldly deliberate, and he could not imagine them with the same deliberation allowing two thousand prisoners to rejoin the insurgent forces.

The trucks began to pull away from the camp entrance. Abruptly a Very light soared into the sky above the tents like a scarlet rocket. Clive threw himself instinctively to the ground, dragging an indignant Frankie with him, but even before he touched the wet grass the machine-guns began to chatter in unison, and the motor-cycle guards outside the barbed wire opened fire with their automatic weapons.

For a few moments the noise of shooting was drowned by shouts and screams from the trapped prisoners, but as the wave of anger and agony subsided he could hear the staccato jabber of the guns going on and on, systematically spraying the enclosure with death. He lay perfectly still, flattening himself against the sodden ground, awaiting the inevitable shattering impact that would bring oblivion.

The firing seemed to continue for an eternity. It takes a long time to kill two thousand men, he remembered thinking. His fingers on Frankie's arm were wet, he noticed, but not from the rain—this was a warm, sticky wetness. He defied an urge to turn his head and look—the slightest movement would be certain to attract a hail of bullets—and because he was so desperately aware of the necessity to lie absolutely still he found his limbs twitching involuntarily. He held his breath and struggled to control his uncontrollable muscles, while all the time cold sweat crawled over his body from fear and strain.

When the shooting stopped they threw in hand grenades—a dozen or more—to finish the job, and then there was the sound of motor-cycle engines starting up and moving away, and the deeper throb of a heavy truck moving off in low gear. The silence which followed was the noisy welcome silence of gunfire beyond the distant trees.

He lay quite still, as if paralysed, for fully ten minutes before daring to turn his head. Frankie was dead, his shapeless boiler suit awash with blood. Raising himself on his elbows he looked around. They might have been two thousand sleeping men, arranged in all postures, comfortably or uncomfortably, sometimes lying together in inert mounds, and a crimson cloud had burst overhead, scattering crimson rain upon them in ugly, jagged splashes. But here and there was movement—the slow uplifting of an arm and the tortuous movement of a leg.

Slowly he pushed himself to his knees, and then to his feet. There are bound to be other survivors, he told himself. Among two thousand men there must be some who escaped death.

He began to tread his way among the massed bodies, seeking signs of life. He was still engaged in his self-imposed task when the first of the insurgent armoured trucks arrived at the entrance to the prison camp.

CHAPTER FOURTEEN

A FTER HIS PERIOD OF QUARANTINE HAD ENDED, DR. VINCENT returned to the underground IVRO Research Centre near Brierley. His place at the recruiting depot had been taken by another doctor, a confirmed BAX type, so that he felt justified in contracting out of further duty of that nature, and firmly insisted on returning to his work in the laboratory.

He was welcomed back by Dr. Youde—a rather sunburned Youde, despite the weeks spent underground. "Ultra violet lamp," Youde explained with a hint of self-conscious apology in his voice. "After all, living in artificial conditions, I thought it advisable, you understand…" He adjusted his concave glasses in a nervous fashion.

"Of course," Vince agreed. Youde was entitled to his sun tan if he wished. "Has there been any progress—I mean, in the nature of a breakthrough?"

"In a way," Youde said. "The Americans have been experimenting with mutation—that is, producing mutated virus strains by radioactive bombardment of selected cultures. The aim is to produce a divergent strain which will be as harmless as the BA type and at the same time confer immunity against the lethal AB."

"BA itself does precisely that."

"Yes—but what they're after is a *stable* BA strain which can't break down into two isomeric forms. In other words, a BA virus which produces only BA cells and never AB."

Vince nodded. "Have they succeeded?"

"They've sent us living samples of a new strain which seems to have most of the characteristics they're looking for. It has a non-isomeric BA structure and is highly virulent. It's called SBA—that is, stable BA."

"Excellent!"

"Yes," Youde agreed, "though we must not be over-optimistic. So far the thing has been confined to the laboratory, and there are certain snags. For one thing, the new SBA virus has a slightly different molecular structure from the BA type which makes it incompatible with the BAX antibody. A reaction occurs which destroys the red blood corpuscles and causes aplastic anaemia."

Vince pushed his pipe into his mouth and lit it. "To what extent? As a BAX type myself I have a vested interest in this new bug."

"We can't be sure. The effect is likely to vary from one individual to another, depending on blood group and other factors. It could, of course, be fatal in many cases. The Americans recommend a complete blood change *before* infection where important BAX people are concerned. That raises a big problem of supply. The new blood would have to be completely virus free so that the SBA vaccine could produce the right kind of antibodies."

"Sounds complex."

"It can be done in a limited number of cases. My own feeling is that the aplastic anaemia will prove to be amenable to treatment. It means, in effect, that the new SBA virus will make everybody immune, but the unfortunate BAX types may be rather ill for a time and a few of them may die. Certain individuals can have a blood change and avoid the unpleasant after effects. On the whole we shall all come out of it rather well."

"Yes," Dr. Vincent said thoughtfully. "Taking a reasonably optimistic view, it will mean that the protected classes can come up from their deep shelters, and the civil war will stop because there's no longer any reason for it to continue."

Youde smiled enigmatically. "That is the theory, at any rate. The insurgents will certainly lose their greatest tactical advantage—the vulnerability of the old Establishment cooped up so helplessly in thousands of shelters all over the country. Whether that will stop the war remains to be seen. Meanwhile we have to go ahead with our plans on the assumption that hostilities will continue."

"What exactly are the plans, Dr. Youde?"

Youde settled himself more comfortably in his chair and explained in greater detail. The IVRO Research Centre, and a number of other sub-centres, were growing cultures of the new SBA virus from the American sample on a crash priority basis, and as quantities of vaccine became available, they would be distributed to the underground virus shelters where the IVRO doctors concerned would make sure that all occupants were infected immediately. It was anticipated that the cycle of infection would require not more than forty-eight hours from vaccination, after which immunity could be assumed and confirmed, time permitting, by means of standard blood tests.

After the two-day lapse, the shelters would be opened and evacuated under police and military protection, and the evacuees would be kept in special transit camps under heavy guard until insurgent activity was quelled. No special effort would be made to spread the SBA infection among the rebels, but it was expected that the new virus would circulate quite rapidly because of its high virulence.

Once the shelters had been evacuated and the Government had surfaced, as it were, an all-out military assault would be launched on the insurgents, who had, after all, only succeeded in making headway because a substantial proportion of the nation's police, troops and militia were pinned down in defence of the shelters.

With the full State security force in attack rather than defence, the insurrection would be squashed in a matter of days.

"What steps are being taken to deal with cases of aplastic anaemia?" Vince asked.

"Blood banks," Youde said. "There will be a nationwide call for donors, though the chances of obtaining virus-free blood are decreasing every day. Most of the hospitals at present specialising in virus cases will be turned over to BAX anaemia therapy. I think we should be able to cope without difficulty."

"And what happens to me?"

Youde took a folder from a drawer in his desk and studied a typewritten sheet. "The difficulty is that if I put you on SBA vaccine development you're liable to have aplastic anaemia trouble before we're fully equipped to cope with it. Frankly, Dr. Vincent, I'd prefer to segregate you for a week or two. I'm sending all the BAX types on the staff to the IVRO sub-centre at Bedford, and I'm hoping to arrange a blood change for them all in a few days, followed by an SBA vaccination."

"What do they do at Bedford?"

"Records and statistics."

Vince put his pipe in his pocket after making sure that it was out. "When would you want me to go?"

"As soon as possible. Tomorrow, if I can arrange for a military escort. Bedford itself is under rebel control, but the town is ringed by troops and in a state of siege. There's quite a lot of guerilla activity to the south, but the military have control over most of the Great North Road as far as Biggleswade. I think a couple of armoured cars should be able to get through to the sub-centre without too much shooting."

"Fair enough," Vince remarked. "I'd better start packing a few things."

"I'll buzz you when I've got some definite information," Youde stated.

Vince left the office and wandered along the corridors in a reflective and rather gloomy frame of mind. The more it changes, the more it remains the same, he thought, translating a half remembered French tag. Authority was still manoeuvring in the same devious way, and yet, looking back, what could any government have done under the circumstances? If it had been possible to protect the living on the same vast automatic scale as had been arranged for the disposal of the dead, then perhaps there might have been no problem.

The sequence of events seemed inevitable, right from the building of the virus shelters and incinerators, through the industrial strikes and rationing, to the insurrection. And now came the equally inevitable anticlimax—the long awaited vaccine that would provide an antidote to the virus. In the course of time historians would shake their heads wisely and wonder why mankind had not possessed the honour and integrity to face up to the virus catastrophe with dignity and courage.

He shrugged his shoulders and dismissed the trend of thinking from his mind. There was no point in trying to take an objective, overall view of the situation when one was inextricably mixed up in it on a day-to-day basis.

He lifted the telephone and booked a call to Dr. Pauline Brant at Zone M45 in Liverpool.

The operator rang back three minutes later. "I'm sorry, sir," she said, "but all lines to Liverpool have been cut. I can route you through Manchester but there's a six-hour delay on bookings, even for priority traffic."

"Never mind," Vince said, hanging up. He refilled his pipe and lit it with an air of dejection.

*

When Pauline went into his office, Captain Villier was thumbing through a sheaf of decodes of teleprinter messages that had just come in over the wire. He glanced briefly at her and smiled.

"Sit down, Pauline," he invited. "I'll be with you in a moment."

She sat down and watched him as he continued checking through the messages. Quite a likeable character, when you got to know him, she decided, and after several weeks of working together as colleagues they had finally achieved first-name terms. Alan Villier had also made a few fairly determined passes and had kissed her three times in all, on occasions when he had seized the initiative offered by surprise and opportunity. But, as she had explained to him with some care, that was as far as he would be allowed to advance, military-wise or any-other-wise, since he was potentially her patient and she, as the doctor in charge of the shelter, had to consider the ethics of her profession. Villier thought this quite a joke.

When Villier had finished reading he gave her one of the decoded messages. It proved to be a lengthy instruction from IVRO head-quarters at Brierley concerning the new SBA vaccine about which she had received a terse preliminary notification some days earlier.

Quantities of the vaccine were now available for distribution to the classified isolation centres and were to be used according to instructions immediately on arrival, the message stated. However, there was a serious problem involved in arranging safe and reliable transport due to the continuing activities of insurgent guerilla bands, and most of the major roads were closed at county frontiers.

It was proposed, therefore, to distribute the vaccine in bulk by air to key zones, using helicopters and other aircraft. Military and security forces would then deliver supplies of the vaccine to those centres which were still accessible. Where opposition from insurgent forces seemed probable, a full-scale military thrust would be arranged in the area concerned in order to get the vaccine to its proper destination.

Forty-eight hours after delivery at a centre, local units of troops and militia, with air support where required, would mount a powerful offensive against insurgent groups and positions. Under an umbrella of covering fire the isolation centres would be evacuated in an orderly fashion. The evacuees would be quickly dispersed in escorted transport to secret dispersal points from where they would be conveyed, by air or road, to special transit camps. There they would be accommodated until the second phase of the operation, an all-out attack on the insurgents, had been successfully completed.

A note at the end added that all food, equipment and arms should be taken away from the centres, or, where time did not allow this, should be destroyed to render them useless to the enemy. Special squads would destroy the centres with high explosives as soon as the occupants had been successfully evacuated.

And finally, all written instructions, coded and decoded messages and so on, had to be burned.

She returned the paper to Villier, saying: "It seems as if they've got things well organised."

"Apparently. The vaccine—will it work?"

"They don't say much about it, apart from the fact that it's a stabilised BA mutation from America. I think it will work. It obviously has IVRO's blessing, and the Government is backing the distribution scheme with troops and escorts."

"Good," he remarked, obviously pleased. "The thought of having to stay in this rabbit warren for another three or four months…"

"At least we've been luckier than those in some of the other rabbit warrens."

"Only because we happen to be bang underneath a strong army depot slap in the middle of Newsham Park, and the Riley mob haven't been able to get any nearer than Edge Hill—but that's not to say they won't. They've got strong support, and a lot of the local army units can't make up their minds which side they're on."

He picked up the sheaf of messages again and skimmed through them. "These are summaries of intelligence reports—all top secret stuff. In London the insurgents are in control of most of the eastern part of the Metropolitan area north of the Thames behind a line joining Hampstead and Waterloo. South of the river they're holding a strip about a mile wide roughly from Greenwich to Battersea. They've set up what they call a Provisional Federal Government which is supposed to be the nerve centre of the revolution throughout the country, and there's a report that the temporary headquarters is located in the underground section of Liverpool Street station. They're calling on the armed forces and security militia to join them."

"Frankly, Alan, it sounds incredible," she remarked.

He read on: "Insurgent forces claim control of many other towns and areas, particularly in the north, including Leeds, Nottingham, Doncaster, Peterborough, parts of Liverpool, parts of Manchester, and about three quarters of Birmingham. In all urban and rural areas where they have established control they are introducing two major economic moves which would appear to be in the nature of an overall policy. First, they are abolishing rationing, and second, they are issuing new currency. The old banknotes are no longer legal tender and only the new notes will be accepted for any kind of transaction. Even silver and copper coins are being replaced by paper money."

"What's the point of that?" Pauline asked in surprise.

"Partly propaganda. They can claim to have ended discriminative rationing. On the other hand, the introduction of new currency is a move designed to keep local populations under stringent control. The old banknotes and coinage are worthless by decree, and there's no question of exchanging them for the new currency at present. In order to live at all, people will have to carry on with their work or join the rebel organisation in order to earn some of the new currency which will buy food and clothing."

"That's not going to be very popular," she commented. "In fact, it reimposes rationing even more severely, and it means that people who've been saving money have lost everything."

"Frozen, I think. The restrictions may be eased in due course, although the insurgents claim that they are starting off their brave new world on a basis of strict equality—by that they mean everyone has to start with nothing at all."

"Except those who own cars and property…"

"They probably won't own them for long, once the so-called Federal Government gets down to a serious job of issuing decrees. According to one report the ultimate object is to abolish money altogether in due course. Food and personal possessions will be donated by a benevolent State on a points system for work done and services rendered."

"And on a jobs-for-the-boys system, too, no doubt."

He shrugged. "There's bound to be the usual corruption, of course. Party members—founder members of the revolution, if you like—will take the pickings and the ordinary uncommitted citizen will find himself in the familiar role of a slave in a totalitarian régime. That is, if the rebels win—which they won't in the long term."

"Have you got a cigarette for me, Alan?" she asked despondently.

He tossed her a packet. She took out a cigarette and lit it, then stood up and leaned, half sitting, on the corner of his desk. His fingers touched her back with infinite gentleness, moving delicately along the ridge of her spine. She trembled momentarily and stood up again.

"Doctor-patient ethics," she reminded him.

"The patient doesn't need ethics," he said, with a cheerful grin. "The embargo is on the doctor, so I can keep on trying as much as I like without feeling guilty. You're the one with the ethical problem to solve."

"It's no problem so far as I'm concerned—or, rather, my particular problems come in different shapes and sizes."

"You mean dark, fair, tall and short, but all wearing trousers."

She smiled ruefully. "Something like that. The point is, Alan, I'm already committed."

"Ah, well," he said with resignation, "I suppose it's better to *be* committed than to *have* committed. There's no future in the past."

"And there's not much future in the future, either," she remarked, sitting on the corner of his desk again. This time he did not touch her.

"How soon is the delivery of the vaccine and the orderly evacuation of the centre, as they put it, likely to take place?" she asked.

Leisurely he blew grey smoke into the air. "Frankly, I don't know. But making an intelligent guess I'd say delivery tomorrow and evacuation the day after. We're well protected in this centre and easily accessible. Barring a major breakthrough by the insurgents there should be no great difficulty. A helicopter could easily land in Newsham Park."

He paused to draw deeply on his cigarette. "All the same, we'd better get things moving. There's equipment to be packed, papers to be destroyed, and food to be crated for transport. And the civilians will need to pack, too."

"The laboratory alone will probably be a twelve-hour job."

"Don't worry about it, Pauline. I'll detail some of my men to do the donkey work. They'll enjoy it, after weeks of idleness."

"Thanks, Alan," she murmured. "You're a good kid."

"You're a good kid yourself," he replied, "but too strong on ethics for my money."

She acknowledged the point with a wry twist of her lips. "It's not your money I need, Alan—just your friendship."

He came over to her and kissed her lightly on the cheek. "How charming," he said, in little more than a whisper. "Friends, but not more than friends."

She stood up, patted his cheek, and went back to the laboratory.

As Captain Villier had predicted, the vaccine was delivered the next day. There was precious little of it—a tiny green phial containing enough yellow paste to cover a shilling, but it was live virus which could be diluted in saline solution or plain serum.

Pauline worked continuously for more than twelve hours administering the vaccine, allowing only short breaks for frugal meals. Meanwhile soldiers packed the laboratory equipment into wooden boxes ready for transport. It was just after one o'clock in the morning when she finally vaccinated herself and went to bed.

During the night there was an air raid on the army base above ground. She was awakened by the multiple concussions of exploding bombs. Dreamily she wondered whether this was a "softening-up" attack to prepare the way for an insurgent advance, but fatigue made the question irrelevant, and soon she fell asleep again, despite the continued bombing.

In the morning, getting out of bed, she shivered involuntarily and promptly checked her temperature. It was over one hundred. For an uneasy moment she wondered whether perhaps the true AB virus had beaten the vaccination, but, of course, that was almost impossible under deep shelter conditions.

During the next few hours she made sample temperature checks among the two hundred or so occupants of the shelter. The pattern was consistent throughout: all had temperatures varying between one hundred and one hundred and two and exhibited the symptoms of a minor feverish chill. The new SBA virus was evidently doing its job reliably and effectively.

In the early afternoon Captain Villier came into the laboratory, which was now just an empty room lined with wooden boxes and packing cases.

"Zero hour is ten o'clock tonight," he announced. "It was to have been four o'clock this afternoon, but the powers that be put it back by six hours in view of the night's events."

"What events?"

"You heard the bombing?"

"Yes."

"The insurgents have gained ground. They've advanced to Kensington and Prescot Road, and they've got tanks at the bottom of Sheil Road, less than a quarter of a mile away."

"Oh," she said. "Are they still advancing?"

"Not at the moment. They've been stopped by tank traps and mortars. On the other hand, they've got command of all the main access roads, except to the north. We're moving out under cover of darkness."

"If we're allowed to."

He nodded. "I think we can hold them for most of the night, though they've got a temporary air superiority."

"But how?"

"You mean how have they gained superior air strength?"

"Yes."

"Defecting Air Force units—and there's a rumour that French aircraft and crews are joining in. It's reported that the French Government has surrendered to its own insurgents, and now they're prepared to assist revolutionary movements in other countries. Italy's gone down, too, they say, but in Germany and Spain the governments seem to be holding their own for the time being."

She closed her eyes for a moment in an attempt to visualise Europe as a kind of enormous cauldron, boiling under the heat of conflicting political pressures.

"I don't think the French have the right to interfere," she said. "It's for each nation to solve its own internal problems in its own way."

"In theory, perhaps—but this is a global catastrophe, and the revolutions going on in practically every country in the world are taking on an international character."

"Like—workers of the world unite…"

"Not exactly. There's no obvious connection with Communism, and the insurrection hit Russia, too, although it was put down promptly and brutally. The whole movement is more fundamental—humanity versus the Establishment, as it were." He hesitated, not anxious to stray from the field of military strategy into the deeper waters of politics. "Anyway, Pauline, the deadline for exodus is ten o'clock, unless there's a further postponement."

"I'll remember," she said.

At the door, about to leave, he turned and said: "How's your temperature?"

"Still high, but falling, I think."

"So's mine. At least that's settled the virus problem. All we need concentrate on now is the fighting."

And that, she thought, was fair enough comment.

The evacuation programme went off quite smoothly, despite mortar fire and an extended bombing raid, but it was worth the risk just to be able to move out of the underground shelter into the open air once more. It was a fine starlit night with a quarter moon hanging low on the horizon, and even in the darkness it was possible to see just why Newsham Park was a major target for air attack. The camp was a vast depot of huts, tents, vehicles and supplies, the latter stacked in tarpaulin-covered dumps. From all sides came the heavy detonations of anti-aircraft fire, while the slender white fingers of searchlights probed the night sky. A stick of bombs whined and exploded on the other side of the park.

There was hardly time to look around before she was climbing a tailboard into a big military truck which had been fitted with bench seats. When some forty men, women and children had been packed into the dark interior, the truck set off, trundling across the uneven ground until it jolted on to the road, where it gathered speed. Canvas flaps had been pulled down over the back of the truck so that it was impossible to see out, but she assumed from the occasional flashing of headlamps that other trucks were following, and probably they formed part of a long convoy escorted by armoured cars.

The journey was cramped and uncomfortable, lasting almost two hours, with frequent stops for obscure military purposes. Sometimes firing broke out close at hand, but it seemed to her that always the convoy answered with the deeper sound of heavy automatic weapons and occasionally the terse explosion of a hand grenade. However, despite the stops and starts, they eventually reached their destination safely.

It was another field with huts and barbed wire perceivable in the darkness. After they had left the trucks they were divided up into groups according to profession, and in due course she found herself being conducted to a particular hut assigned to IVRO staff. This was unexpected but welcome, the more so when she discovered twenty or more colleagues, some of whom she knew quite well, relaxing in the hut with the aid of coffee and biscuits.

She attached herself to a man named Rogerson whom she had met on several occasions at Brierley, and asked the inevitable questions.

He grinned amiably. "I'm really as much in the dark as you are, Pauline. All I know is they're collecting the IVRO medical staff together from the various shelters as they close down, and they're going to send us back to Brierley headquarters."

"I thought most of the main roads were closed."

"So they are. We're flying."

"I see. Where are we now?"

"About two miles from Speke Airport. There's a plane standing by to take off just as soon as we've got a full complement."

"How soon will that be?"

He shrugged. "It depends on how the evacuation programme is progressing. So far things seem to be pretty well under control, although a few of the convoys had to fight a running battle with the rebels. Three IVRO people have been killed tonight."

"It all seems so pointless," she said with a sigh.

"Opportunity knocks but once," he pointed out. "Never in the history of the human race have revolutionary forces had such a wonderful chance to seize power while authority is buried beneath the ground. But they've left it too late, in my opinion. They've already lost."

"I hope so," she murmured, "but sometimes I wonder."

Four more IVRO staff doctors arrived during the next two hours. Soon after three a.m. they were all driven to the airport where the plane, a twin-engined aircraft of military type converted to carry passengers, took off within the half-hour, rising to seventeen thousand feet and flying in a straight line towards London.

Soothed by the vibration of the engines, Pauline fell asleep, but despite physical and mental exhaustion the sleep was restless and tormented by incoherent dreams. She awoke finally to the familiar and depressing noise of explosions. For a moment she was disorientated, imagining herself in the underground shelter in Zone M45; then, as memory came flooding back into her mind, the aircraft lurched violently, almost hurling her from the seat. Came another grinding explosion and the cabin seemed to twist in a fast tortuous circle. Excited voices could be heard above the roar of the engines. "Fasten your safety belts," someone was shouting.

In a momentary panic she clipped the broad strap round her waist and secured the buckle. Through the small oval window dawn was discolouring the black night sky with a tenuous grey stain. The ground below was invisible, but bright points of incandescence cast intense shafts of blinding light into the air, and anti-aircraft guns belched flame in minute erupting spots. Shells were exploding around the aircraft—too far away to be totally lethal, but too close for comfort. Again the aircraft lurched—and again.

Now she was in the grip of a cold, positive fear. Stark paralysis seemed to take possession of her limbs so that she could do nothing but stare through the window of the aircraft at the flashing lights in the sky and on the ground. Her ears clicked abruptly at a change in atmospheric pressure.

"The starboard engine's had it," somebody said. She looked across the cabin to the windows on the other side of the fuselage and saw streamers of flame licking jet-like from the wing, tearing away frantically in the slipstream, glowing orange and blue. An instant later the door to the flight deck swung open and a member of the crew, perhaps the navigator, stood swaying in the opening, his face sallow in the subdued light.

"No cause for alarm," he shouted in a mechanical voice that was by no means reassuring. "The starboard engine's been hit by flack, but we can probably make it on the port engine. We're about five miles from Northolt airfield, which is in Government hands. If the worst happens we may have to crash-land in open country, so make sure your safety belts are secure. There's no real danger."

Having finished his recitation he disappeared into the flight deck again, slamming the door behind him. Pauline sat perfectly still as the plane lost altitude, watching the spurting flames from the blazing engine creeping along the wing. The ground below was quite dark and featureless in the pallid grey light of dawn.

At the first touch-down the aircraft veered to one side, tilted dangerously, then zoomed aloft again with an angry surge of power. The second contact was a vicious bounce that strained her body against the retaining grip of the safety belt. And then the aircraft was bumping like a bouncing ball across open grassland, to crash through a thorn hedge and slew round, ploughing a wing-tip into soft soil. It came to a shuddering halt with the tail high in the air and the nose buried deep in the moist earth of a corn field.

Somebody opened the fuselage door near the tail of the plane, but the ground was more than twelve feet below. Two or three men had already jumped out before the navigator announced that the escape hatch in the flight deck was open, offering easy access to the ground. Pauline took her place in the queue and presently found herself being helped through a curved trapdoor in the perspex canopy of the flight deck. In a few seconds she was standing on trampled corn.

"I figure we're somewhere between Rickmansworth and Ruislip," said the pilot.

"Rebel territory or home?" someone asked.

"I don't know. We'd better assume it's home. Let's get the luggage unpacked."

They had opened the luggage bay in the tail and were in the process of throwing out cases when a spotlight glared suddenly from across the field. A whistle sounded shrilly in the air. Seconds later the thin metallic voice of a loudhailer announced:

"Line up, all of you. Put your hands in the air."

A Sten gun fired a tentative burst above their heads.

"Don't move if you want to stay alive," the voice went on. "You're all prisoners of war, only there ain't no Geneva convention this time, so watch out."

From beyond the blinding spotlight a score of shadowy figures began to advance purposefully towards the wrecked aircraft and its apprehensive passengers and crew.

CHAPTER FIFTEEN

THE MAN NAMED ROGER SNELL WAS A SQUAT, THICK-SET individual with black oily hair brushed straight back from a pair of heavy horn-rimmed glasses. He looked like a clerk or a company secretary, Clive thought, except that he was wearing an old khaki battledress with a broad red armband on which had been inscribed the letter "A" as an insignia of rank. "A" stood for area commander, Clive understood. Snell was ostensibly in charge of the entire insurgent organisation in the London area and parts of the Home Counties.

Although the man did not appear to possess a noticeably commanding air, he had a certain indefinable administrative solidity, like an intractable trade union leader. There was stubbornness in the curved underslung lines of his prominent jaw.

The room was large and comfortably furnished. It was part of a first-floor suite in a hotel near Russell Square which had been taken over by the insurgents. Clive had spent two days in a small bedroom in the same hotel recuperating from the effects of physical and mental shock. He had been looked after by two young women, presumably qualified nurses although they wore no uniform, and an elderly doctor had examined him with a taciturn air on three occasions. Medical supplies seemed to be adequate. His physical injuries were slight but painful—the facial wound, the bayonet puncture in his thigh (which had turned septic), and the grenade fragment embedded in his shoulder.

Here at headquarters insurgent discipline and organisation was clearly on a much higher level. The people around him were reasonable human beings, even possessing traces of genuine human-ity and compassion. Inevitably he was interrogated by men who were obviously insurgent officers, but there was no further brutality.

He had been adequately briefed by the nurses for the interview with Roger Snell. A shrewd man, they had said—a born leader with a mind like an encyclopedia. He's one of the founders of the revolutionary movement. You play ball with him and he'll play ball with you.

On the surface Snell certainly seemed to possess the qualities of a father image. He had the gift of authority in the set of his features and in the resonance of his gravelly voice.

"Mr. Brant," Snell said formally, referring to papers on the table before him, "I understand that you are not, in fact, one of us at all."

Clive nodded.

"But nevertheless you were taken prisoner by the militia and you were one of the five people who survived the massacre in Regent's Park. That experience would hardly endear you to the so-called defenders of freedom."

"No. On the other hand, I was even less endeared to the drunken insurgent louts who raped and murdered my fiancée."

Snell inclined his head sympathetically. "I'm sorry about that. There are always drunken louts of all political complexions. The black militia would have raped her just as brutally, given the chance. When law and order break down, licence has its way. You're an intelligent man, Mr. Brant. Surely you can appreciate the difference between hot-blooded rape, even if it results in death, and the deliberate cold-blooded murder of two thousand helpless prisoners."

"They are both criminal offences in any civilised society," Clive pointed out.

"A society torn by civil war is hardly civilised," Snell said with a sigh. "One has to distinguish between murder which is authorised as part of a deliberate policy of ruthless tactics, and capricious acts of violence and lust performed without any kind of authority—on the whim of an individual, drunk or sober."

"It's the old story," Clive commented sourly. "Authorised atrocities versus unauthorised atrocities. I find myself unable to defend either, any more than I can defend the systematic murder of the people in the underground virus shelters."

"That is a question of politics rather than policy," Snell explained, with a half smile on his lips. "There is a point at which we have to be realistic rather than sentimental. The purpose of any revolutionary movement is to erase the existing authority as quickly and as economically as possible. Authority—and by that I mean not only the Government, but also the higher echelons of executive industry and commerce—conveniently buried itself in vaults. Our purpose is to make sure that it stays buried. In the long run it will shorten the war and save innumerable lives—not that life counts for much now that it has been devalued by the virus." He paused, leaning across the table intently. "You see, Mr. Brant, we are determined to win. In fact, we *are* winning. The end justifies the means."

Clive stared at him doubtfully, but said nothing. Snell spread out his hands appealingly. "Let's face the facts. Governments all over the world have discredited themselves by combining survival with class privilege. But the privileged class consists of ordinary people like you and me, and the Government derives its authority from a constitution which is supposed to protect the fundamental rights of ordinary people like you and me. When those in authority abuse their power, ruthlessly and selfishly, then we, the ordinary people, have the right to deprive them of that power in the only way possible. We have the right to contract out, to refuse to recognise the régime which refuses to acknowledge the basic human rights."

He produced a packet of cigarettes and offered it to Clive, who took one with grateful alacrity. It was his first cigarette in several days.

"That's all very well..." Clive began, then paused to light the cigarette. At the first inhalation of smoke his brain began to spin, the floor swayed, and his thoughts drifted dreamily into an invisible grey cloud. "What I mean is, neither side can hope to gain the support of the mass of the population by committing atrocities."

Snell smiled knowledgeably, puffing at his cigarette. "At this stage we don't need support, only non-intervention. The uncommitted masses should remain uncommitted—unless they wish to join us, of course." Carefully he placed the cigarette in an ashtray on the table. "I must point out, Mr. Brant, that we are not a rabble, although some of our members may act like barbarians in time of stress. We do have a plan and a policy, and we are acquiring a competent leadership. You may in these early months accuse us of ruthlessness, but in fact we are merely being single-minded."

"I suppose so," Clive admitted. "The two are very much akin."

"History will decide in due course. What I want you to appreciate is that there is a significant shift in the balance of power throughout the world. It is as if a miracle has happened—that authority everywhere should bury itself simultaneously, abdicating, as it were, and leaving the way wide open for revolutionary movements."

Clive sucked at the cigarette and inhaled the smoke. The dizziness had given way to a feeling of torpor. "Supposing you win," he asked, "what then?"

"No supposing about it, Mr. Brant. We must win because we have decided on a rigid, cold-blooded strategy. I was an officer in the last war, and when they trained me to be an officer I was taught to recite, before beginning a field assault exercise, 'We shall advance and destroy the enemy.' That is precisely what we intend to do. We shall erase completely the existing authority protected in the virus shelters, and then we shall start again from the beginning and create a new State based on new principles—currency reform, moral reform, new concepts of social responsibility, the principle of reward for utility, that a man should have a standard of living reflecting his true contribution to society. One enters the world with nothing and departs with nothing. We believe that everything a man acquires between those two points, birth and death, should result from his own personal usefulness to human society."

Clive suppressed a cynical smile. The theory was pretty enough on the surface, but he could foresee serious problems in its application.

He said: "Who is going to decide how useful any individual is—how much his efforts are worth? There are various kinds of productivity. A composer writing one symphony in five years may be as productive in his own way as a screw-cutter turning out twenty-thousand or more screws in a working day."

Snell blew cigarette smoke through his nostrils. "With a population cut down to half, our primary need for the next twenty years will be screws rather than symphonies. We have a big programme of industrial development in view, and I'm afraid culture will have to take care of itself. I rather think that the would-be composers will be writing their symphonies in their spare moments between factory shifts. Culture is a luxury we shall not be able to afford for a long time to come."

"I suppose that will be the situation whatever happens," Clive said with resignation. "Any government of whatever colour would be committed to restoring industry and commerce as top priority. But candidly, I don't quite see how I could fit into your brave new world."

Snell twisted his lips sardonically. "Nobody has asked you to fit in."

"Then—why the cordial treatment?"

"We are cordial people, except when we're being uncordial. Frankly, I think you might fit in very well. We are always open to receive recruits of the right type, provided they have the right attitude of mind."

"Here and now I haven't any attitude of mind at all, except that I hate everybody. Even that's not true. I just don't care any more."

"Well, that's a good start," Snell remarked, turning over a number of papers on the table. "The original act of creation took place in a vacuum, and look at the result. Even God makes mistakes." He selected one particular paper and studied it for a few seconds. "I see you have top level newspaper experience, and a useful appreciation of international affairs."

"Yes," Clive agreed.

"We could probably use you in our intelligence system—in a small way at first. In due course we plan to set up a kind of Ministry of Information, and take all channels of communication—newspapers, radio, television—under State control. We shall need people with solid journalistic training and public relations background. We are looking ahead, you see."

"And if I were to decline?"

"Then"—Snell spread out his hands in a gesture of withdrawal—"you would remain a prisoner of war with, I fear, a relatively low survival value. Prisoners are passengers, and we can't really afford to carry passengers for very long."

"What would I be required to do if I joined you?"

"We would determine that in due course. At first you might assist in our intelligence work by interrogating prisoners and helping to interpret information received from various sources—such as intercepted radio transmissions and tapped teleprinter lines."

He touched his moist lips thoughtfully. "It could be, for instance, Mr. Brant, that in the long term you might be appointed editor of your own newspaper, the *Daily Monitor*—or you might be put in charge of television news services. I believe you have had some kind of experience in that kind of work."

"Yes," said Clive wistfully, "I have had experience."

"Well, then, it's up to you."

Snell regarded him benignly, interlacing his fingers and propping his elbows on the table. Clive, avoiding his eyes, considered for a while. In a disintegrating world it was dangerous to take sides, to commit oneself to a definite policy—on the other hand, it was equally dangerous not to take sides at all. In his mind there was no longer any problem of allegiance; the things and symbols that had lent significance to his life in the past had been destroyed, so that even his own name and identity seemed meaningless, as if he had become a nameless shadow in a monochrome surrealist landscape that was functional but always changing, and possessing no solidity. But the important thing, even for a shadow, was to survive, to be on the winning side—provided one could be quite sure which *was* the winning side. The world of Mr. Snell and his kind, if they were destined to succeed, would be bleak and austere; but it would be the same, anyway, whatever political clique seized power, after the ravages of the Hueste virus. The process of rebuilding a shattered economy would take many years and involve hard living for the majority, and it was possible that a single-minded dictatorship might achieve a successful economic recovery more quickly, even if more ruthlessly.

Clive found himself staring at Snell in a dreamy, thoughtful manner, trying to assess his character. He was typical enough: the methodical, unimaginative organiser, dedicated to his cause, objective and dispassionate in outlook, but nevertheless shrewd enough to secure for himself an administrative post in which he could exercise authority in a comfortable non-combatant way by signing papers and originating orders. He would probably sign a document authorising the destruction of shelters containing hundreds of protected men, women and children with the same matter-of-fact equanimity as he would endorse a cheque—in the new currency, of course. And his defence, as always when atrocities are planned at administrative levels, would be that of merely implementing policy determined at even higher levels—in other words, obeying orders.

"Well?"

Clive collected his straying thoughts. "I'm a practical character," he said. "I held executive status in the old society, and I can see no good reason why I should not hold an equivalent status in the new, if it's possible. Seems to me it's only sensible to recognise that the world will never again be the same as it was. If I were to say no, in the belief that the old order would come back some day—well, it would be wildly unrealistic."

"And wildly foolish," Snell interjected.

"On the other hand, I'm not fully convinced that the revolution can succeed. I'm thinking internationally rather than nationally. Once the virus problem is over, the true crisis will be political. It could be that the governments of the world, the United Nations if you like, will combine forces in an all-out counter-attack against insurgents on a global basis."

"Sound thinking," Snell acknowledged with a nod. "In fact, we have some evidence that this is a possible step. How would you like to see Britain invaded by troops of a Continental Federation, or by Africans, or even Americans?"

"I wouldn't, but I suppose it is not impossible."

"I'll put it more strongly, Mr. Brant. How would you like to see our principal cities atom-bombed by missiles, and then have the country taken over by a UN force of mixed nationalities and races?"

Clive shook his head. "I don't think things could ever get to that stage."

"They could, quite easily. We have intercepted a number of signals which give no cause for complacency. They suggest that plans are in hand for a counter-revolution on a world-wide scale, once the virus is quenched. And that may be sooner than we imagine. We have reason to believe that some kind of antivirus drug or vaccine is already being distributed among the enemy and the protected classes, because shelters are being evacuated in a mass military operation. That is why we must act quickly and ruthlessly."

"I see," Clive said, his doubts and misgivings returning. Even so, one had to act on a short-term basis, however much it might conflict with the long-term view. Snell was the man in command here and now, and Snell had to be kept happy and reassured about potential recruit Brant—in Brant's own interests, of course.

Snell placed his bunched fist gently but firmly on the table. "We have to be in absolute control of the country within three weeks, so that we, too, shall be able to use all military resources in self-defence. We shall not be without allies."

"What allies?"

"We already have the support of other countries where the revolution has succeeded. At this very moment units of the French

Air Force are operating over here on our side, and we have had promises of military aid from other European countries."

Clive eyed the other man with dubious uncertainty. "The entire business seems to be much bigger than I had imagined," he remarked.

"In due course it will be bigger than even I can imagine. Now I put it to you, Mr. Brant—either you are for us or against us. Do you want to play an active part in establishing the new order, or are you inclined to back the old order?"

"It sounds as if you are offering the choice of life or death."

"Not in the way you think. We don't murder our prisoners as the militia do."

"You mean, outside of hotel bedrooms. Well, I hold no brief for the behaviour of either the rebels or the militia, but I never did support the Government's virus policy. I don't like the way they handled rationing and I don't like the militia. In other words, I'm with you. I'd like to do some useful work in your intelligence and information services."

Snell nodded, watching him keenly. "All right. I'll give you a chance to make good. You'll be assigned to our field intelligence staff under a man called Vaughan. You'll take your orders from him. Your job will be to dig as much information as possible out of prisoners, particularly those who have some official status and are likely to know something of enemy plans. Vaughan will show you the methods we use. They're humane, but one mustn't be too squeamish. After all, this war is a matter of life and death for all of us."

"I understand," Clive said, with some reluctance.

Snell stood up and came round the table. "In that case I'll hand you over to Vaughan without delay. We have quite a number of prisoners to deal with."

*

"Interrogating prisoners is not simply a matter of asking them questions," Vaughan stated blandly.

He was a small man of mild manner, probably in his early fifties, with a pallid pinched face and wearing rimless glasses. His suit was expensive and immaculate, in dark grey, so that he possessed an elegant, professional air, as if he were perhaps a doctor or something fairly important in the City. He smoked a cigarette with the aid of a small silver holder, and had an irritating habit of rubbing the tips of his fingers with his thumbs, as if judging the sharpness of his nails.

His office was small but neat, with a tidy glass-topped desk and comfortable chairs. On meeting Clive he promptly offered him a cigarette and poured sherry for both of them. Mr. Vaughan was evidently a man fond of civilised amenities, however much they were in short supply.

"Interrogation is a science," Vaughan continued in a pedantic manner. "During the last war I was an agent in Norway—I had lived there for many years. In due course I was taken by the Gestapo."

His lips shaped a phantom smile of tired irony. "I learned the science of interrogation the hard way. The course of instruction lasted nearly three years. They were very good—very thorough. When I told them all I knew, they would start all over again three times, four times, just to make sure there were no discrepancies. Sometimes, for the fun of it, they would invent discrepancies and then spend days forcing me to explain an error of which I knew nothing."

He shrugged. "That was a long time ago, and one forgets very quickly."

Clive said nothing. The other man stood up and began to pace slowly across the room behind his desk, smoking his cigarette and not looking directly at Clive, rather as if he were rehearsing a lecture. He walked with a noticeable limp, Clive observed.

Vaughan said: "There are a number of psychological factors to be taken into consideration. The interrogator must be a man of education, culture and poise. He must also have a sympathetic manner and the ability to reassure the prisoner, who will already have been roughly treated by his guards before the interrogation. The prisoner must be made to feel relaxed and more secure, so that he will be willing to co-operate with his interrogator."

Clive sipped his sherry, making no comment.

"There are certain qualifications, however," Vaughan went on. "The prisoner has to be made to feel inferior to the interrogator, even though he may be a man of high academic or social standing. Therefore he has to be humiliated and stripped of all the things which lend him self respect. The higher the status of the prisoner and the greater his potential knowledge of military affairs, the more he needs to be demoralised."

"Just how do you do this?" Clive asked.

"Oh, the usual techniques," Vaughan said in a blasé manner. "We do it in a civilised way. None of your Gestapo brutality. We clean him out with emetics and purgatives, then starve him and deprive him of sleep for three or four days. That is usually sufficient. He is not allowed to shave, of course, and if he shows signs of resistance we may take all his clothing away and shave off his hair. No question of torture or sadistic cruelty, just a simple scientific matter of reducing him to the lowest common denominator and sapping his physical vitality so that he becomes depressed and apathetic to the point of unconditional surrender."

"Isn't that being—rather inhuman?"

Vaughan smiled vaguely. "We can hardly afford to be otherwise. We use the minimum of tough tactics. Humiliation is invariably more effective than pain, and the methods we use are considerably more humane than, say, the Gestapo electric soldering iron or rubber hose. In any case, these preparations take place before the prisoner is brought to the interrogator, so that one does not feel personally involved."

He spread out his hands deprecatingly. "After all, Mr. Brant, a few days of fast, a few nights without sleep—many innocent people have to endure these things in time of war. They leave no scars, either physical or psychological. On the whole, from my own experience, I think it is good for the human physiology—tends to toughen it up, increase its powers of endurance. So far as the shaven head is concerned—well, they do say that the new growth of hair is much stronger. The nakedness is neither here nor there, except in so far as it is a humiliation. We are all born naked."

"And what happens if a prisoner proves difficult—refuses to talk?"

"That is something the interrogator does not need to consider. He merely makes his report, and others take over responsibility for persuading the prisoner that co-operation is desirable. I can't recall having to interrogate any one prisoner for more than four sessions. You must bear in mind that each question and answer period may continue for as long as forty-eight hours, sometimes more. We work in relays, about three hours at a time, and of course we use women interrogators as well as men. Quite frequently the women are more successful."

"You mean that it is more humiliating for a male prisoner when stripped naked to be interrogated by a woman?"

"And vice versa, though we don't normally have many female prisoners, and, of course, they do not, generally speaking, have much useful information."

"I see," was all that Clive could say. He was too busy fighting a deep sense of revulsion to think coherently. One had to remain rational and matter-of-fact, to imitate Mr. Vaughan's suave unconcerned manner. The thing was reciprocal, anyway. Probably the rebel prisoners were undergoing even more severe treatment in the hands of the militia. You couldn't fight a civil war wearing kid gloves.

Vaughan stopped pacing around and peered at him through his rimless glasses. "I think, perhaps, the best thing would be for you to sit in on a few interrogations," he suggested. "Then you could make your own independent report, and we could assess your ability. You would be allowed to ask questions, of course."

Clive nodded. Oddly enough he thought he could detect a gleam of sardonic humour in Vaughan's eyes.

"We have a new batch of prisoners from IVRO," Vaughan went on. "They were shot down in an aircraft which made a crash-landing. There are fifteen men and five women. They were captured about three days ago, and between them they could have a great deal of information. We know, for instance, that they have all been evacuated from virus shelters, and they all have symptoms of a mild virus infection, but not the usual AB or BA type. This, we believe, is very important, and ties in with reports we've had about a new antivirus vaccine. It's up to us to find out, Mr. Brant—that is, you and me and about a dozen other experienced interrogators."

"Whatever you say," Clive agreed.

CHAPTER SIXTEEN

THE TELEPRINTER MESSAGE BEGAN WITH THE OMINOUS WORD *Airloss,* and continued: *Flight B34 IVRO Liverpool London shot down insurgent territory. Passengers crew believed prisoners. Names follow.* And among the names was Dr. Pauline Brant.

For Dr. Vincent the message was an unexpected shock; it brought the violence and insecurity of the outside world into the peaceful routine of the IVRO sub-centre at Bedford. He took time off to make himself some coffee, then went to see the administrative head of the sub-centre, an elderly man named Derringer.

"I chanced to see this signal as it came through the cypher department," he explained, putting the teleprinter decode on the other man's desk. "One of these people is a very close friend of mine. I'm wondering if it's at all possible to obtain further information."

Derringer made a doubtful noise as he studied the terse wording of the message. "I could try Brierley, if it's all that important."

"It is most important," Vincent emphasised.

"All right. Leave it with me. I'll let you know."

Four hours later Vince was summoned to Derringer's office. The old man sat passively behind his desk, drumming his fingers impatiently on the polished top.

"I've been on to Youde, and then Caplan," he said. "There's little to add. The plane crash-landed near Rickmansworth. There were no casualties, but everyone aboard was taken prisoner by an insurgent patrol. It's believed they are being held at Harrow in an empty school near Wealdstone main line station, but by now they may well have been moved to more permanent quarters."

"I would like permission to leave the sub-centre," Vince said.

Derringer registered surprise and adjusted his bifocal glasses.

"That would be most unwise, Dr. Vincent. I understand that the insurgents are now in possession of the greater part of London, particularly north of the Thames. What could you hope to achieve?"

"I'm tired of sitting round on my backside analysing statistics and filing punched cards. The real struggle for survival is going on in the world up above. I'd rather join in than just wait and wait and wait—in the hope that things will sort themselves out."

Derringer made a noise in his throat which sounded like hrrmph. Clearly he disapproved of such a belligerent attitude. An IVRO doctor had no part to play in the struggle for power taking place in the world on the surface; one had to remain strictly neutral, to pursue one's calling whatever the political climate.

"I'm a BAX type," Vince went on, "so I've nothing to lose. If I run into aplastic anaemia then I'll have time to seek medical attention. I'm prepared to take a chance."

"Aren't you being just a little impetuous?" Derringer asked. "What good can you possibly do out there? You may have a friend who has been taken prisoner, but all that will happen is that you will become a prisoner, too."

"It's a calculated risk."

"The answer is no. We at IVRO are aligned with the Government, and we must conform to Governmental policy. It is not within my power to sanction what is, in effect, the abdication of a member of my staff."

"Not even if I resign?"

Derringer removed his glasses, wiped them with his handkerchief, and replaced them.

"Dr. Vincent," he said, "I can quite understand that you may be deeply concerned about the fate of a colleague or friend who is in the hands of the insurgents, but I urge you not to be precipitate. Let a day or two go by. Pause and consider. I am sure that you will realise the utter futility of your present demands."

"I've spent too much time pausing and considering," Vince said. "The net result has been nothing—absolutely nothing. I have the right to leave if I so wish, and if necessary I shall resign."

"Twenty-four hours," Derringer said, raising an admonishing finger. "Twenty-four hours in which to think it over."

"No. I've thought it over and my mind is made up."

"Twelve hours, then. Four hours." Derringer hesitated, his hands fluttering in uncertainty. He pointed to the telephone. "Speak to Dr. Youde. He is a shrewd man. He could give you very sound advice."

"I don't need advice. All I want is authorisation from you to have the airlock opened so that I can go out."

Derringer's indecision was painful to observe. Finally he said: "If you're quite determined, Dr. Vincent..."

"I am."

"Then perhaps you would be kind enough to write me a formal memo, just for the record. It might simplify matters if you were in fact to resign, in a purely nominal way, of course. It would clear me in so far as administrative discipline is concerned, and there would be nothing to stop you from withdrawing your resignation at a future date if you so wished."

"I'll do that," Vince promised.

A few hours later, having committed himself to the rash and rather irresponsible course of action he had outlined to Derringer, he began to have misgivings. It was one thing to feel frustrated and bloody-minded because Pauline was a prisoner in the hands of the rebels, but quite another to go out into the hostile world, unarmed, vulnerable, with no clearly defined plan of action. In some vague way he imagined he would find Pauline, perhaps by making a desperate journey to Harrow and allowing himself to be taken prisoner, but cold logic told him that the idea was impracticable. Nevertheless, having made up his mind, he was fully prepared to go ahead and face the consequences; it was only necessary to be hard, single-minded and ruthless—qualities which on the whole were alien to his easy-going personality.

He was allowed to leave the shelter shortly after midnight, via the airlock, taking with him nothing but the clothes he was wearing and some chocolate ration wrapped in polythene. As the steel door closed behind him he felt suddenly alone. The night was cold and crisp, with the stars gleaming brilliantly in the black sky and the smoky band of the Milky Way glowing luminously above. He was in a copse on a hillside, with the main road to London not more than a quarter of a mile to the east. He started walking over the brittle grass.

At the road, some ten minutes later, he waited, squatting in the shadow of a thorn hedge. The moon, rising to the west, was in a cold quarter phase, casting pallid shadows on the monochrome ground. There was no traffic, and the air was still apart from the remote barking of a dog. The sky to the south flashed with staccato orange lights, and presently came the sound of attenuated explosions. He continued to wait.

This was enemy territory, he told himself. The rebels had consolidated their grip on Bedford, extending the area of their control, and although his particular zone was a kind of no-man's-land there was little doubt that the insurgents were in the ascendancy.

Half an hour went by. Abruptly twin headlights emerged over the unseen horizon, a mile away, perhaps. They vanished in a declivity, then reappeared, much closer. He stood up and advanced into the road, waving his arms.

The vehicle stopped with a snarl of brakes. It was a small open truck loaded with wooden crates, and the man at the wheel was wearing a black beret and a red armband. Vince formulated his policy in a fraction of a second.

"You going to London?" he asked.

Two men got down from the truck, one of them holding a revolver, the other a flashlight. They searched him methodically and went through the contents of his wallet.

"Bloody IVRO doctor," one said.

"I was," Vince stated. "I've deserted. I got tired of being kept underground. I've got a wife and children to consider, and I want to be on the winning side."

"That's *your* story, mate."

"I've been wasting my time," Vince went on earnestly. "Seems to me doctors are needed on the surface, not underground. Take me prisoner if you like, so long as I can do something useful."

"You sound too bloody good to be true," said the man with the gun.

"Would I be likely to stick my neck out in this way if I didn't mean what I say?"

"Maybe—maybe not. You'd better get in. We're going to Watford area HQ. They'll know how to deal with you there."

Vince climbed into the front of the truck, firmly sandwiched between the two men, and they set off at breakneck speed along the deserted road in the direction of London.

There was little in the way of conversation—a few desultory

questions and answers. Six times the truck was forced to stop at
road blocks, but all were manned by insurgents, and it came to
Vince gradually that revolution was practically a *fait accompli*. Two
of the road blocks were manned by troops in khaki uniform—a
disconcerting fact which indicated the true strength of the insurgent
forces. If the rebels were backed by the military then the battle
was virtually over. Even the militia could hardly hope to maintain
a reactionary balance of power.

They ran into an air raid at an industrial estate some five miles
from Watford. The driver stopped the truck for ten minutes, switching the lights off, while planes dropped incendiary bombs and high
explosives on dark buildings less than half a mile away.

"Munition factory," the driver said in a subdued voice. "They
make hand grenades and mortar shells."

As if in confirmation a tremendous explosion leaped incandescently into the night sky, blinding the stars with orange flame.
The blast came in a shock wave that made the truck shudder on
its hard tyres. And then, abruptly, the air raid was over, and the
driver resumed his journey. The red glow in the sky fell back to
the rear.

Watford itself was deserted and blacked-out. Their destination
proved to be a printing works on top of the hill a few hundred yards
past the station, but the machines were idle and there was a fine
film of dust over the benches and stones. The composing room and
the machine room were stacked with wooden crates containing,
so far as Vince was able to judge, ammunition and canned rations,
and the truck was presumably adding to the store.

He was escorted at gun point down a corridor to a glass door
on which was painted: *Works Manager*. Inside was a small room,
austerely furnished, in which three harassed looking middle-aged

men sat around a battered old desk. They glanced up simultaneously as Vince was escorted in.

The truck driver said: "Picked him up south of Bedford, Commander. He's an IVRO doctor. Said he was trying to escape 'cause he wanted to do something useful on the surface."

The three men stared at him for quite a long time, as if he were an unwelcome intrusion into a placid discussion of long term strategy. Then one of them waved a hand curtly, and the driver and his mate left the room.

"What's your game?" demanded the man in the middle, a flabby individual with a spaniel-like face and suspicious grey eyes.

"No game," Vince stated. "I'd like to join some of my colleagues."

"What do you mean by that?"

"During the past two or three days an aeroplane was shot down in this area. There were some twenty IVRO doctors aboard, and they were taken prisoner. I'd like to join them."

"You would, would you? You think this is a kind of old pal's club, or something?"

"I am already a prisoner," Vince said in a reasonable tone of voice. "All I'm asking is that I should be allowed to join my fellow prisoners."

"Is that all? Then what was all the crap about wanting to do something useful on the surface?"

"It would be useful, from my point of view."

The man in the centre of the desk stood up wearily. "Turn out your pockets," he ordered. "Let's find out who you are."

When they had gone through his wallet and his personal possessions, the man said: "You're obviously a nut case, Dr. Vincent. You could be worse—a spy or a saboteur. But no secret agent would hand himself over to the enemy in such a naïve fashion. What's your angle?"

"I'll tell you the truth," Vince said. "We're all human beings of the same race, so perhaps we can understand each other. One of your IVRO prisoners is a woman whom I'm going to marry. I'd like to be near to her, if possible, until this whole rotten business is sorted out."

The three men grinned, and one said, "How sweet."

"You ought to remember that the IVRO people are mainly doctors, first and foremost," Vince went on. "Whatever our political views, our first duty is to humanity, regardless of colour or creed. I think, perhaps, we merit confidence."

"You mean like we should trust you and in particular let this doctor tart of yours and you get together?"

Vince suppressed a surge of anger. "Couldn't the insurgents use a score of experienced virus doctors? None of us would deliberately withhold our services in the strictly medical sense. All we ask is to be treated as responsible adult human beings."

"Speak for yourself, chum. You're not in a position to ask for anything at all. We're all responsible human beings when it comes to the point."

"Are we?"

The man in the centre eyed him coldly. "We can use doctors, of course. But what good are they? Do you know any doctors who can cure the virus?"

"Yes," Vince said firmly. "Here and now I do."

"Well, I'll tell you something, chum. I'm a BAX type—all three of us are—so we're not particularly worried. All the same, you can have your wish. In the morning I'll send you down to Harrow for interrogation. You'll probably be put with the other IVRO prisoners. Whether you'll get to see any of them, I wouldn't know—it all depends on Mr. Snell. If I were you I'd talk like hell and co-operate to the limit. That way you might get a kind of reprieve and even manage to see your girl friend. It's the best I can do for you."

"Thanks, anyway," Vince said, with due sincerity.

"You'll have to spend the rest of the night in what they call the Monotype casting room. It has no windows and a very solid door, and there are other prisoners in there. It's uncomfortable, but you're a big boy and you'll live."

"Thanks," Vince repeated.

The man in the centre spoke into an internal telephone, and thirty seconds later two insurgents wearing red armbands arrived to escort him with the aid of a long-barrelled revolver towards the casting room.

Early in the morning he was brusquely wakened and bundled into the back of a small covered truck with an armed escort for company. The guard was a young man with an amiable, bearded face, and he spoke with a Welsh accent. He offered Vince a cigarette and lit one up for himself.

"You'll be all right, mate," said the guard. "You're getting V.I.P. treatment. Reckon they know doctors don't want to cause trouble. Some of the other prisoners—proper bloody-minded sods they were, so they got it rough like you'd expect. It never occurred to them that the war is nearly over."

"There's still the virus to fight," Vince pointed out.

"Not so much now, there isn't. Most of us have had the mild attack, so we've got nothing to worry about. It's on its way out. Another week or two and it'll be a dead duck."

"Yes," Vince said thoughtfully. "It has certainly passed its peak."

The guard leaned forward; he seemed to be in a confidential mood. "I'll tell you, mate—we're not worried about the virus any more. All our commanders and top men are the whatsit types…"

"You mean BAX?"

"That's right. So they can really get down to the job of sorting things out—chopping up the resistance and forming a new government. Course, things'll be tough for a time—bound to be—but you mark my words, mate, this old country's going to be a bleeding utopia one of these days."

At least the adjective was correct, Vince thought with irony. A lot more blood would be shed before the conflict was finally resolved, and even then it wouldn't be a utopia.

"They was talking on the radio this morning," the guard went on. "The enemy, I mean. They said they'd got a vaccine and that we should all have a cease fire and play happy families while they fiddled with their vaccine and started up a new plague—only this time antivirus." He laughed sardonically. "What they don't seem to know is that most of us don't give a monkey's about the virus any more. What do we want with a vaccine?"

"You'll get it regardless," Vince stated. "The antivirus is just as infectious as the other, if not more so." But he did not elaborate further. The threat of aplastic anaemia was rather like a gun that could fire both ways.

Within fifteen minutes the truck turned into the playground of a school. Part of the perimeter wall of the ground had been removed to form a wide opening, and the area had been converted into a parking bay for insurgent vehicles of diverse types.

He jumped off the back of the truck and was promptly seized by two burly men with Sten guns strapped round their shoulders. The escort handed over a blue envelope containing a typewritten sheet of paper—probably a commitment document, Vince decided.

At least there seemed to be some signs of order and method in their procedure after the earlier wave of irresponsible violence and atrocities, and that was reassuring enough.

They took him into the school, which had evidently been converted into a prison, up a flight of stone steps to the first floor, and along a corridor to what might have been the headmaster's study. Here again was the inevitable office with the paper-strewn desk, and the shirt-sleeved man with the red armband looking bored and faintly perplexed.

He answered the routine questions that concerned identification and motives. The other man examined the commitment order, then said:

"You've wasted your time, Dr. Vincent. The chances of your seeing any of the women prisoners is nil." His voice was smooth and educated, contrasting strangely with his unshaven face, shaggy hair and dirty clothes.

He went on: "Who is this woman doctor with whom you have some kind of association?"

"Dr. Pauline Brant."

"Ah, yes. Well, the position is that the men and women prisoners are completely segregated, as you might expect. There can be no point of contact, unless, of course, certain individuals join the insurgent forces and are therefore in a position of trust. Is that your intention?"

Vince hesitated. "Candidly, no."

"Then what *is* your intention?"

"I have no intention other than to find Dr. Brant."

"But you have found her. She is here, in this prison. That is as near as you will get."

"If I could be allowed to talk to her for a few minutes…"

"The answer is no," the other man said firmly. "At some future date, possibly, but you have a busy time ahead of you talking to our interrogating staff, and learning how to adapt yourself to the new kind of society in which you are to live." He stood up and lit a cigarette. "However, you can certainly join your male colleagues from IVRO. There are fifteen of them—I beg your pardon—fourteen. One died last night. But talking is out, I'm afraid."

He placed his hands on his hips and regarded Vince with eyes that were almost melancholy. "Get this firmly fixed in your mind, Dr. Vincent. Prisoners may only talk to insurgent officers and personnel. They are not permitted to talk to each other under any circumstances. That is an inflexible rule which we enforce very severely. Do you understand?"

"I understand, but can't see the point."

"The point is obvious. Without communication there can be no organisation. And, frankly, Dr. Vincent, we prefer to have our prisoners unorganised—as individuals. If we could isolate them from each other we would do so, but we have neither the space nor the facilities. Therefore we have to compromise."

"Is it necessary to be so severe with doctors? After all, we are really non-combatant."

The other man smiled. "Doctors are human, and all humans are combatant in one sense or another, even if it is only a question of attitude. In fact, the IVRO doctors are treated with more consideration than other prisoners, but there are still policy regulations which have to be imposed and enforced. This is not the Savoy Hotel, Dr. Vincent."

"I realise that."

"Well, then..." He signalled the two guards standing silently near the door. They came over to Dr. Vincent and took his arms.

"Put him in room eleven, with the other IVRO prisoners. The usual procedure."

"Yes, sir."

He was escorted from the room, along the corridor, and up another flight of steps to the second storey. Here a wide corridor bisected a row of classrooms with big windows which had been boarded up from the outside so that it was impossible to see whether they were occupied or not. Two armed guards patrolled the length of the corridor, at the end of which was a double door opening into a big hall-like room which had probably been a physics or chemistry laboratory at one time. Four benches, each fitted with a small sink and tap, still straddled the room, but all apparatus and equipment had been removed. A partition of angle-iron bolted together in a strong lattice separated the main body of the laboratory from the smaller area where a raised platform had in former days supported the science master's desk. It had been replaced by a plain board table bearing an automatic carbine and a box of tear gas bombs. The guard was a young man with a high forehead, wavy blond hair, and an intelligent manner. He put away the paper-backed book he was reading as Dr. Vincent and his escorts entered the room.

Vince looked around. The IVRO doctor prisoners, all fourteen of them, were sitting or squatting on the floor around the walls of the room, each with his hands behind his back. The reason for their unanimity of posture was not apparent until the guard produced a pair of handcuffs from a wooden crate under the table and snapped them on to his wrists, after first pulling his hands behind his back.

"Just a restraining measure," he said in a bored fashion, as if he knew the words by heart. "Each of you can be released individually for essential functions such as eating, drinking and sanitation, but not all together. That way we won't have any trouble. If you want anything, you ask me. That doesn't mean to say you'll get it. All you have to do is sit around, like the others. If you want to walk around for exercise, you've got to ask permission."

He took a small green-backed book from a drawer in the table, and opened it, then produced a ball pen.

"Name?"

Vince gave all the details of identification that were asked for as the guard wrote them down. Presently the guard closed the book with a sigh.

"I was almost a doctor myself," he confided. "Fifth year medical student when the virus struck. I expect that's why they put me in charge of you lot."

He paused to light a cigarette. The two escorts stood silently to the rear.

"You'll find it all right, here, Dr. Vincent. A bit dull, of course, and rather uncomfortable, but if you obey the rules you won't come to any harm. Now if you'd like to find yourself a place to sit down by the wall…"

He made a sign to the escorts, who promptly took Vince's arms and propelled him through a narrow gap in the lattice partition, around the benches, to a blank space against the right hand wall which faced the tall windows overlooking the road outside.

"Sit down," one of them said. "You're not allowed to be nearer than six feet to any other prisoner. And no talking—get it?"

Vince indicated with a nod that he had indeed got it. The escorts left the room, and after a quick glance around at the prisoners, the guard continued reading his paperback.

For the next two days and nights Vince remained in the same room, always sitting by the wall and, when sleep became a matter of desperation, slumping to the hard planked floor. Food was supplied twice daily—simple food that consisted of a watery vegetable soup into which potatoes had been mashed, with a hunk of stale bread—but even that became welcome after the first few hours and proved to be something to look forward to. Sanitation was primitive, for security reasons. In a small room annexed to the laboratory were two white enamelled buckets. The prisoners were detailed in turn to empty and wash the buckets in the school lavatories as necessary, but always under escort, of course. And occasionally the guard, or his relief, who had also been a medical student, would tire of reading and address the prisoners on various aspects of insurgent plans.

"You must realise that our society is rather upside down at the present time," the guard preached on one occasion, patting his thick wavy hair into place. "You men should not be in the position you are, with your knowledge and experience. On the other hand, while the civil war continues, the old values and standards don't apply. But you won't have long to wait. It will soon be over."

He lit a cigarette and said apologetically: "I'm sorry I can't hand them round. I expect many of you would like a smoke. One of these days you'll be able to make up for it. In any case, think of the money you're saving. Cigarettes cost the earth these days."

That was pure cynicism, Vince thought. The insurgents were probably supplied with looted cigarettes.

"We've taken London," the guard went on. "Also Manchester, Liverpool, Birmingham—most of the principal cities. We have the fighting Services on our side, with the exception of some Navy units, a few Army camps and not more than half a dozen Air Force squadrons, but they're all quite powerless because they can't get fuel or food and we've cut off water supplies and communications. The old Government has been chopped in half. Most of the Cabinet are either prisoners or dead, and the Prime Minister as was is hiding out somewhere, if he hasn't left the country. Sir Ralph Betenguel has been proclaimed provisional president of Federal Britain, and there are moves to set up a European Federation with a common political and economic policy."

The name Betenguel meant little to Vince, who had not delved deeply into pre-civil-war politics, but he recalled that the man had at one time headed a break-away ginger group of the Labour party before he had resigned to form a new party, known popularly as the Economicals (the full title, he thought, was Economic and Labour Federation) whose policy was to introduce drastic reform in the financial organisation of society—the abolition of money, as such; the rejection of gold as a standard of currency in favour of a rather nebulous concept of "unit output" in terms of productivity per adult person; the establishment of the principle that every individual was only entitled to as much in the way of civilised amenities and standard of living as he was prepared to contribute to society as a whole in the form of physical labour and inventiveness of mind, in other words, brains and brawn. Central government as such was to be abolished; instead, the country would be divided up into a large number of small economic zones loosely linked in a national federation. The requirements of each zone would naturally differ, depending on whether it were rural or urban, agricultural or industrial, and the individual zones would be assessed in terms of productivity to the gross national product of the State as a whole. Subdividing and subdividing, the local area authorities would finally determine the required productivity of individuals. Those who failed to achieve the standard required would enjoy, if that was the word, a lower standard of living. Those who exceeded their productivity index would receive the various extras that made life more pleasant and lent one a "status symbol". In such a way society would re-adjust itself to a logical economy divorced from the artificial and arbitrary standard of gold—the source, it was alleged, of all economic evils.

"The virus threat is nearly over," the guard went on. "It did a great deal of damage but it also brought good. Without it there could never have been a complete social revolution. You've got to accept that life has changed for all of us. There'll be no going back to pre-virus days. It will take time to get things organised, perhaps ten years, perhaps twenty, but in the long run we're all going to be much better off."

Vince, listening sceptically to the optimistic monologue, was faintly startled to hear whispering from his right. He glanced round briefly. His nearest neighbour was a grey-haired and rather plump prisoner who promptly winked briefly and solemnly, and whispered again without moving his lips.

"Don't look round. This is the only chance we get to talk. What's your name?"

"Vincent," Vince replied, keeping his lips motionless.

The other man's whisper was difficult to distinguish under the noisier blanket of the guard's peroration, but he was able to construe the sense of what he was saying.

"I'm Carter. We're all IVRO here. Are you?"

"Yes. I'm IVRO too."

"All we have to do is sit tight and wait. The SBA virus will finish them off."

"Not all of them."

"Most of them. All the BAX types."

"You mean aplastic…"

"Every one of them. They won't be able to treat more than just a few. They'll die like flies."

"Are you sure?"

"Positive. Best thing is to co-operate. Do as they say. We've all agreed on that. In a week or two things will be different…"

Vince was suddenly aware that the guard had stopped talking and was staring straight at himself and the man named Carter. "You two," he said in a flat, impassive voice. "You were talking."

"Nonsense," said Carter. "I've got a wheezy chest, that's all." Vince remained silent, uncertain of the situation.

"I heard you quite distinctly," the guard stated. "You know the rules."

He pressed a bell push which had been rigged up by the double door of the room.

"Get up, both of you," he ordered.

As he struggled to his feet, hands still pinioned behind his back, he heard the other man whisper: "Bad luck. This is my third beating in four days."

A moment later two guards entered the room and took them away.

Some time afterwards, Vince decided that the beating itself was not so bad. The fear and the helplessness combined to neutralise the pain. The worst part was the soreness and discomfort that seemed to stiffen his whole body for hours afterwards so that even the simple inactivity of sitting down became a prolonged torment. But, he told himself, it could have been worse. It could have been a steel bar instead of a length of rubber hose.

Philosophically he settled down to wait for his aches to dissolve. The blackest shadow darkening his mind was the threat of the antivirus which, if Carter were right, would prove to be far more ominous and widespread than Dr. Youde had said, though in all fairness to Youde, he had no doubt assumed that immediate treatment would be available for IVRO staff who developed aplastic anaemia—but not IVRO men who voluntarily handed themselves over to the enemy.

CHAPTER SEVENTEEN

A T FIRST CLIVE WAS PUZZLED BY THE LENGTHY, DETAILED way in which Snell and his assistants pursued their interrogation of prisoners, particularly those who quite clearly possessed no useful information. In due course he realised, however, that the purpose of interrogation was not simply intelligence, but also to ascertain the prisoner's political affiliation and his attitude towards the insurgent forces and policies. Sometimes the question and answer routine was varied so that the session became a discussion—a rather one-sided discussion in which the interrogator attempted to change the views and beliefs of the prisoner in a kind of indoctrination procedure.

Snell explained this by pointing out that all prisoners were potential recruits for the insurgent movement. "Only a small percentage will have information of military value, and even then it may be difficult to extract without an extended period of brutality and brainwashing. Frankly, it's hardly worth the trouble. The revolution is progressing so quickly that details of enemy deployment would almost certainly be out of date by the time the prisoner was forced to reveal them. If we regarded prisoners only as a source of information we should be wasting both time and material."

Elaborating on this, he said: "Most prisoners are hostile. It doesn't make them any less hostile to treat them well. They have to be deprived of hope, reduced to a state of apathy. They have to be made to examine their beliefs so that they can discard those which are of no immediate practical value to them. They must be made to modify their attitudes so that finally they will accept conditions imposed on them, even if it means accepting a new system of beliefs."

In practice the method worked very well. Snell estimated that about two thirds of all prisoners eventually overcame their prejudices and accepted the new régime, even if only as a matter of expediency at first. "What starts as expediency soon becomes permanent policy," he concluded, and Clive recognised the basic truth of the assertion.

During the first few days he sat in on interrogations of a miscellaneous selection of prisoners, some of whom had been badly treated and bore visible signs of applied violence. A few were undergoing Snell's "full treatment", with shaved heads and stripped of all clothing, but these were the defiant ones for whom the only effective treatment was one of complete humiliation. Sooner or later they would break down, but it would take time.

It was surprising how quickly one became habituated to violence, Clive thought. Violence at second hand, at least. To witness the succession of prisoners with their bruises, wounds and broken limbs, and the cases of emaciation and semi-starvation, was rather like watching the intake of a big general hospital. After the initial sense of shock and distaste, one became objective and impersonal about it, and one stopped trying to imagine the cold-blooded horrors that had produced the injuries in question.

Those prisoners who were prepared to switch their allegiance and join the insurgents were sent to special training units where, under strict supervision, but with more humane treatment, they were screened for rehabilitation in the new society. The majority were assigned to non-combatant duties such as labourers, engineers, mechanics, and so on, for the primary need of the new State was to get the wheels of industry and commerce turning again as soon as possible.

Meanwhile, the anticipated large-scale counter-attack had not materialised, although there had been vicious and sporadic fighting in dispersed areas of the country, particularly in the Midlands. The picture built up by intelligence was sketchy and unreliable, but indicated the changing trend from day to day. The south of England was quiescent; opposition had largely collapsed. In the Midlands and the north the process of evacuating the underground shelters under military protection was still going on, and it was significant that the decay of enemy resistance seemed to follow the successful evacuation of such zones.

It was as if, Snell pointed out, the protected ones and the Establishment generally were moving secretly to an unknown rendezvous. Much air traffic was recorded. Furthermore, Army and Air Force units were also moving out by sea and air to destinations undetermined. Reports seemed to indicate a substantial build up of reactionary forces in Ireland and parts of Norway, but in the absence of direct communication with these countries it was impossible to confirm them. There was also reason to believe that the Americans, who had apparently emerged from both virus and attempted revolution intact, were building up substantial military strength in Ireland. All this was indicative of an imminent attack on a large scale—a full-scale invasion, in fact—but Snell was of the opinion that it could not work. The opportune moment had already passed, and as each day went by the rebel defences became stronger and more co-ordinated.

Medical intelligence reports showed that the new antivirus was spreading rapidly throughout the country, conferring immunity on those who had been fortunate enough to escape Hueste infection so far. Clive himself suspected that he had contracted the SBA virus, for there had been a day when he shivered slightly from mounting temperature, and there had been a sensation of fever accompanied by a headache and muscular stiffness, but there was no way of checking without a full blood test, and the necessary clinical facilities were not available.

There was a darker side to the picture, however, in a rapidly increasing number of illnesses of mysterious origin, many of which were resulting in death. Because the insurgent organisation lacked a central medical headquarters there was a considerable delay in correlating the many clinical reports from various hospitals and centres, and even now the central intelligence department was only just beginning to realise that something strange was happening. All the affected cases were BAX types, which in itself was odd, and the disease took the form of acute anaemia in which the red blood cells were rapidly destroyed by some invisible agent which had not yet been identified. Zirconium and transfusion treatment was possible, but simply could not be administered on a large enough scale to cope with the rising trend of patients.

At first there had been wild surmises: bacteriological warfare, nuclear radiation, atomic fallout, some subtle poison gas injected into the atmosphere. But it was now becoming apparent that the new disease was related to the SBA antivirus, due to some interaction of antibodies in the blood, and that it would spread rapidly among all the existing BAX people—the so-called immune ones.

The problem was being tackled at the highest level, Clive understood. Snell told him that the Federal Government had set up an emergency medical committee to organise countrywide treatment centres in temporary hospitals that had previously been used for Hueste virus cases.

It was as if the virus had struck all over again, Clive thought, with the prospect of more and more millions of bodies to transport and consign to the incinerators. But there was time, at least, to do something about it, even if only on a small scale. The aplastic anaemia victims took a week or two to die, so that treatment and cure was possible for a selected minority. As to the basis of selection—no doubt it would operate in exactly the same way as before, when the privileged few had been chosen for protection in the virus shelters. Survival for the new bosses, the new insurgent Establishment, for anyone who knew the right people and could pull the right wires.

Ironically enough, Snell himself was one of the first to succumb to the new infection. The lethargy and paleness came slowly, over the course of a few days, and Clive assumed that the symptoms were due to overwork, but when Snell's oxygen-starved brain blacked out during the course of an interrogation, he realised that something was organically wrong. A subsequent blood count in the headquarters clinic revealed the truth. Snell, a BAX type, had contracted SBA virus and was already in the grip of severe, debilitating anaemia. He was rushed to hospital for treatment, being in a sense a fairly important member of the rebel Establishment.

Clive promptly assumed full responsibilities as an independent interrogator in his own right, and it was in these circumstances that he came face to face with Pauline and Dr. Vincent.

Details of prisoners were entered on index cards, and each day these were distributed among the interrogators on an apparently arbitrary basis. Thus, one morning Clive was issued with four cards, one of which bore the name of Dr. Vincent, though this held no particular significance for him.

One of his colleagues, however, an experienced interrogator named Howell, said to him as they walked along the corridor away from the administrative offices: "Hey, Clive, what do you know? I've got your namesake."

He held out a card bearing the name *Dr. Pauline Brant*.

Clive, taken aback, needed a second or two to plan his reaction. No point in pretending coincidence, that there was no connection between himself and the prisoner. They would find out sooner or later, and any attempt at subterfuge would be dangerous.

"My wife," he said in a tone of suitable surprise. "Or rather, my ex-wife. It's a small world."

"She's with IVRO?"

"Yes. That was why the marriage broke up. Her IVRO job kept her in Japan, and I was left in London. I'm surprised she's still alive."

"You want to see her again?"

Clive shrugged. "You mean, in the role of interrogator? Hardly the best kind of reunion."

"Well, you can probably get more out of her than I could. It's a great help in this game if you know your prisoner."

"All right," Clive said dubiously. He took the card from the other man and gave him one of his own in exchange.

It could be a trap, he thought. It's the kind of thing Snell would do, to test my loyalty. He wouldn't give me Pauline's card direct, that would be too obvious, but he would arrange for it to be passed on to me in an innocent fashion. On the other hand, Snell was in hospital, and the whole thing could have been coincidental—or could have been pre-arranged. Brant the interrogator and Brant the prisoner. Only a fool could miss the connection.

On the journey to the prison in Harrow he studied the details typed on the cards in his possession, and so was confronted with the second surprise and problem of the day. *Dr. H. Vincent, the card announced. Male. Age 37. M.D. and Ph.D. Virologist at IVRO HQ, Brierley. Served as staff medico at Barnet militia recruiting centre. BAX type. Transferred to IVRO Statistical Centre, Bedford. Surrendered voluntarily to Federal authority. Reason given—to make contact with Dr. Pauline Brant, another prisoner with whom he claims to have liaison. Behaviour in prison—good, but punished once for infringement of regulations. Note—potential useful recruit. Brant woman can be used to exert pressure.*

There was no abrupt change of attitude within him, but just a slow awakening of retrospective acknowledgement of the fact past and present. In relation to Pauline, Dr. Vincent was placed and pigeon-holed. My successor, Clive thought with irony. The opposite side of an equilateral triangle. Then bitterness clouded his mind. Not so long ago it had been a rectangle rather than a triangle, with Noelle and himself forming two of the sides, but those days were over, and now it was a triangle again, but with himself as the base, in the strongest and most fundamental position.

By the time the car reached the prison he had already made up his mind. Dr. Vincent was to be the first to be interrogated, and Pauline next. Here, at last and finally, was the chance to sort out his own personal and matrimonial problem once and for all, regardless of Snell and insurgent policy.

A series of small rooms on the ground floor of the school had been earmarked for interrogations. The room assigned to Clive was at the end of a corridor, overlooking what had been the school playground. Originally it had been part of a classroom, but hardboard partitions had been erected and the desks had been removed. The room was quite bare, apart from a small table and a chair. A bell push screwed to the side of the table could be used to summon a guard, if necessary, and in addition, Clive had been issued with an automatic revolver on arrival at the prison.

He sent for Dr. Vincent.

It was obvious from the moment Vincent was escorted into the room that he was ill. There was a considerable lethargy and weariness in the pallid lines of his face, and he walked with a slight limp—no doubt a souvenir of a dose of prison punishment. As there was no chair for him, he remained standing, and Clive stood up, too, because he felt vaguely embarrassed in a sitting position and preferred to face his man on equal terms. He waved the escorting guards out of the room. Their presence was optional, depending on the character of the prisoner and the whim of the interrogator. Vincent, his hands still handcuffed behind his back, clearly posed no threat.

When the guards had left, Clive said quietly: "Dr. Vincent, you are a rather unusual type of prisoner. I understand you surrendered voluntarily."

"Yes."

"For the reason that a certain Dr. Pauline Brant was also a prisoner, and you hoped to establish contact with her in some way."

"That is substantially true."

"Did it not occur to you that the insurgent authority would hardly adapt their procedure to suit your personal convenience?"

"I'm afraid I didn't really think about it in any detail."

Clive squatted on the corner of the table, and waved a hand towards the chair. "You can sit down if you like."

Vince shook his head. "I prefer to stand. I've been sitting down for several days."

"I want you to understand," Clive said, "that I am not part of the disciplinary set-up. My job is simply to talk to you, ask you questions, find out your attitude towards the new régime, if you have an attitude."

"I have no attitude. I am a doctor."

Clive nodded and lit a cigarette.

"What precisely is the relationship between you and Pauline Brant?"

"We were to be married."

"But Dr. Brant is already married."

"She would have divorced her husband by now, if it had not been for the virus."

"In other words, marriage is out of the question until a divorce is obtained, and in the present chaotic state of society a divorce as such may not be on the cards for a year, two years, five years…"

"I'm prepared to wait."

"But meanwhile Dr. Brant, who is, I understand, a person of rather orthodox views, might choose to be reconciled with her husband."

"I don't think so."

"Why not?" Clive asked with a disarming smile.

"Well, there was a great deal of incompatibility. He let her down rather badly. In any case, we had an understanding."

"You astonish me," Clive remarked. "The world has turned upside down and practically half the population of the country is dead or dying, and yet you can still think in terms of what you call an understanding. Have you bothered to consider your own personal immediate future as a prisoner?"

"I am hoping I shan't be kept imprisoned for very long."

"You mean that you are prepared to swear allegiance to the new Federal Government."

Vince hesitated. "Without committing myself politically, I am prepared to serve humanity as a doctor."

"That is not enough," Clive stated. "It is impossible to be neutral in the world as it exists. The neutral is the enemy of both sides."

"May I put it this way? I don't give a damn who's governing the country. After a major crisis there are bound to be difficult times ahead, whatever the colour and creed of the leadership. As a professional man I can play a modest part in helping to restore civilised society."

"With the aid of Dr. Brant, I suppose."

Vince shrugged. "That is a personal matter."

"It is more personal than you imagine," Clive said, without elaborating. He looked at Vincent's pale, drawn face and remembered that he was marked on the index card as a BAX type.

"Do you feel fit?" he asked.

"Reasonably fit."

"But tired?"

"Yes."

"As an IVRO doctor you must know about the new SBA antivirus."

Vince nodded. "I know something of it."

"Has it occurred to you that you may already have contracted antivirus infection?"

"Yes, it has. I realise that the chance of obtaining treatment is pretty remote. If I were free, and able to join the staff of a hospital…"

"That's a big 'if'. The fact is, you're rather out on a limb, aren't you? I personally can do nothing to help. My job is simply to report on your attitude. I have no control over clinical matters, even if they involve life and death. One thing is certain—if the authorities suspect you have SBA anaemia your chances of survival are nil."

Vince looked at him despondently. "Then what do you suggest?"

"At the moment there's nothing I can suggest. I propose to adjourn the interrogation. I'll talk to you again later."

"But you haven't given me much of a chance to explain…"

Clive pressed the button on the table. "You'll get your chance later. For the present I have other things to do."

The guards came in a moment later and took Vincent away. He waited until he had finished smoking his cigarette and then sent for Dr. Pauline Brant.

There was no surprise in her eyes when she saw him, just a cool bitterness. He was shocked at her appearance. Her clothes were torn and dirty, and her hair was matted and awry. Her complexion, without cosmetic, looked sallow in the grey light from the windows.

"Hello, Pauline," he said, after the guards had left.

"Good old Clive," she responded. "True to form. Always on the winning side."

He offered her the chair. She accepted wearily.

"I had little choice," he explained. "I was taken prisoner as a neutral and I preferred to stay alive."

"Naturally."

He looked at her uneasily, noting the irony of her voice and the accusing hostility of her eyes.

"They've treated you badly," he said.

"Yes."

"I'm sorry about that," he said, shuffling nervously on his feet. "The fact is, I'm supposed to interrogate you, to report on your political views and attitude. I think they know you're my wife, so I have to be careful. I have no influence and no security."

"Poor Clive," she murmured. "How dreadful life must be for you."

"I've talked with Dr. Vincent," he said.

Her expression changed—became momentarily startled, then slightly incredulous.

"You mean…"

"He's a prisoner, too. He was in here just a few minutes ago."

Her hand fluttered uncertainly to her mouth. "How is he?"

"In fair shape. He gave himself up to the insurgents in the hope of seeing you."

"I see. Does he know…?"

"He doesn't know who I am, but I know about him and you. I've got something to tell you, Pauline."

"Well?"

He hesitated, not knowing quite how to phrase the words that tumbled in his mind.

"The position is this. Vincent is going to die. He's a BAX anti-virus case and he's already showing the symptoms of the SBA type of anaemia."

"Oh," she said quietly. "Isn't it possible for him to have treatment?"

"Not as a prisoner."

She remained silent and sullen.

"How much does Vincent mean to you?" he asked.

"Not everything, but a great deal," she said after a pause. "I had contemplated marrying him. It was an acceptable future."

"There's something else I have to tell you, Pauline."

She eyed him pensively, without great interest.

"Noelle is dead. She was murdered by rebel troops. So, you see, my future was chopped up, too. We're back where we started, both of us."

She shook her head slowly. "No, Clive, we're not."

"Listen to me," he went on, moving closer to her and speaking with quiet urgency. "The revolution is won for all practical purposes. I was lucky enough to work myself into a position of trust, and I know I can go on up the ladder if I do things in the right way. I could take you with me, Pauline, if you were loyal to the new régime. As my wife they would accept you. We could pick up where we left off…"

To his astonishment she laughed in his face, and the laughter was genuine.

"I'm serious," he insisted. "I know things went wrong between us, but that was just a phase. I've lost Noelle and you've lost Vincent…"

"Not yet."

"He's a dead man. He has no future."

"What's the matter, Clive? Is your conscience troubling you at long last? Let me tell *you* something. *You're* the dead man with no future, not Vincent. You think you're well established in the brave new world of Federal Britain and perhaps Federal Europe. Well, maybe you are, but it's not going to last for long. The forces of reaction are too strong and too co-ordinated and they'll strike back long before you can get your feet on the next rung of the ladder."

"Nonsense," said Clive, without conviction.

"Why do you suppose there has been no major counter-attack so far, why there's a big air-lift in progress moving military forces and supplies out of the country to Ireland and elsewhere, why all the top people evacuated from the shelters are being flown overseas? Do you imagine authority, and I mean the real authority, not your petty rebel dictators, is abdicating or surrendering unconditionally?"

"All right. You tell me."

"There's nothing to tell. It's perfectly obvious. The counter-revolution could not be fought from underground shelters. It is being organised on a world basis, and the target will be every country where the rebels have seized power. Most of the rebels are BAX types by now, and the new antivirus will practically wipe them out. Then will come the invasion by the old Establishment. It will all be over very quickly, perhaps with the aid of a few atomic bombs."

"No," he said, "it would never come to that."

"By the time the virus and the antivirus have taken their full toll of humanity, about ninety per cent of the world's population will be dead, Clive. Those of us who survive will have to start all over again. We shan't need the big cities and the factories and the lines of communication. We shall revert to the land, to an agricultural economy, for sheer survival. Imagine Britain with only five million inhabitants. You could dispense with London and any or all of the major cities—they wouldn't make any difference. That's why there will be atom bombs, because they won't affect the basic situation."

Clive lit a cigarette. "I think you're wrong," he said. "I think the revolution was the logical and inevitable outcome of circumstances. The Establishment betrayed the common people, and now the common people have taken over. Things are still chaotic, I agree, but gradually a policy is emerging and there is an entirely new pattern of thought, a new concept of man's function and purpose in society. The old ideas are dead and they will never come back. Not even atom bombs will bring them back."

"You talk like a rebel," she said, "but you're not a rebel."

He pondered that for a while, and then grinned. "Pauline," he said gently, "you're the only woman who ever really understood me."

*

A plan was forming in his mind, although it was vague and ill defined. The day had been fruitless. Talking with Pauline and talking with Vincent during a number of so-called interrogation sessions had achieved nothing; if anything his own self-assurance had been steadily undermined. Pauline had certainly made it perfectly clear that she did not wish to jump on the Clive Brant bandwagon, and she did not attempt to conceal her hostility and hatred for the insurgents. Vincent's sincere and conscientious neutrality was pathetic in view of his condition: how could one be neutral in the face of death, Clive asked himself. But perhaps the most disconcerting thing was the feeling that he himself was wrong, morally and ethically, in some obscure way—and yet he could not see why.

I've always been practical, he told himself. That is, I've acted according to circumstances and have never been obsessed by abstract ideologies. Nevertheless, I have principles of a kind; even Pauline would admit that. I'm not a coward, and I'll fight, if need be, with the best of them, but I have no false gods. I believe in survival. No principle, however noble, is worth suicide.

But he still felt dissatisfied. There was something wrong in his personal make-up, though it defied definition. It seemed to him that he lacked something which both Pauline and Vincent possessed in different ways. Integrity, perhaps, but what was integrity—just one of those words that lost its meaning the more you thought about it.

In my own way I have integrity, he decided. I had it when I first told Pauline about Noelle, and I had it when I shot those murderous raping louts at the Astoria Hotel, and I had it when I punched that supercilious militia officer on the nose at the Regent's Park prison camp, and I had it when I ploughed through those two thousand dead bodies looking for survivors after the machine-guns and the hand grenades had done their worst. But in some odd way it's the wrong kind of integrity, not like that of Pauline or Vincent. It's a practical, personal integrity, operating in accordance with principles that only I seem to be able to understand or appreciate. But I think it's honest enough for all that.

He began to examine and assess the plan that was crystallising in his mind. Certain realities had to be faced. For one thing, Pauline could not be allowed to remain a prisoner a moment longer than necessary, and Vincent was going to need medical treatment which could not be obtained outside a hospital. Consequently, he too would have to cease being a prisoner. It was expected, of course, that the insurgent Government would in due course declare an amnesty for all prisoners once they had consolidated their hold on the country, but that might not occur for weeks or even months, and in the event of a counter-revolutionary invasion would not happen at all.

That left only one practicable solution—escape. But to where? Well, there were still pockets of resistance left, particularly in the north, and it was known that the big IVRO centre near Brierley and a number of satellite units were still surviving independently under heavy guard, although the latest intelligence reports on enemy troop and transport movements suggested that a massive evacuation programme for IVRO staff was being prepared. That set a time limit. A day or perhaps two days. If Pauline and Vincent could be bulldozed through the rebel and enemy lines to rejoin IVRO, there was a reasonable chance that they would be in time to take part in the evacuation.

The idea was ridiculous, of course. It could never work in a thousand years, and yet it persisted in his mind, haunting his conscience. He decided to pigeon-hole it overnight so that it would either mature or disintegrate under the severe scrutiny of his subconscious mind.

Late in the afternoon he left the school and returned to the administrative headquarters. He made an interim report to the man named Vaughan who was acting as deputy intelligence officer. He thought it advisable to plunge straight into a confession in order to establish his loyalty and honesty of purpose.

"I had a fascinating time interrogating my ex-wife," he said. "Also her boy friend. I take it the set-up was planned that way."

Vaughan's eyes were pale blue and rather fish-like. His mouth made a twitch which may have been intended as a smile.

"Not officially, Brant. Snell was rather amused by the idea. He wanted to spring it on you as a surprise. In the end I switched the cards to Howell because I didn't think it so funny. I see you switched them back."

"Howell and I talked it over and did a swop. The point is, Vaughan, this could be useful. She may be guessing, or she may have some definite information, but she made reference to an American-backed invasion using A-bombs."

"That's not so incredible."

"More than that. The SBA antivirus is being used to play a positive part in the counter-revolution. A figure was quoted—a reduction of the population to ten per cent. Also a return to an agricultural economy."

"I don't think we need to take that very seriously," Vaughan said.

"Perhaps not. On the other hand, she is with IVRO, and she may have heard things over the grape-vine—added to which she's more likely to be informative to me because of past liaisons than in a formal interrogation with a stranger. I think it's worth pursuing."

"What do you suggest?"

"Nothing sensational. I'd like to continue the interrogation tomorrow. Perhaps Vincent, too. There are possibilities of playing one off against the other."

Vaughan placed the tips of his fingers together in an effeminate fashion. "I shouldn't waste too much time on it if I were you, Brant. We're quite accustomed to sensational claims from prisoners. Generally speaking they're exaggerated, and in any case our intelligence system is fairly comprehensive. Of course, if you get hold of anything definite…"

"That's what I'm hoping."

"Do what you think best." Vaughan stroked his lips with an air of remote contemplation. "As a matter of fact, we can easily fix your ex-wife up in our medical organisation, if she's prepared to be co-operative. It's just a question of wire-pulling."

"I'll bear that in mind," Clive said. "How about Vincent?"

"That rather depends on how you feel about Vincent."

Clive shrugged. "He's neutral and prepared to co-operate."

"Well, then, if you put a formal recommendation through the usual channels, I imagine action will be taken in due course. Sooner or later we expect to have all the IVRO doctors working for us, but it will take time. They have to be broken in."

"I'll see what happens tomorrow. Before making any recommendations at all I'll let you have a full report, just in case there should be any difficulties of policy."

"Fine," Vaughan said with a stifled yawn.

Clive went to his room, where he spent a restless night trying not to think of the escape plan buried deep in his mind.

CHAPTER EIGHTEEN

A T FIVE A.M., UNABLE TO SLEEP ANY LONGER, HE GOT OUT of bed and dressed, and began to prowl around the room. Dawn was already a pallid blue glow in the eastern sky. Presently he went downstairs to the basement kitchen of the hotel in search of coffee, but the place was in darkness and deserted.

He returned to his room and began to pace up and down, striving to cast off the mood of stark depression that possessed him. One was always depressed at dawn, particularly after negligible sleep. At the same time, one was in a more logical and matter-of-fact frame of mind, and the wild enthusiasms of the day tended to evaporate. The escape plan, for instance, was sheer idiocy. Best thing for Pauline was to join the insurgents, and as for Vincent—well, there was nothing much one could do for him.

But his thoughts continued stubbornly in a groove of fantasy. I'm unarmed, he told himself, but at the prison they will issue me with an automatic revolver. That is a start, at least. There are two guards patrolling the corridor with carbines. They could be taken by surprise and shot dead. There would then be three weapons. Three determined people with three weapons might make progress. It would not be impossible to smash the planks from the boarded windows and drop into the playground where the vehicles were parked. A fast truck, two carbines and a revolver—two men and one woman…

Impossible, he thought. A snowflake's chance in hell. And anyway, why should I cut my own throat for the sake of an estranged wife and her lover? I'm accepted in the insurgent administration, and there's a future of some kind for me in this strange new world. Why should I throw it all away? In the course of time Pauline will be released and find her own place in the pattern of things. Vincent will probably die, but so will many other millions who deserved better.

Speed was the essence of the operation, he realised. To get Vincent and Pauline into the interrogation room together, to brief them quickly and accurately, to call in the two patrolling guards on some pretext, to shoot them in cold blood, to seize their weapons and crash through the windows, to destroy all opposition.

Supposing we got through, he thought—what about me? I'm not an IVRO man, but they might take me with them. They could hardly in all conscience reject me, abandon me. After all, I am Pauline's husband…

The mood evaporated and gave way to speculation. On the surface the insurrection is nearly won, he mused. In this new anarchistic kind of society I could build a career of a kind. On the other hand, if Pauline is right, and a massive counter-revolution is being planned, it would be better to remain uncommitted—better to be a neutral prisoner, like Vincent. In the changing flux of political systems one needed to be flexible and adaptable. One needed the practical mentality of the Vicar of Bray.

His mind switched again. A vehicle was essential. It might not be possible to obtain an ignition key, but there was a quick method of short-circuiting the ignition switch wires behind the dashboard. For that one would need a sharp penknife, and that he had, attached to a key ring. A tiny knife admittedly, but capable of slicing through the average twisted-strand insulated wire.

Step by step the details shaped themselves in his mind, so that by seven-thirty the scheme had acquired an unwelcome quality of imminence. Now there was movement in the building, so he went down to the canteen for coffee and an austere breakfast of toast and margarine.

By the time he was ready to collect his interrogation cards from the office he was so withdrawn and gloomy in manner that Howell commented on it. Clive promptly made an effort to appear cheerful, offering toothache and a restless night as the reason for apparent despondency. During the journey to the prison he kept up a laconic conversation with the other man, although most of the time he could have hardly defined what he was talking about.

The routine at the prison was the same. Purposely he chose two other prisoners for interrogation on arrival, leaving Pauline and Vincent until later in the afternoon. He took the opportunity to explore as much of the school building as possible, without intruding into other sealed classrooms where presumably prisoners were being questioned.

The cloakrooms and lavatories at the end of the corridor on the first floor seemed to offer the best possibility of escape. Reserved for the use of the staff, and not prisoners, they had a number of small windows which had been left unboarded, overlooking flower beds bordering the quadrangle in which the vehicles were parked. The windows were of the metal frame type, opening outwards, and the drop to the ground was fifteen feet—but into soft soil. Not more than a few paces away from the flower bed was an adequate selection of cars and trucks parked in line, and as he watched a small utility van backed into a vacant space in the car park.

During the rest of the day he found it difficult to concentrate on the tedious routine of question and answer. He found himself talking informally to the prisoners with no definite policy in mind, while another part of his brain pondered the potential difficulties and dangers of escape. All the time he kept putting off the moment when he would send for Pauline and Vincent, until, at four-thirty, he realised that he could delay no longer.

They refused. It was as simple as that. For a while he was conscious of an immense feeling of relief until an even bigger problem began to cast its shadow across his mind.

He sent for Vincent first. After the guard had left the room he told him bluntly that he was Pauline's husband. Vince registered no surprise, only apathy. He seemed considerably worse, Clive thought. His complexion was nearly chalk white and there was a weary brittleness in his body. He stood quite limply, hands still manacled behind his back.

"In a moment I am going to send for Pauline," Clive went on. "Although we're estranged, I'm naturally not anxious for her to be held here as prisoner any longer than necessary, and because of your special relationship with her—well, the same applies. In any case, you need some pretty urgent medical treatment."

Vincent nodded.

"I have a plan which will need full co-operation from both of you. I'll put it to you together when Pauline arrives. Meanwhile I propose to go through the routine of interrogation for about fifteen minutes to make things look right."

In due course he sent for Pauline. There was an awkward moment of reunion when she and Vincent met, awkward because of the tenseness, the silence and the suppressed emotional reaction. Clive felt very much of an outsider. Then she said: "Hello, Vince," and he said: "Hello, Pauline—long time, no see," and the reunion was over.

Clive put the proposition to them quite briefly. There was a reasonable chance of acquiring some automatic weapons by force and breaking out of the building via the cloakroom window before the alarm could be properly raised. After that it would be a relatively easier task to steal a vehicle and drive desperately to Brierley to crash through the insurgent defence lines. It might work, it might not; it would be a calculated risk.

Pauline said: "I don't think it's a good idea. I couldn't use a gun, not even to save my life, and Vince wouldn't be much use while he's handcuffed."

"We can soon deal with the handcuffs."

"Just how?"

"A saw, or perhaps we can get a key. At the worst one can shoot through the chain."

"I never knew a lead bullet that would cut through a steel chain."

Clive shrugged. "The point is they can be removed in *some* way. It's a point of detail, that's all."

"A very important point of detail, Clive. Why are you doing this, anyway? You're comfortably installed with the insurgents—why throw it all over?"

"For once I'm not considering my own skin," Clive said with a wry twist of his lips. "We know there's a military operation being planned to evacuate the IVRO headquarters and satellites. If I can get you back there in time…"

"There are others besides us," she pointed out. "Perhaps I'm being foolish, but I don't feel I can run out on them."

"That goes for me, too," Vince remarked. "There are twenty IVRO people involved, men and women. Seems to me that if you're planning an escape for two, you might as well make it twenty."

"That's rather unrealistic."

"Well, it's unrealistic, anyway. At least we're alive and there's no immediate threat of death."

"Vincent," Clive said sourly, "for you the threat of death is more than immediate, but I can see your angle. You don't want Pauline to run the risk of being shot and killed while escaping."

Pauline said: "It's not just a question of life or death. Nobody would like to get back to Brierley more than me, and for Vince it's a matter of urgency, but, frankly, it sounds like one of your wildcat schemes. Wouldn't it be better to plan the thing on a larger scale, to release all the IVRO prisoners; and any others who may be in the school? It's a difference of quantity, not quality."

"What would be the use of fifteen handcuffed men?" Clive asked, at which Pauline smiled.

"Why, only a few minutes ago you were dismissing handcuffs as—what was the expression?—a point of detail."

"In fact," Vince said, "it would simplify matters to release the other IVRO prisoners. We could get the handcuff key from the guard and at the same time pick up a carbine and a crate or two of tear gas bombs. That would give us a strong advantage."

Clive made a doubtful grunt. "Where are the IVRO prisoners?"

"The men are on the floor above in what was probably at one time the school physics or chemistry laboratory. The women are on the top floor in a much smaller room."

"Under the supervision of a male guard, also with a carbine and tear gas," Pauline put in. "But we're not handcuffed—yet."

"I hadn't visualised an operation on such a large scale," Clive said. "The trouble is there isn't time to stop and plan. I can't reasonably come here again tomorrow to interrogate you two. It would begin to look suspicious. So whatever can be done has to be done here and now. The three of us might reasonably make it because

I've worked out a plan. As for the others—it would mean acting off the cuff, by instinct."

"Look," said Vincent in a flat voice, "any course of action that surprises you must surprise the enemy, too—that is, if you regard them as an enemy. For myself, I don't care—as you so aptly said, for me the threat of death is more than immediate, but I'm not the only one. At least four of the other IVRO men are BAX types suffering from antivirus. As a doctor I can hardly leave them to their fate in order to save myself."

"I'm not concerned with medical ethics," Clive said with a sigh. "We three are linked together in a certain way, quite by chance, if you like. The fact that you and Pauline happen to be doctors has nothing to do with the situation. So can we forget the IVRO *esprit de corps* for a while?"

Pauline said: "Perhaps you would tell us just what you planned to do, step by step."

Clive outlined his plan to call in the two guards from the corridor, overpower them or kill them if necessary, seize their weapons, and escape through the cloakroom window. When he had finished Vince said: "Why stop at that point? Why not proceed down the corridor, classroom by classroom, shooting the interrogators and releasing the prisoners one by one, and gathering what weapons are available at the same time. Even a handcuffed prisoner can fire a gun from behind his back. It might not be very accurate, but it would be demoralising."

"And then what?"

"Clear the floors one by one. Release all prisoners, and get the handcuff keys from the guard. Let's face it, the more there are of us, the less likely any one of us is to be shot dead. In the end we could outnumber them."

Clive thought of Howell, probably in the next room. "I don't think I could kill my own colleagues—I mean, people I know on the interrogation staff."

"What's the difference?" Pauline asked. "You kill a guard, you kill an interrogator. They're all human, and war is war."

Better to abandon the idea completely, Clive thought. It had gone beyond all rational limits. At the same time he recognised that one is always tied by human relationships and responsibilities. It would be easy enough to bow out, but not so easy to leave Pauline as a prisoner, without possessing the power to intervene. About Vincent he did not care much, except in so far as Pauline was involved. It was one of those crossroads in life where one has to make a quick, snap decision, for better or for worse, whatever the consequences. He thought deeply and despondently for five seconds and then made up his mind.

"All right," he said, "we'll storm the Bastille, from inside. The three of us—a rebel, a woman and a handcuffed man. Agreed."

"Long odds," Pauline said after a while, "but I'm game."

Vincent tugged hopelessly at the handcuffs. "I'll do the best I can," he promised. "The important thing is to get the key from the guard and set the other IVRO prisoners free."

Clive nodded. "We'll do that. There's one thing we have to agree on. This is a military operation. We have to be single-minded and ruthless, and we have to shoot to kill if necessary."

"Yes, we may have to do that in self defence," Pauline admitted reluctantly.

"Okay," Clive said. He pressed the button that would summon the guards.

In retrospect Clive never quite forgave himself for the events of that afternoon, but the entire operation went off with smooth efficiency, just as if it had been rehearsed over and over again. He clubbed the guards in a moment of squeamishness against cold-blooded murder, but as one of them rose again with his Sten gun at the ready he was forced to shoot. Blood squirted and splashed to the wooden floor.

The worst moment was when he had to kill Howell, but it was clearly either Howell or himself and there was no time for sentiment. By the time they had reached the end of the corridor the party was six strong and adequately armed, though four of the men were handcuffed.

The stairs to the second floor were unguarded. They reached the laboratory holding the majority of the IVRO prisoners without incident. The rather intellectual guard with the blond wavy hair surrendered immediately, and even volunteered to remove the handcuffs from the prisoners. He then submitted to being handcuffed himself to a radiator pipe, which would keep him immobile, and seemed, if anything, rather pleased to have been let off so lightly.

The party was now seventeen strong and armed with automatic weapons and tear gas bombs, but time was running out. By now a general alarm would have been raised and reinforcements would inevitably be speeding towards the school from the nearest insurgent depot.

Half a dozen of the men raced to the third floor to locate the remaining women IVRO prisoners. Another group went through the boarded-up classrooms one by one in a search for further prisoners. Clive left them to it; accompanied by Pauline, Vincent and two other men he took possession of the staircase and began to proceed slowly downwards. From above came two individual revolver shots followed by a short burst of Sten fire. As they by-passed the first floor landing they were rejoined by some of the other prisoners from above.

It was at the bend in the staircase leading down to the ground floor level that they ran into organised opposition. A machine-gun clattered like a road drill. Bullets chipped plaster from the brick walls. Clive stopped and fired an answering burst, but he was unable to see his target.

A well modulated voice called from below: "This is the prison commandant. You can't get any further. Better surrender quietly before we smoke you out."

"Nothing doing," Clive replied. "We've already won the day. Call off your men if you want them to stay alive. We're coming down, anyway."

Again the machine-gun chattered and bullets smashed into the nearby wall.

"You want to try? Go ahead. We're waiting."

Clive turned to Vincent, who was standing just behind him. "You stay here with the others," he ordered. "Just hold the position. I'll take two men. We'll get out through the cloakroom windows and work our way round to the main entrance at the foot of the stairs. Don't advance until you get the word from me."

He selected two of the IVRO doctors and went back up the stairs to the first floor. The party now assembled was much bigger than he had anticipated; in addition to the IVRO personnel there were about a dozen other prisoners, making a total of over thirty, and all adequately armed so far as he could judge.

In the cloakroom he outlined the plan to the others. First he would drop through the window with a carbine and provide covering fire, if necessary, while the others followed him. Then they would follow the wall of the building round to the main entrance to the school where the machine-gun party would be installed at the bottom of the staircase. Surprise was the important factor: there would be no second chance.

But, in the event, he changed his plan completely the moment he had dropped to the ground. Only a few yards away from him, with his back turned towards the building, an insurgent was loading cardboard cartons into the back of an armoured truck. As he watched, the other man went round to the driving seat, got in, and started the engine.

Clive went after him without hesitation. There was no necessity to kill. The rebel surrendered instantly at the sight of the carbine and came out of the vehicle with his hands well in the air. By this time the two other IVRO men were on the ground, advancing stealthily from the rear. Without instruction one of them clubbed the driver with a reversed carbine, and a moment later all three men were sitting side by side on the bench seat of the vehicle.

Clive took the wheel and engaged the bottom gear. As the truck began to trundle forward, he said:

"Next best thing to a tank. At least we'll have some protection, and the advantage of speed. I'm going to crash straight through the main entrance. Be ready to shoot at anything that moves. We can't afford to fail."

He swung the truck in a wide circle around the quadrangle, gathering speed and changing up to second gear. No point in changing up further—he might need the power in due course. The school entrance came into view, a wide arched porch with a flat three-inch step like a stage in front of a proscenium. The doors were wide open, and in the gloom of the foyer he could discern the movement of men.

"This is it," he stated, squeezing the accelerator.

The armoured truck hit the edge of the step at nearly twenty miles an hour. A tyre burst with a violent explosion as the vehicle lurched and bounced. And then, astonishingly, they were inside the entrance hall, and the roar of the engine was reverberating hollowly from the walls.

Clive aimed the vehicle at a group of some twelve armed men clustered near the foot of the ascending stairs, his foot poised above the brake ready to make an instant stop. The demoralisation of the enemy would have been comic if the circumstances had not been so desperately urgent. They scattered as if a bomb had exploded among them. From the floor, half lying on his back, an insurgent fired a burst at the truck, and bullets ricocheted wildly from the steel-plated sides.

And then the IVRO men were firing too. The windscreen shattered into an opaque spider-web of fragmented glass. Clive stamped on the brake and clutch simultaneously and thrust his carbine through the windscreen, knocking a shower of white crystals on to the flat bonnet of the truck.

The shooting continued for another moment, and then it was all over. The remaining insurgents, four of the dozen or so lying scattered and motionless on the floor, had raised their arms in surrender.

There was no further problem. The survivors were bundled into one of the boarded-up classrooms and locked in. Within a minute the rest of the prisoners, led by Vincent, had descended the stairs, and the great exodus was on.

They chose four small armoured trucks from the wide variety of vehicles in the car park. There were faster cars available, but speed was not so important as protection. Without doubt the insurgents would present obstruction and opposition on the twenty-mile journey to Brierley, and the safest means of travel was as a military convoy.

Clive, Pauline and Vincent decided to split up on the grounds that if they made the journey in different vehicles they stood a much better chance of getting through individually. With some eight people to each truck, the loading was adequate but not excessive. Clive surrendered the wheel of the leading vehicle to an IVRO doctor who knew the route to Brierley intimately, but he sat beside him nursing the carbine. As a precaution they had smashed the windscreens of all four vehicles—the glass was not bullet-proof, and it was better to have the wind in one's face than encounter a milky sheet of glass atomised by a bullet.

The short-circuiting of the ignition systems wasted valuable minutes, but in the end the convoy started moving in crocodile formation. It was remarkable how deserted the roads were, Clive thought. They passed a few other vehicles and a number of insurgent patrols without opposition. In the absence of any briefing the enemy would probably assume that the convoy was simply carrying out a rebel assignment.

The first obstacle came into view just south of the Barnet by-pass. A big lorry straddled the road close to a roundabout, and gunfire opened up. At last they're on to us, Clive thought, and from now on we can expect trouble.

"Faster," he said to the driver, levelling the carbine through the windscreen and firing an aggressive burst at nothing in particular. "On to the verge and round."

The grass verge bordering the road was wide enough, but the ground was soft through recent rain. For a frantic moment the wheels skidded in the damp soil, while bullets beat a murderous tattoo on the armoured sides of the vehicle. They were shooting from behind the hedge and from the protective bulk of the lorry, but there was answering fire from the convoy. In a few seconds it was all over. The obstructing lorry was falling back, and the following trucks were still behind, keeping their distance.

The next obstruction occurred several miles ahead on the three-lane road leading north to Hatfield. Railway sleepers had been spread across the road, and for a moment Clive's heart sank as the vehicle reduced speed and the familiar rattle of gunfire started up.

"Hold on to your hats," said the driver. He changed down into bottom gear with a smart double declutch.

"Keep shooting," Clive shouted above the noise.

They took the sleepers in a series of lurching, bouncing jolts that shook the truck to the point of disintegration. Clive fired at the hedgerow to the left, and others were firing, too, from the rear section of the vehicle. A hand grenade exploded a dozen yards behind them, scattering shrapnel into the front of the second truck. The driver beside him struggled with the clutch to force the vehicle over the next sleeper, but the engine finally gave up the unequal fight and stalled. Amen, Clive thought, this was how it was bound to end.

The three following vehicles had pulled into the side of the road, nose to tail, and to Clive's astonishment prisoners were leaping into the road, armed with revolvers and automatic weapons, jumping the ditch bordering the hedgerow and crashing through into the field beyond. Another hand grenade exploded not more than a few feet away. The driver uttered a curiously strangled sigh, and looking round, Clive saw with horror that a jagged hole, spurting blood, had been neatly punched into his face just below the left eye.

He seized his carbine and leapt from the truck to join the spontaneous assault on the insurgent unit beyond the hedge. It was a "sights down" manoeuvre, the obvious course of action when you paused to think about it, the only military way of dealing with an enemy obstruction when there was no possibility of finding a protective screen behind which one could deploy the attacking force. He pushed his way through the thorn hedge to find himself in the middle of a savage gunfight. The insurgents were screened behind two heavy lorries, and they had a Bren gun and hand grenades, but the IVRO men had the advantage of single-minded determination—they had nothing to lose and everything to gain.

The battle was over in a few minutes, but not without heavy casualties. Of the dozen or so rebels involved in the ambush only three survived. They surrendered unconditionally as soon as they realised that the fight was lost. Seven prisoners had been killed, and three were seriously wounded. Clive himself escaped injury, but Vincent suffered a flesh wound in his left shoulder from a grenade fragment.

They tied the three defeated insurgents to the wheels of one of their trucks, and then held a rapid conference. At least one advantage had emerged from the incident: they now had a Bren gun with a reasonable supply of ammunition, and two full boxes of hand grenades. There was no time to attend to the dead; survival for the living was a matter of top priority.

It was agreed to mount the Bren gun in the first of the armoured trucks and distribute the hand grenades among all four. There would be further attempts at ambush, no doubt, and it was decided as a matter of policy to avoid the main road, so far as was possible, and travel via parallel second class roads; but in any case fire power would be used instantly and ruthlessly to break down any opposition.

They went back to the trucks. The women were still safe, but one had sustained a minor wound from a fragmenting hand grenade. The driver of the first truck, the man who had sat next to Clive, was not actually dead, but seemed to be dying quite rapidly. They moved him into the back of the truck and made him as comfortable as possible, but there was nothing more they could do for him. He was quite unconscious.

Clearing the railway sleepers from the road wasted precious minutes, but in due course they were ready to move on. A new driver took over—a big, burly man who called himself Dr. Dick Reeves. The muzzle of the Bren gun swung in a wide arc above the driving cab and fired one brief burst by way of practice, or perhaps by accident. And then they were moving again, driving in convoy along the A1.

They took the first available by-road on the left, even though it might mean a tedious and circuitous diversion, and continued without incident for nearly half an hour. It was then that the helicopter came into view, swooping from the west at high speed, slowing as it came overhead. Clive leaned forward and pushed his head through the gap where the windscreen had been. The helicopter was hovering now, following the convoy as it pressed ahead at a steady forty-five miles an hour along the narrow winding road, and probably transmitting a radio pin-point to insurgent ground forces.

Clive withdrew his head and tapped on the rear window of the driving cab, making a sign to the Bren gunner. The vibration of a long series of bursts of gunfire shook the vehicle, but the helicopter merely soared aloft and flew away to the east.

Brierley could not be far away now, Clive thought. Soon they would come upon the northern perimeter of the insurgent defence line around London, and beyond that would be a few miles of no-man's-land bordering the heavily armed IVRO zone which was still under the control of the old Government. That would be the real testing point—once they had broken out of insurgent territory there would be no further trouble.

The convoy turned east, back towards the main road to the north. The helicopter was still in sight, a black dragon-fly silhouetted against the grey sky, well out of range of the Bren gun. Clive gripped his own carbine more firmly, aware of a sense of growing uneasiness and heightening tension.

In a few minutes they joined the Great North Road again, quickening speed on the smoother surface of the wide carriageway. Still no traffic, and no sign of insurgent barriers. And then, mounting the brow of a hill and looking down a stretch of wide grey road sweeping into a valley, Clive saw the first indications of barbed wire stretching across the fields. Scanning the panorama of the countryside he saw military huts and the slender masts of transmitting aerials. He spoke tersely to the driver and called the convoy to a halt.

It was a moment for observation and reflection. Clive got out of the vehicle and joined a group of IVRO men who were standing by the verge studying the road ahead. About half a mile away, perhaps more, the road curved round to the right, and even as they watched a tank trundled slowly into view, to be followed half a minute later by another one. They took up positions side by side, blocking the road with a solid barrier of steel.

"How far are we from the IVRO zone?" Clive asked.

"About four miles—possibly five," one of the prisoners replied.

Clive glanced quickly at the darkening sky. "I don't think we can get any further by road. We're not equipped to fight tanks. At the same time, it's still too light to trek across country."

"We'd never make it," said the other man. "Even at night it would be a suicide trip."

"They'll have seen the trucks by now," somebody else pointed out. "They'll be waiting for us, whatever we do."

"We'd better go back about a mile," Clive said. "We'll turn off the road and drive across country for as far as we can. If we can get among trees, so much the better. As soon as it gets dark we shall be out of sight of the helicopter and we can advance across open ground, keeping away from the rebel encampment."

"What about the wire?"

"There's a way of crawling under barbed wire—flat on your back, pushing up the strands as you go. It will take time, but they won't know exactly where we're going to break through, so we may have time enough."

"Isn't there any other way?"

"None that I can think of. We'd better get moving. Reverse the trucks back over the hill until we're out of sight, then turn round and head the other way. Those tanks are on the move."

It was true enough. The tanks were lumbering forward, side by side, at a speed which at that distance appeared to be a crawl, but was probably faster than anyone realised. Quickly the group dispersed and returned to the vehicles. A moment later the convoy was moving backwards over the brow of the hill and then, one by one, the trucks swung in a tight semicircle on the wide road and accelerated back towards London.

Well within a mile they came upon a narrow side road that was little more than a cart track, and turned into it, bumping across the uneven ground at bone-shaking speed. The track narrowed until the thorn hedges on either side were brushing the sides of the vehicle. Abruptly it terminated in a wide wooden gate beyond which lay a fallow field receding to the dark trees of a distant copse.

"Straight through," Clive instructed.

The driver changed down and went straight for the gate at a steady pace. It broke up on impact into flailing bars of old wood which catapulted into the air and on to the ground. The wheels bumped violently over the remains of the gate, skidded for a moment on the damp grass, then renewed their grip. The truck kept on, followed by the others, lurching and jolting towards the distant wood. And still in the evening sky the helicopter hung inquisitively, observing their movements and presumably reporting back to base.

At the fringe of the copse the convoy split up, each vehicle pursuing its own tortuous path among the trees until it became impossible to advance further, and at that point the journey was over. The prisoners abandoned the trucks and assembled silently under the protective trees.

Clive found himself gravitating towards Pauline, who was beginning to show signs of strain. Vincent was a few yards away, talking to some of the other IVRO doctors. There was an atmosphere of subdued depression, as if pessimism had replaced the earlier optimism of the day.

"Cheer up, Pauline," he said. "The worst is over."

She attempted to smile. "The worst hasn't even started yet, Clive."

"Don't you believe it. Once it gets dark we shall be able to move fast and unseen." He glanced round at the others. "How many of us are left?"

"Twenty-three, I think. Two more have died since that ambush, and there are two men with serious chest wounds. They will probably die too."

"It's the luck of the game," Clive remarked. "It turned out to be quite a party—much bigger than I'd expected."

"Clive," she said, then hesitated for a moment. "Clive, I think perhaps I was a bit unfair to you earlier—but I've had reasons to feel bitter."

"Forget it," he said, slightly embarrassed.

"If we should get through this lot alive, perhaps we could talk about things."

"You'd do better to talk with Vincent, wouldn't you?"

"I want you to understand about Vince. I owe him a certain obligation. We've always been good friends but there has never been any question of love…"

"This is neither the time nor place to talk about love," Clive said. He looked anxiously backwards, through the trees towards the big field with its smashed gate. No sign of the tanks so far.

"I think we ought to move on," he continued. "We'll talk about other things when it's all over."

Slowly, supporting the injured men on either side, the group threaded their way through the trees into the darker interior of the wood. The Bren gun had been left behind because of its weight, but between them they carried all the portable arms and the hand grenades, and their pockets sagged with ammunition. At least, Clive thought, we can keep up a running fight for quite a long time, if it comes to the point, and the rebels have more reason to surrender or retreat than we have.

At the far side of the copse, where the trees thinned out into a grassy declivity bisected by a stream, they made their final plans and waited for the condensing twilight to thicken into night. Of the helicopter there was no further sign, and the evening air was quite still. If the tanks were coming we would hear them, Clive thought, but the thought was premature. Within a few minutes the distant sound of powerful engines reached his ears, and he knew that the time had come to move on.

They formed a long crocodile, with a gun party carrying automatic weapons at both front and rear and the women and the two injured men in the middle, and set off across the open field, making for a tall hedge on the rising ground at the other side of the small valley. The stream was shallow and proved to be no obstacle. Beyond the hedge was a field of rotten and withered corn which had not been harvested, and beyond that a neglected potato field thick with weed. Keeping always close to the hedgerows they followed the chequerboard of fields in a north-easterly direction, and presently the darkness became solid and impenetrable.

It began to rain—a fine drizzle that was hardly more than a mist floating in the air but which seemed to be all the more wetting because of that. Somebody called a halt suddenly. One of the wounded men had died. In the dark they concealed his body in a ditch as a substitute for a grave, and continued on their way, covering the ground slowly but with steady progression.

Several times they heard remote gunfire, and once searchlights stabbed the sky as an aircraft flew by at high altitude, but there was no anti-aircraft fire. And so, in the course of time, perhaps some three hours after they had left the copse, they reached the wire. Beyond it lay no-man's-land and the promise of freedom.

It was a double roll of wire in tight coils, pegged to the ground at intervals, but manoeuvrable enough for a man to crawl under, head first, lifting the barbed strands from his face and laboriously unsnagging trapped clothing. The quickest method of passing the wire, Clive decided, was for half a dozen men to crawl under it and raise it up as high as possible so that the remainder of the party could wriggle through the tunnel at higher speed. Even so, the operation was laboriously slow, and the wet ground was cold and uncomfortable. Clive, as one of the tunnel party found his arms aching intolerably with the strain of holding the wire high above his head.

The women went through first, and then the injured man was dragged through, suffering scratches and torn clothing in the process. The rest of the men followed on, one by one.

The exodus was nearly complete, with four more men to pass through, when a dog growled audibly in the middle distance. Clive, still flat on his back under the wire, supporting the roof of the escape tunnel, thought he could hear mumbled voices. A moment later came the sharp crack of a pistol, a second of silence, and then a blinding light appeared about two hundred feet above his head, swinging and descending gently beneath the canopy of a small parachute. Another explosion, and another flare. In an instant the night had been switched into day.

In the confusion it was impossible to discern precisely what was happening. There were men and dogs at the fringe of the circle of light, and crimson tracer bullets flashing above his head and through the wire. The four men left inside the wire had dropped to the ground and were already shooting back, but for the six men trapped under the wire any form of defence or retaliatory fire was virtually impossible.

Clive shouted at the top of his voice to those who had already passed through. "Keep moving. Run like hell before they shoot you down." He released the wire, which promptly snapped back into his face, tearing his mouth, and fumbled inside his shirt for the carbine. With great difficulty he twisted to one side, dragging the weapon through the restraining strands of wire, and took aim, firing desperately and inaccurately at the advancing shapes.

"Run like hell," he repeated. He fired another burst, and kept on firing until the ammunition ran out, at which point he abandoned the gun and began to struggle with the wire again.

The grenade exploded only a few feet away, it seemed. A hot iron stabbed his shoulder, running right through into the base of his neck. The pain was a transient thing. It was immediately obliterated by numbness, and in a fraction of a second the numbness gave way to unconsciousness.

CHAPTER NINETEEN

"You're a fool, Brant," Vaughan said. He was sitting on a chair beside the austere canvas bed, his pale blue eyes peering fish-like through his rimless glasses. Near the door of the room stood a guard, a revolver stuck in his belt. The small window above the bed was screened by a latticework of iron bars. The rickety table on the other side of the bed from Vaughan supported a plastic mug half full of water.

Clive attempted to push himself into a sitting position, but remembered abruptly that his left arm had been amputated. He abandoned the effort. Even now, three weeks after the fragment of shrapnel had shattered his shoulder joint, the illusion that he still possessed an arm deceived him, and he could frequently imagine sensations of movement and touch in ghostly fingers.

"You're a fool because your future with us would have been bright," Vaughan went on, rubbing his thumb against the tips of his fingers in his characteristic fashion. "We are now fighting our worst enemy, the antivirus, and it's a battle most of us are going to lose. All the people who thought they were immune have suddenly become vulnerable again. But not you, and not me, and not some ten or fifteen per cent of us who managed to miss the Hueste virus and catch the SBA type instead. True, we can cure about a third of the aplastic anaemia cases, but it's a long haul, and they're out of commission for weeks, sometimes months. Many of the key executive positions are already vacant. Sir Ralph Betenguel himself is a victim. You could have gone up in the world, Brant, if you hadn't been such a fool—a treacherous fool at that."

"I did what I had to do," Clive said.

"You did it extremely well. Your wife got clear, and most of the IVRO doctors. But it was a waste of time and effort. A few days later it was decided to release all prisoners who were prepared to co-operate with the new régime, particularly the antivirus types. We need such people to build up our strength."

"What strength? The virus won in the end, didn't it?"

"We haven't reached the end yet, but you have."

Clive said nothing. He had no wish to ask the inevitable question.

"You were responsible for many deaths," Vaughan went on. "You were responsible for the escape of a number of prisoners who might have had much to contribute to our new society, but who have now rejoined the enemy. I don't think there can be any doubt as to the verdict of a military tribunal."

"If you intend to shoot me, why didn't you do so when I was recaptured?" Clive demanded. "Why go to the trouble of amputating my arm and keeping me in hospital to recover?"

"One does not execute a man without a trial…"

"But you have done in the past, you and your insurgent friends."

"In the early days of the insurrection the rule of law did not always apply. Today things have settled down, and things must be done in a civilised way. We are not unreasonable people, Brant."

"You tried to trap me by bringing me face to face with my wife," Clive accused. "In the end I did what any other man would have done."

"It was not a trap—just a simple test of loyalty. One can not have two loyalties that conflict with each other. I'm afraid you failed to pass the test."

"I have no loyalty to anyone or anything," Clive said. His voice was flat and bleak. "I swear allegiance to nobody, and because of that I am free."

Vaughan's lips formed a cynical smile. "Free? As you are now?"

"Free in my mind, because I've always acted according to my own standards, and not somebody else's."

"You mean that you have always allowed yourself to be blown about by the prevailing wind."

"I believe in survival, but not if it means being pushed around."

Vaughan stood up. "Survival for yourself, of course—not others. Well, Brant, I'm afraid your belief in survival has brought you to a sticky end. I'm sorry, in a way. I have no personal feelings in the matter."

"Nor have I," Clive said.

Vaughan walked towards the door. "I may not see you again. I believe your trial is due to take place in about four days. You should be fit enough by then. Good-bye."

The guard stood to attention as Vaughan left the room, and then he went out, too. A key turned in the lock.

A firing squad, Clive thought. Or perhaps a hangman's noose. Abstract and rather macabre ideas that seemed to have no basis in reality. It wouldn't come to that, of course—something would turn up in the next few days. His luck had never really let him down yet.

The invasion, for instance. Three weeks had gone by since the mass break-out from the prison and in that time the antivirus must have wrought havoc in the ranks of the insurgents. Even the imperturbable Vaughan had betrayed anxiety about it. And, of course, it would affect the opposition, too, but with support from America and other nations they would have numerical superiority. And the Establishment had been preserved, apart from the small percentage that had been deliberately destroyed in the deep shelters.

By now, he persuaded himself, the military build up in Ireland and Scandinavia must be considerable, and it can only be a matter of time before they launch the attack. They can't afford to fail, nor can they afford a long drawn out battle with high casualties. It will be a swift, sharp steam-roller operation to seize the key cities and lines of communication. It could be over in a matter of two or three days.

The trend of his thinking changed. I'm glad Pauline got away, he told himself, and Vincent, too—not that I hold any affection for him. One of these days we'll sort out the situation once and for all. Bad luck about Noelle. Somehow that interlude was never more than a dream.

He got out of bed and walked around the room for a while, his movements slightly unbalanced. Strange how a missing arm could upset one's equilibrium. It was almost like learning to walk all over again.

A good thing it happened to be the left arm, he thought. At least I can still write, and still use a typewriter for that matter. When the world got back to normal there would still be room in Fleet Street for a one-armed journalist—or, preferably, a one-armed foreign correspondent.

He sat down on the edge of the bed, staring into space, reviewing incidents from the past, and it was as if the tortured world beyond the four walls of the room did not exist—had never existed. Indeed, for all practical purposes it was so, and if his only journey from the room was to be to a court room and from there to a brick wall, then the outside world no longer had any reality. It was what he imagined it to be.

In this relatively peaceful frame of mind, untroubled for the moment by worry, he lay back on the bed and allowed himself to fall into a calm reverie, and presently he fell asleep.

★

The trial had been short and to the point. It had not really been a trial at all in the proper sense of the word, but simply a recital of his misdemeanours couched in officialese and military jargon. The tribunal of three insurgent officers had listened impassively, asked him a few questions, and had finally sentenced him to death. The whole thing had taken no more than ten minutes and in retrospect it seemed like a fantasy from some up-to-date version of *Alice in Wonderland*. "Off with his head," they might have shouted with as much plausibility.

It was the kind of thing the mind refused to take seriously, perhaps because some defensive mechanism deep in the subconscious would not admit the finality of the sentence. Even when he was taken to a small stone cell and locked in he remained faintly incredulous. It was to be a firing squad at eight o'clock the next morning, he told himself, rather as one might report that Martians had landed in Battersea Fun Fair. But as the hours crept slowly by, his brain began to assimilate the full significance of what was to happen to him, and sickness began to curl and quiver inside him.

They gave him a fairly substantial meal in the early evening, but he was unable to eat much of it. He stood in the middle of the cell, staring at a section of brick wall visible through the high grating. Occasionally there were remote noises of traffic going by, so that he assumed he was somewhere in London, but in some strange way it was frustrating not to know exactly where.

I ought to leave a message for Pauline, he thought. They could hardly refuse to have a final message passed on in some way, and yet, what was the use, and what was there to say? It was a concession to sentiment at a time when sentiment was futile.

My God, he realised suddenly—*they've* finally beaten me! By *they* he meant the world at large and men in general, not just the insurgents. Somehow he had always managed to pull the right strings at the right time in order to arrange the pattern of his fate, but now *they* had taken over and *they* were going to pull the strings. For perhaps the first time he was depressed by a sense of utter defeat. Clive Brant—finally and irrevocably beaten.

Night came and his depression increased. Now it was a caged feeling of complete helplessness; not only defeat but annihilation. Annihilation before the event. In the blackness of the small cell it was as if he were already dead—buried alive. The sickness modulated into cold panic.

He had no way of knowing the time, but he supposed it was around two a.m. Six hours to go. Six hours of consciousness left. Perhaps the most important six hours of one's life, and yet there was nothing a man could do with them, and the seconds ticked impassively by amid a torrent of incoherent and uncoordinated thoughts. Somehow one ought to come to terms with oneself, with the fact of death, with God. A fine time to turn to God, he thought with irony. To renounce one's agnosticism through sheer physical fear and spiritual cowardice. On the other hand...

The explosions were far away, like distant thunder. His thoughts stopped dead for an instant, and now his mind was concentrated like a sensitive radar system on the unexpected noises of the night. A siren wailed forlornly, and then another took up the lament, and within a few seconds a whole chorus of sirens filled the air with their plaintive moaning. More explosions—louder and nearer.

For a while he was quite incapable of thought, but his mind reacted instinctively to the incredible significance of the noises. It was an air attack, and it could be the start of the invasion. The realisation triggered his half-paralysed brain into action again. Optimism deluged him. This was how he had always known it would happen. His luck was still holding. How stupid to lose faith even for just a few minutes. He was going to be all right. They hadn't defeated Clive Brant after all.

The bombing was music to his ears. Through the metal grating he saw the incandescent glow of incendiaries reflecting from the brick wall outside, like dawn sunlight, but a different kind of dawn from that he had been anticipating. A bright dawn—a warm glowing dawn after a very dark night. The darkest of nights brings the brightest of dawns, he said to himself, repeating the sentence over and over again until it began to acquire a mystical quality.

The noises of the air raid began to subside, but soon a fresh wave of bombers came over, and the floor of the cell shook in violent agitation as the high explosives did their work. The incendiary dawn became brighter, flickering with the orange light of unseen leaping flames. Somewhere nearby debris fell with a great rolling crash. He heard excited voices, remote and muffled, and the far off jangle of an ambulance bell.

He sat on the hard bunk in a state of hypnotic fascination, trying to see the pattern of the future, for there had to be a pattern, Clive Brant's pattern, and the strands were interweaving intricately as each bomb fell. But the air raid quietened down and an hour of silence followed. Soon the orange light beyond the grating faded into darkness once more.

They'll come back, he assured himself. They had to come back. It was part of the pattern, the mystical design which had determined his life in the past and would guide it through the menacing and uncertain future. And sure enough they did come back, in greater strength than before. A new dawn flashed into being beyond the grating, and the bombs crashed ferociously into the city, tearing it apart. But his cell remained intact. He knew it would, of course. The bombs were not meant for him; they were the means to secure his survival.

The attacks continued intermittently throughout the night until the blue-grey light of the true dawn discoloured the view through the grating. And then there was peace for a while.

They brought him coffee and a breakfast of thick porridge at seven o'clock. There were two of them, mature middle-aged men, gruff in manner but not unfriendly.

"Rough night," one said. "The bastards gave us a caning."

"Yes," Clive said passively.

"You're the lucky one if you did but know," said the other guard. "This is just the start. They mean business. You'll be out of it and I reckon you won't have done so badly for yourself."

Clive said nothing, but there was just the ghost of a knowledgeable smile on his lips.

"Never seen anything like it," said the first guard. "I went right through the bombing of London in the last war. Never seen anything like it at all. They must have had thousands of planes."

After the guards had gone, Clive ate his frugal breakfast with a genuine hunger and a sense of deep satisfaction. There's plenty of time, he told himself. Very soon they'll come back, more and more of them. It's daylight now. They've got air superiority and they can see their targets. They may even try an air assault with paratroops. It would be easy enough. They've already got these rebel swine demoralised and on the run.

He finished his breakfast and drank the coffee, then sat quite still, just thinking. His instinct had not failed him. Soon the distant roar of aircraft could be heard again. The timing was precise, just as he had anticipated.

They came for him at five minutes to eight, four of them, rather young men, tough looking, and businesslike in their attitude.

"You know the procedure," one said, advancing on Clive.

The thunder of the aircraft became louder. Clive looked at them in surprise. "You're not really proposing to go through with this…"

"Don't make things difficult," one said. "We've got to carry out our orders."

"But the air raids…"

"So what? Life goes on just the same."

They formed up in front of him and behind him, then pushed him forward and marched him through the open door of the cell, down a stone corridor and through another heavy door into a flagged yard surrounded by a high wall. He walked blankly along, in a stupefied frame of mind. They didn't understand. Clearly they just didn't understand.

In the yard, at one end, four men stood with automatic carbines slung over their shoulders. Not even rifles, he thought. An automated firing squad. At one side an officer in shirt sleeves stood with hands in his pockets, smoking a cigarette.

They escorted him to the opposite wall and put him against it. One of them produced a white cloth and started to tie it around his eyes.

"No," he said abruptly. "No blindfold."

"Suit yourself," the man said.

He looked up at the sky. They were coming over like a flock of birds, hundreds of them, perhaps thousands, and an incredible thing was happening. Tiny black blobs were cascading from the planes, twisting and turning as they fell towards the ground. Bombs, he thought, more bombs. But they were not bombs. Fabric spilled away from the shapes like ectoplasm, convoluting and contorting for an instant in the rush of air, then billowing out into parachutes. Thousands of parachutes like a snowstorm in the morning sky.

He looked at the firing squad. They had already raised the guns to their shoulders, and the officer had put out his cigarette and was grinding it under his heel.

"Wait!" Clive shouted. "Wait—invasion! They've come…"

He glanced once more towards the sky. The aircraft were almost overhead and the snowstorm had thickened. It was the most incredible thing he had ever seen in his life.

"Wait!" he shouted again. "You can't do this…"

The officer's smooth face was cold and patient. He said: "You think they arranged all this just to rescue you?"

He turned to the waiting gunmen and said, "Fire."

Clive started to run forward, but the impact of the bullets rocked him back. He twisted, doubled up, collapsed on the ground. His blank eyes continued to stare at the descending snowflakes.

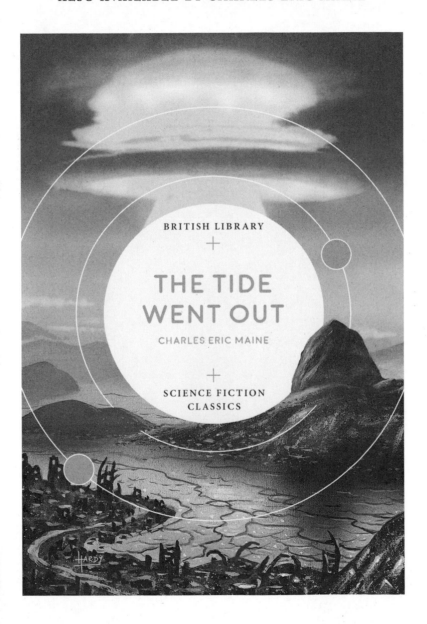

BRITISH LIBRARY

✛

THE TIDE
WENT OUT

CHARLES ERIC MAINE

✛

SCIENCE FICTION
CLASSICS